C000263720

The Threlfalls
By: Barbara Phipps
ISBN: 978-1-927134-73-3

Bluewood Publishing Ltd
Christchurch, 8441, New Zealand
www.bluewoodpublishing.com

For news of, or to purchase this or other books please visit.

www.bluewoodpublishing.com

The Threlfalls

To Lyn,

by

with best wishes,

Barbara Phipps.

Barbara Phipps

This page is intentionally blank.

Chapter One

Susan Joanne Fletcher entered the world at 8.30 a.m. on Saturday, 14th day of August, 1948. She was slapped on the back, weighed, washed, wrapped in a blanket and handed to her mother. The midwife smiled for the first time, her job done. It had been a long night.

"You can come in now," she called.

Charlie had been waiting in the corridor all night in a sour mood. He begrudged leaving his business. Siobhan had screamed and sworn, at no-one in particular, for hours. It was all quiet now.

The first sight of his wife and daughter took him aback. There was nothing unusual about the room. It was a picture that could be seen in any maternity hospital, anywhere in the world. Susan slept in the crook of her mother's arm. Siobhan looked up for a moment, smiled at her husband, and returned her gaze to her baby. Charlie's own reaction took him by surprise. The love in that confined space was palpable. Peace surrounded the little family like a veil. Siobhan was relaxed, content, fulfilled, beautiful, loving with that unconditional love of a mother. Charlie stood by the bed. After watching his daughter for a while, he looked at Siobhan.

"I love you, Siobhan Fletcher."

It was only a flash, a split second, but her eyes spoke. Her eyes shouted in disbelief, a fear; a distrust.

"You never said that before, Charlie."

"Maybe I didn't know until now." He kissed her forehead and then touched the pink cheek of the new life. His daughter. He was in no doubt about his love for Siobhan.

Her dark hair stuck to her temples with the sweat of childbirth. Her pale skin seemed luminous. She was beautiful.

Siobhan's eyes filled with tears, tears for the past, tears of joy; tears of love. She didn't look up, as her gaze was fixed on her baby. There was a fear, too, that if she looked at Charlie, he might change his mind. Charlie had said he loved her, and she wanted it to stay like that. She wanted everything to stay just like this moment. If she moved, it might break the spell.

"I have to go, Siobhan. I have to see to business."

"Look at her, Charlie. Look at little missy. She yawned."

Charlie looked and smiled at the miracle before him. Siobhan pulled the blanket away a little to reveal soft, pink hands. The perfect fingers wrapped themselves around Charlie's little finger. He should be going, but his feet wouldn't take him away. Warmth spread through his body, his every nerve tingling from the top of his head to the tips of his toes.

"I think she is like you, Charlie. Just look at the line of her jaw, her nose."

He'd heard people say that new babies looked like one or the other parent. He had never believed it before, but even he could see it. She did look like him. The knowledge gave him a sensation of elation and shame simultaneously. He had not wanted this child. When Siobhan told him she was pregnant, his first instinct had been to fix her up with an abortion. To be fair though, the thought hadn't lasted long. The memory shamed him.

A nurse broke the spell, bustling up to the bed, straightening blankets that were already straight.

"You should go now, Mr Fletcher. Your wife needs to rest."

"See you this afternoon, Siobhan. Look after our beautiful baby. I love you both."

Siobhan looked up. He had said it again. It must be true. He held her free hand and squeezed it for a few seconds, kissed her on the cheek, and left.

Charlie had to keep walking. With every step, he wanted to turn round and go back to that little room. He reached the main entrance door and stepped outside. He paused on the top step, pulling himself up to his full height. At five feet and four inches, he usually felt his lack of height acutely, but not today. Today he was ten feet tall. Today he was a father. To the best of his knowledge, he had no other children. He had always avoided any sort of commitment. Until half an hour ago, he had felt uncertain about having married Siobhan. Those thoughts were quickly banished from his mind. Charlie was good at discarding shameful memories. He had done the honourable thing. He had married her two months ago at the registry office. No photographs, no guests, no party. He took a deep breath, and went down the steps with the light movement of joy, his short, fat body floating along the streets with the weightlessness of a butterfly. Charlie knew the streets of Leeds well enough, but this morning it was as if he hadn't seen them before. This was at least in part because he didn't usually see Leeds much before eleven o'clock. He was in bed until ten-thirty most mornings. He smiled at people and they smiled back. He raised his trilby hat to the ladies, almost bowing to the mothers with their prams. Newspaper vendors on the street corners shouted the headlines in an effort to attract customers. Something about the London

Olympics and Iron Curtain countries. Athletes refusing to go home. Such things had never interested Charlie, but he bought a paper anyway. He would keep it for Susan and give it to her on her twenty-first birthday. His thoughts were beginning to wander back to his real world, the world of Charlie Fletcher the publican, when he suddenly stopped. A pram in a shop window had caught his attention.

Lavells was a posh shop. He never went into any shops if he could avoid it, but the sight of the Silver Cross pram captured him. He had never been in Lavells, but before he knew it he was in the revolving doors. Charlie was ejected into the shop and hit by a wall of perfume.

"Can I be of assistance, sir?" The woman before him wore a brightly coloured dress and a lot of makeup. The image of a pantomime dame flashed before Charlie's eyes. He struggled to reply but no words came out. This was another first. Charlie Fletcher was never lost for words.

"Is sir looking for some perfume for his wife?"

Charlie could no more say 'No' than fly to the moon. The next thing he knew he had bought a bottle of Chanel, as recommended by the pantomime dame, before asking the way to the pram department.

"That would be the sixth floor, sir. You could take the lift, which is to your left, or the escalator, over there." She pointed with the red talon of her right forefinger.

Charlie said, "Thanks," and turned to the escalator. He wondered how she could work with nails as long as that. She wouldn't even be able to wear gloves in winter. He had never been on an escalator before. Another first for Charlie Fletcher. By the third floor, he was getting used to it, despite the way his hand travelled slightly faster than his feet. He was fascinated. He knew the shops were filling up again after the war years, but clothes were still rationed.

How do they manage to sell this stuff? he thought. It was all Christian Dior and the 'New Look'. The clothes seemed to use as much material as possible, just because they could. *Fair enough*, he thought. *Rationing won't last forever.*

Charlie had done quite well out of the war. He wasn't a conscientious objector. He was a coward. He exaggerated the effects of a crooked spine and stayed in Leeds. Landlord of The Threlfalls Hotel and entrepreneur. Little bit of this, little bit of that. He had a very simple philosophy when it came to business. *Always make sure you are selling what people want to buy.* Foolproof. If you wanted something, Charlie Fletcher could get it. It made his pub very popular. It made Charlie popular. His customers looked up to him, in a manner of speaking. He smiled at the thought.

Sixth floor. Cots… Blankets… Sheets… Nappies… Prams! Charlie was horrified. Susan had nothing. Why hadn't Siobhan bought all these things? She should have told him. He could have got it all on the cheap. NO! Nothing cheap for Susan. She would have the best of everything.

"Can I help at all, sir?"

Charlie was startled. He turned quickly to the voice, regaining his composure as quickly as he could. He had not heard the assistant approach. She was different from the pantomime dame on the ground floor. This one actually looked real.

"I—er…I—umm… My wife has just had a baby and—erm—and I saw the pram in the window." Charlie waved vaguely in the direction of the escalator. He had no idea which way the window would be. With all that going round and round the floors and escalators, he had lost his sense of direction. Not that it mattered.

"Congratulations, sir. A girl or a boy?"

"A girl, a beautiful girl…Susan. We decided on Susan before she was born. A boy would have been Richard…" Charlie was babbling. He couldn't get the words out fast enough. "Siobhan—my wife—I bought her some perfume…but we don't have anything. I mean anything for Susan. Nothing. We need everything."

The assistant smiled. "Don't worry, sir, you're in luck. We just had a delivery. No doubt we'll be sold out again soon."

Charlie stared at her blankly.

The assistant continued. "So many babies… the end of the war." His mind was working ahead. He could hear what she was saying, but his head was in his business.

"A shortage of prams?"

"The baby boom, sir. Have you heard of it?"

* * * *

Charlie was first in the ward at visiting time. Susan was fast asleep, replete from her feeding. He looked at the baby with disbelief. She was his daughter, and she was perfect. He sat at the side of the bed chatting away, holding Siobhan's hands in his. Siobhan was watching his face. She heard his voice, but not what he was saying. It was strange. This morning, she hadn't dared to look at him at all, yet now she was staring at him. As he talked, she slowly realised that she had never seen him smile much before, not like this. He had never talked to her this much either.

"So it's all sorted out."

Siobhan continued to stare, her lips sealed.

"Siobhan? Are you alright?"

"Yes, yes, sorry, Charlie, what did you say?"

"I said it's all sorted out." The blank look on her face worried Charlie. He felt a twinge of impatience. "The nursery. The pram, a cot, clothes, nappies. Two dozen I bought. Everything. All best quality. Nothing but the best for our Susan, eh, love? All delivered tomorrow from Lavells. The Sister told me you will be home on Tuesday. It will all be set up. I got Billy Oldroyd painting your old room. All pink. What do you say?"

It took a while for Siobhan to say anything. As her eyes filled with tears, she whispered, "I say you are a good man, Charlie Fletcher." When he gave her the perfume, she was lost for words, and tears of joy streamed down her pale cheeks.

* * * *

The doors of the Threlfalls Hotel opened at six o'clock each evening. There were always two or three customers on the doorstep. Charlie knew most of his 'earlies' by sight, if not by name. Strictly speaking, it wasn't a hotel anymore. There were no rooms to let. It was a big city centre pub with an air of faded glory. Standing on the corner of Briggate and Thompson Square, the entrance was still impressive. The ornate carvings around the doorway and mullioned windows were typical of their day. The Yorkshire stone blackened with soot from the mill chimneys, the same mills that had created the prosperity of the city.

As the clock struck the hour, Charlie unlocked the tall mahogany doors. He latched them to the floor with heavy brass bolts.

First in was Tom Hicks, the barman. Charlie liked Tom. He was reliable and worked for a pittance, and would open up if Charlie was away on business. He even stayed after closing time and washed the glasses. Tom was followed into The Threlfalls by Johnnie Frogget, and a couple of other 'earlies'. They followed him across the hallway and left into the tap room. By the time they reached the bar, Charlie was standing on his board and pulling the first pint. The board was four inches high and ran the length of the bar. Enough to make him feel he could look people in the eye. Tom never needed to be told not to stand on it; it would have made him appear taller than the boss.

Charlie had a favourite spot behind the bar. From here he could see all of the tap room and most of the 'best' room. He liked the feel of the curved mahogany and inlaid brass as the bar swept from one room to the other. The 'best' room had originally been the dining room. Ceiling roses added to the grandeur of the dusty chandeliers. Oil paintings, dulled by tobacco smoke, hung in the recesses either side of the mahogany fireplace. The skirting boards were over a foot high, stained and varnished. Even Charlie had to admit they were somewhat battered, the carpet a bit worn. Siobhan had done wonders with the cleaning though.

"What's t' big smile fo', Charlie? You got lucky wi' t' 'osses?" Johnnie asked.

"Not me, Johnnie. Not a one for the gee-gees. You know that." Charlie pulled another two pints. With his back to his customers, he rang the money in the ornate till. Turning as he shut the drawer, he said, "I'm a dad, Johnnie.

Siobhan had a baby girl early this morning. We named her Susan."

The three men simultaneously raised their pints.

"Congratulations, Charlie!" They drank deeply from their glasses.

Johnnie slammed his down on the bar. "'Ave a drink thissen, Charlie. This un's on me."

Charlie had never known Johnnie to buy a drink for anyone; he always just had a pint and went home. The only other time he had had a second pint was when Charlie had introduced him to Siobhan. That was on the first day she worked in the bar. Charlie felt obliged to accept.

"Very kind, I'm sure, Johnnie. I'll join you in a pint." As he pulled the beer, Charlie was aware he was breaking his own rule. 'Never drink behind your own bar.' His conscience said it was wrong, but his hands pulled the pint anyway.

"An' 'ere's afe a crown fo' t' babby."

Charlie was staggered. The two other men each added a half crown to Johnnie's.

"What tha's ter do, Charlie Fletcher, is ter oppen a Post Office book fo' young Susan. This'll start it off. It's not fo' thee, y'old bugger. It's fo' babby Susan."

This was the longest speech Charlie had ever heard from Johnnie. The other two drinkers muttered in agreement. Charlie put the three silver coins in a tankard at the side of the optics. By the time Johnnie left, the bar was getting busy. Alf Lawrence had arrived. You could set your watch by Alf. Seven 'clock. Alf. Half a pint of Tetley's.

Tom and Charlie were kept busy. The hot weather was good for trade. They would both be pulling pints until closing time.

When Charlie called 'Time', it wasn't only the skirting boards that were looking a bit battered. Charlie's beaming smile had attracted comments all night. Each comment had warranted a further announcement of Susan's birth. Each announcement had resulted in another pint being bought for the proud father.

Chapter Two

Siobhan was awake, but her eyes were still closed. She listened with simple delight to the noises of the ward. The newborn cries. The footsteps of the nurses. The hum of voices. She lay there for a minute or so, luxuriating in the warm bed. Her eyes opened slowly to focus on the cot at her side. She had never been happier. Charlie had married her. Susan was born, a perfect little girl. Charlie loved her, and he loved Susan. It was a far cry from the day she had stepped off the boat in Liverpool. She had landed on her feet all right when she met Charlie. There was a murmur from the cot. Siobhan climbed out of bed, reaching down to her daughter.

"Now, Mrs Fletcher, let me help." For a moment, she didn't realise the nurse was speaking to her. Siobhan was still not used to being called Mrs Fletcher. "You sit on the chair here, and I'll hand your baby to you. She'll be hungry."

Susan sucked at Siobhan's breast greedily. She could hardly believe how it hurt, but that didn't matter. How could pain be a pleasure? Siobhan smiled. Susan's face moved rhythmically as she took the milk.

Siobhan's thoughts wandered lazily to her own childhood. Had Pa beaten her brothers and sisters for her disappearance? Had he beaten Ma? She wondered how long it had been before he missed her. Did he care? One less mouth to feed. That was how it had worked in their house. You couldn't call it a home or even a house really. It was a poor structure, but for all that, no different to the others in Kilmain. Other families laughed together despite the poverty but not in their house. If one of them did a wrong thing, another was beaten for it. That was how Pa kept them in line. But all that was gone for Siobhan now. By the age of sixteen, she had had enough. She had travelled with the gypsies to Dublin and worked until she had enough money for the ferry and a bit to spare.

Charlie never showed any interest in her past and that was the best way to keep it. She shuddered, the warmth of the hospital temporarily banished by the memories flashing through her mind. She would never go back to Ireland. She would have liked Ma to see Susan, though. Ma loved babies.

Old Mrs McMahon from the village had told her about Leeds, and what a fine city it was. Siobhan liked listening to Mrs McMahon. She would tell Siobhan of the time she went on the boat to Liverpool with her father.

"Liverpool is as bad as Dublin. Full of whores and drunken sailors," she would say. Siobhan didn't know what a whore was, but the way Mrs McMahon said it, told Siobhan they were not nice. Siobhan learned about whores and sailors in Dublin. Mrs McMahon had been right.

"Now Leeds is something quite different. A fine city."

"Tell me about Leeds."

Mrs McMahon would repeat her memories. "There's honest work in Leeds, Siobhan. Hard work, but honest work. The mills are the best. You're dry and warm in the mills."

Siobhan's thoughts took her further back in time, to the day she boarded the boat in Dublin. She'd never been on a boat before. Despite the warm sunshine of early summer, it had been a rough Irish sea that carried her to Liverpool. She felt horribly sick. Standing on the deck, she watched the Liver Buildings grow before her eyes as the ferry approached Pier Head, where it would dock. The huge clock faces on the towers, and the liver birds, with their wings outstretched, were frightening. The water of the Mersey rose and fell between the ferry and the dockside. Ropes were thrown with ease and secured to the worn capstans. The noise of the river and the shouts of the crew and shoremen filled the polluted air of the dockside. The landing deck swayed as she walked with the other passengers to England. Even if Mrs McMahon hadn't done such a good job of putting her off, she wouldn't have stayed in Liverpool. Siobhan knew that if her father looked for her he would look in Dublin. Then he might go as far as Liverpool, but no further. Siobhan didn't want to be found. She asked for directions to Lime Street Station. Up Water Street, onto Dale Street, then turn right into Crosshall Street and on towards the station. It was late afternoon when Siobhan saw the stone frontage of Lime Street Station. It didn't impress her. She was oblivious to such details; she simply wanted to get on a train to Leeds.

"Single to Leeds, please."

The man in the ticket office didn't look up. Siobhan passed her money though the criss-cross grille, and he pushed the ticket back over the worn wooden counter, scraped of varnish by the years of coins being passed through the gap.

Siobhan liked the train, better than the boat anyway. She took a seat by the window and put her bag by her side. There wasn't much in it, just a spare shawl, blouse and skirt, a hair brush and a piece of ribbon. Down at the bottom, there was a piece of cardboard, under that was a purse, and what was left of her money.

No one else entered the compartment. She opened the window a little and sat down, glad to be alone. The carriage didn't have a corridor; each compartment had a door to the platform. The porter slammed the doors. The guard blew his whistle. With a loud whistle from the engine and a huge puff of black smoke, Siobhan was on her way to Leeds. As the train set off, Siobhan felt safe for the first time. The rhythmic movements and sounds were somehow comforting.

The train slowed as it passed through Rainhill, St. Helen's Junction, and Newton le Willows. The first stop was Salford, then Stalybridge.

To her relief, Siobhan remained alone in the compartment. She saw the chimneys of the Lancashire cotton mills bellowing their black smoke, giving a haze to the air. The next stop was Manchester. The bustle of the station had Siobhan spellbound. So many people. She peered through the carriage window, her eyes wide in amazement. A smartly dressed man opened the door and sat in the opposite corner to Siobhan. He wore a beige coloured raincoat with a belt. His shiny brogues were tied tightly, his hair slicked back with pomade. He made no effort to look at Siobhan, as if he hadn't seen her. He opened his newspaper, and she turned her face to the window. The train huffed its way out of Manchester and on towards Yorkshire, labouring up the gradient of the Pennines.

Without any warning, there was a huge bang. Siobhan screamed in terror as the carriage was plunged into pitch black darkness. The dim lights of the compartment came on slowly.

"You alright, love?" He put his newspaper down and shuffled along the seat towards Siobhan. She felt a twinge of fear.

"What was that?" she asked, holding her little bag tightly on her lap.

He sat opposite her now, leaning forward, his short fingers spread across his knees. She knew he'd heard the panic, and the Irish accent. "A tunnel. We're under the Pennines."

Siobhan's blue eyes grew wider. Mrs McMahon hadn't said anything about tunnels.

"There are about four of them. They're the Standedge tunnels. When a train goes in a tunnel it pushes the air through. It makes a bang. After the last one, we will be in Yorkshire."

"Good," she whispered.

She didn't understand about the air in the tunnel. It didn't matter. They were out now and in daylight again. The landscape had changed to the bleak moorland of the Pennines. She returned her eyes to the window and the passing countryside.

"Where are you going?" he asked.

"Leeds. I'm going to Leeds. I'm going to get a job in a mill." Siobhan tried to sound confident. She held her chin up and looked the man in the eyes. She didn't want him to think she was afraid. He was older than her, but not old. Siobhan thought he was probably in his twenties. He seemed nice enough, but you could never tell.

"Hard work that, in the mills. Hard work and long hours. Which mill are you going to?"

Siobhan felt her stomach lurch and drop. She had no idea which mill she was going to. She didn't even know the name of a mill. She shuffled her feet and looked to the floor.

He sat back with a sigh, resting his head on the back of the seat. "Don't worry. I won't turn you in," he said.

She relaxed a little. She was in Yorkshire now, and could see the woollen mills.

There was a finality to the hiss of the engine as the train stopped.

"All change, all change. Leeds City Station." The porter threw the doors open, banging them against the side of the train. Siobhan remained in her seat. Tears welled up in her eyes. She had nowhere to go. Her travelling companion stepped down to the platform. He paused and then turned towards her. "What's your name?"

"Siobhan." Her voice was no more than a whisper.

"And how old are you, Siobhan?"

"Nineteen," she lied.

"Well, Siobhan, I think you had better come with me."

She stood up, clasping her little bag in front of her defensively. He walked away down the platform. Siobhan followed, handing her one way ticket to the inspector at the end of the platform. What choice did she have? He didn't turn round until they were out of the station.

"My name is Charlie, by the way. You can stay at my place tonight if you like."

Siobhan nodded. Just a slight inclination of her head, it was almost imperceptible.

"Come on, Siobhan, I won't bite." Charlie held his arm out to her, bent at the elbow.

They crossed the road, arm in arm, and walked along Boar Lane, then left into Briggate. The electric trams clanked their way along the busy street.

A man called out, "Evenin', Charlie." Siobhan saw him cast his eyes over her. He was about to say something when Charlie cut him off.

"Evenin', Billy. Can't stop, see you later." They continued to walk without a pause.

Siobhan was beginning to feel more relaxed. He hadn't lied to her about his name, and he was known here.

"Here we are." Charlie guided her through the doors of The Threlfalls Hotel. Straight in front of them was a sweeping staircase with a rope across the lower steps. Charlie turned left into the tap room.

"Evenin', Charlie." There was curiosity in Tom's eyes, one side of his mouth slightly curled in a faint leer. Customers turned to see who had come in.

"I'll be out in a few minutes, Tom. You carry on here, I won't be long." Charlie lifted the wooden flap at the end of the bar, and signalled for Siobhan to follow him. They went through a door at the back of the bar and into a dark passageway, then through another door, and into the kitchen.

"D—do you live here, then?" Siobhan looked around in amazement. She had never seen such a huge kitchen. It was bigger than the whole house she had left behind in Ireland.

Charlie was filling a kettle. "I do that. This is my pub." He took a box of matches from the shelf above the gas stove, placed the kettle on the stove, and lit a gas ring.

Siobhan sat down on a wooden chair next to a large pine table.

"The tea is in that tin, next to the teapot," he said, pointing to another shelf. "You can help yourself. There is some bread and jam in the cupboard behind you."

Siobhan turned to see cupboards that ran the length of the room.

"I have to go work in the bar. I'll pop back when I can and show you your room for tonight." Without waiting for a reply, Charlie left the kitchen, and Siobhan was alone. She could hear muffled voices from the bar and the occasional laughter. She thought she could make out Charlie's voice but wasn't sure. The kettle started its low noise. Siobhan stood up and went to the cupboards. There were dozens of everything. Plates of all sizes, cups and saucers, soup bowls, salt and pepper pots. She took a cup, saucer and a small plate and put them on the table. Opposite the cupboards, there was a kitchen range. It didn't look as if the fire had been lit for a long time, the gas oven having taken its usefulness. There was an armchair to each side, one more worn than the other. Siobhan assumed the worn one was Charlie's chair. She made her jam sandwich and cup of black tea and sat in the other one. When she finished, she took the dishes to the sink, washed and dried them, put them back in the cupboard and returned to the armchair, stifling a yawn as she sat down. The ticking of the clock was like a lullaby; Siobhan was asleep in seconds.

* * * *

As luck would have it, both the tap room and the best room were busy that night. When Charlie returned to the bar, Tom gave him a quizzical look.

Charlie just said, "Don't ask."

Tom didn't ask. He knew his boss well enough. Charlie didn't like being asked anything unless it was to do with 'business' and you were a customer.

Charlie had had a good day in Manchester, set up a few new contacts. As he pulled the pints, his mind darted between his business deals and the young girl in the kitchen. The chat and banter with the customers was part of the job. The weather, the football, rationing, some even talked politics, but Charlie tried to avoid that particular subject. It wasn't good for trade for a publican to hold strong political opinions. He knew that much.

"Last orders, please, gentlemen." It was 10:15; closing time was 10:30. 'Drinking up time' meant it was 10:45 when Charlie locked the doors. He was a stickler for time. There was the usual rush for drinks, and then gradually the bar emptied. Tom collected the glasses and stacked them on the bar, ready to take them through to the kitchen.

"Just leave them there, Tom. I'll see to them tonight."

Tom gave Charlie a knowing look.

"I know what you're thinking, Tom Hicks, but let me tell you now, you're wrong."

Tom smirked. Charlie pretended he had not seen the look on his face.

"Goodnight, Charlie."

"Goodnight, Tom."

Charlie let Tom out, then locked the doors again. He turned and leaned his back on them. With a sigh, he closed his eyes. He had found himself, or more truthfully, put himself, in a tricky situation. After a minute or so, he opened his eyes and walked back through the bar and into the kitchen. Siobhan was stirring from her sleep.

"Sorry I didn't come back sooner. It's been non-stop in the bar. Have you had something to eat?"

"Yes, thank you."

"You had better come upstairs, then. Come on, this way."

Siobhan followed obediently.

He unhooked the red rope on the stairs and laid it to one side. The stairs gave way to a wide landing with a passageway to one side and double doors to the other.

Charlie continued up to the next floor, turned to the left and then pointed to the first door on the right.

"That's my room. I get up at ten thirty, so don't make any noise before then." He walked on. Opening a door on the left, he switched on the light. "You can sleep in here."

Siobhan stepped past him into the room. There was a dressing table and a small wardrobe. The single bed had blankets, a pillow and an eiderdown folded up on it. The dark green velvet curtains were held open by heavy cords with tassels. The street lights gave a golden light to the room. She walked to the window and looked out onto Briggate. Turning slightly, she simply said, "Thank you." It seemed inadequate, but she didn't know what else to say.

"There's a linen cupboard further down the landing. Help yourself to whatever you need. The bathroom is over here. There's another one down the steps at the end of the passage." Charlie pointed to a small flight of stairs. "We'll talk about getting you a mill job tomorrow. I'm going out on business now. Goodnight, Siobhan. You're quite safe here."

After Charlie said goodnight and left her in the bedroom, she sat on the edge of the bed, listening to his footsteps receding along the landing, and then down the stairs. A door banged and she rushed to the window but there was no sign of him. She unhooked the cords and drew together the curtains. The room had a slightly musty smell, not damp exactly, just not fresh air. There was a little table to the side of the bed with an ornate lamp on it. The base was a carving of an elephant; the shade had deep red fringing. Siobhan went out onto the landing and into the first bathroom. It was a big room with a bath, a toilet, and two washbasins. Each washbasin had a large mirror with a gold frame. There was a razor beside one of the basins. On the shelf above was a jar of pomade, a hairbrush, and a comb. She picked up the razor and quickly put it down again. She didn't know why, but it felt all wrong to be in this room, as if she were trespassing. She left quickly, closing the door behind her, turning to her right and down the landing. The other bathroom was quite different to Charlie's. It was very small, though it did have a bath. The toilet and washbasin were side by side on the right. Straight in front of her was a small window which had been left open. Siobhan shut it quickly. There was no soap or towels in the room. She turned on the hot tap of the bath. The water sputtered and coughed its way out, running a dirty brown colour at first, then warm clean water. She put in the plug. To Siobhan, it was the height of luxury. She looked at herself in the tiny mirror.

"You look a proper mess, Siobhan," she said out loud. "Better find that linen."

She opened a couple of bedroom doors before finding the double doors of the cupboard; it was stacked high with dozens of sheets, pillowslips and towels, bars of soap and face cloths. All the bedding and towels were pure white, neatly folded and stacked. Siobhan took two sheets and a pillowslip. She left them on the bed. Taking her hairbrush from her bag, she went back to the cupboard. With a large towel over her arm, some soap and a facecloth, she returned to the bathroom. Siobhan stripped off and stepped into the bath. The water was like silk on her skin as she lay back in the enveloping warmth.

She had never slept in a bed with sheets before. The cold, smooth cotton felt strange; as soon as her body warmed the linen, she sank into a dreamless sleep.

* * * *

As he locked the gates of the back yard behind him, Siobhan was erased from his mind. Charlie Fletcher was out on business. He was feeling rather smug about his latest little venture. It had been a good day in Manchester. The solicitor had all the papers ready for him to sign. The house in Leeds was his now. A nest egg if ever there was one. Charlie liked to keep his dealings in Manchester, the legal and the illegal.

Next morning, Charlie woke up slowly and stretched. All was well with his world. Charlie opened one eye to see it was already twenty to eleven. Time he was up. There was a lot to do today, people to see. He staggered sleepily to the bathroom. He was lathering up his face for a shave when he thought he could smell something. A cooking smell.

"Oh, Christ!" he said to his reflection. "I'd forgotten about her."

He quickly finished shaving, tamed his hair with pomade, and got dressed. As he hurried down the back staircase, he remembered all the glasses were still stacked up on the bar.

"Bloody hell, what was I thinking of?" he muttered as he headed for the kitchen. Siobhan stood up quickly as he entered the room.

"Siobhan! The glasses haven't been washed! Will you do them, I—?"

"I did them already. I did it real quiet so as not to wake you."

He rushed through to the bar. The glasses were washed and put away. The tables wiped, chairs neatly under them, ashtrays washed and put out, one on each table. The bar looked spotless. He turned to see her standing behind him.

"You don't mind that I did it, then? I had nothing to do. I thought it might help," she said. "There's some sausages cooked. I found them in the refrigerator."

Charlie followed her back into the kitchen, and sat down at the table. Siobhan served him a breakfast of sausage, bacon and egg, toast, butter and marmalade, and a cup of tea. Charlie ate in silence, and when he had finished he sat back in the chair, wiping his mouth with a handkerchief.

"You're a good cook, I'll say that much, Siobhan."

She smiled weakly.

"Listen," he said, "I don't have time to take you to the mills today. I've a lot to do. Business, you know?"

Siobhan didn't know. How could she?

"You stay here. You can do some cleaning if you like. There's plenty needs doing. You'll find a cupboard under the stairs with all sorts of stuff in, dusters and that. There's more under the sink. I have to be off. I'll be back for opening time at twelve."

Charlie grabbed his coat and was gone. A door banged, a clock struck eleven, and silence fell on the kitchen.

* * * *

Siobhan lost no time in starting her cleaning. She polished the big brass beer pumps until she could see her reflection in them and then started to wax the woodwork. The smell of the polish combined with the stale beer and tobacco to give a strangely sweet odour. When it was almost twelve, she took her dusters into the kitchen, along with the mail from the worn coconut mat in the doorway. She put the kettle on. Charlie returned just as she put the last of the breakfast dishes away. He hung his coat on the hook in the corner.

"No time for tea, Siobhan. You drink it. I have to open up." He walked quickly through the kitchen to the bar. She had collected the mail; his letters were stacked neatly on the table.

Siobhan didn't know what to think, or what to make of it all. She made herself a jam sandwich and a cup of tea. She was warm. She wasn't hungry. She had slept in a comfortable clean bed. No one had shouted at her. No one had hit her. Things were looking pretty good so far.

By the time the pub shut at three o'clock on that first day, she had scrubbed the pine table, black leaded the old range, and washed the paintwork on the cupboards.

"Nice, very nice," was all that Charlie said as he looked round the kitchen. He made himself comfortable in his chair and fell asleep. Nothing was ever said about Siobhan staying on at The Threlfalls Hotel. She just did. He never mentioned the mills again, and Siobhan was more than happy to stay.

A routine established itself. Siobhan cooked and cleaned. The big fireplaces in the bar and the best room had not been used for some time. The grates were full of old coal ash, cigarette ends and cigar butts. She found a bucket and cleaned them out, then wiped the hearths and polished the brass fenders. Charlie showed her how to work the vacuum cleaner and the carpet started to show its colours again. When the pub was open, she cleaned in the kitchen and prepared Charlie's meals. The refrigerator and pantry were always full of fresh food. Subconsciously, she began to think of the bedroom Charlie had given her as 'her' room. The chair opposite Charlie's in the kitchen was 'her' chair. She had never been happier. She wasn't stupid, though. Her curiosity had led her to have a good look round upstairs one afternoon when Charlie was out. On the first landing, she turned right and went through the double doors. There were cloakrooms for 'Ladies' on the left and 'Gentlemen' to the right, their gold and red paintwork faded with age. Straight ahead, there was another set of doors with the word "BALLROOM" etched in opaque glass. Siobhan pushed one of the heavy doors just far enough for her slim body to slip in sideways.

Green velvet curtains like the ones in her room were drawn across the windows. Here and there, a shaft of sunlight came through. Dust floated in the air, highlighted by the rays, yet invisible where the sun didn't pierce the darkness. She could see lots of boxes on a little stage. Round the edge of the ballroom there were all sorts of things. Bicycles, radios, bedsteads, mattresses, blankets, pillows. All brand new. She walked to the centre of the dance floor and stopped. She turned round slowly, taking in the splendour of the room, ignoring the array of goods. She held out her arms to an imaginary dance partner. She hummed lightly as she danced around, the floor creaking beneath her light steps. At the end of her dance, she turned to the stage and gave a small curtsy before applauding the imaginary band. She then climbed the two steps of the stage, and peeped inside one of the open boxes, taking care not to disturb anything. Silk stockings. In other boxes she found lipstick, make up, hair brushes and combs, hair curlers and clips. There was crockery and cutlery. Siobhan knew all this had to be black market stuff. The war was not long over and all these things were rationed, or you just couldn't get them. She might be a simple Irish girl, but she wasn't daft. Standing on tiptoe to look out of one of the windows, she could see a yard with beer barrels stacked up. There was a fire escape which led from somewhere at the back of the hotel. Siobhan was getting really curious now; it didn't take long to find the door at the far end of the room, to the left of the stage. She pushed gently at first, then harder. As it gave way, she stepped onto a little platform. The cast iron staircase led to the yard; it also led upwards. There were two more storeys to the hotel, the bedrooms on the next, then the steep steps of the fire escape continued to the top storey. Stepping back inside the ballroom, she crossed the floor swiftly and went out on to the landing. Charlie could be back soon. The top storey would have to wait, she didn't want to get caught snooping about.

She had been there for three weeks and two days and was dozing in her chair when Charlie came into the kitchen. She glanced at the clock. Five past three. The bar would be closed.

"Siobhan, you need some new clothes. Get that old shawl of yours, we're going shopping."

She ran upstairs, gave her hair a quick brush and grabbed the better of her two shawls. They went out the back way. She had not been out of the Threlfalls since she had arrived with Charlie three weeks ago. It had been dark then. She had no recollection of the shops she must have passed that night. They walked briskly and in silence, Charlie leading the way. He took her arm through his as they entered the 'British Home Stores.' With their arms still linked, he held her hand, as if he was afraid she would run away. They were an odd looking couple. She, in her bedraggled skirt and blouse; her best shawl was a poor piece of cloth, her shoes all scuffed and worn. He, in his smart raincoat and shiny shoes, his trilby hat attempting to make him a little taller.

An assistant approached. There was a note of suspicion in her voice when she spoke. "Can I help?"

It was Charlie who replied. "This is my niece from Ireland. She needs some new clothes."

Siobhan shot a sideways glance at him. He squeezed her hand to silence her. Not that she would have spoken. Siobhan knew all about keeping her head down and her mouth shut. She was hardly going to argue with a man who was about to buy her some new clothes.

"Do you have any coupons, sir?" the assistant asked. Charlie was irritated by the question. Of course he had coupons, he was Charlie Fletcher. Siobhan felt the momentary tension, but when Charlie replied, there was no hint of it in his voice.

"Yes, I have plenty of coupons."

This time the assistant didn't need to speak, the suspicion was in her eyes.

Charlie continued. "I have been saving them. I knew she would need clothes when she got here." He was obviously annoyed that he felt the necessity to explain. "Please follow me," The assistant said, as she turned towards the ladies department.

They left the store over an hour later. Siobhan had three dresses, a jacket and a coat, three cardigans, underwear, nightdresses and a dressing gown.

"We don't need to buy any stockings or gloves, there's plenty of that sort of stuff in my store, but you need some shoes."

"Charlie, I…"

"Don't say anything, Siobhan."

She forced back the tears that threatened to run down her cheeks, instinctively knowing he wouldn't want a fuss here in the middle of town. Siobhan was bewildered. Why was he doing this? They went to 'Stead and Simpson' and he bought her two pairs of shoes, both flatties. With their hands full of shopping bags, there was no opportunity to link arms now. The shops were closing as they walked back to the Threlfalls. They had been out all afternoon and Tom had opened up the bar. Charlie and Siobhan walked through the bar and carried the bags up the back stairs to her room.

"Right, Siobhan." His tone was brisk, businesslike. "I want you to get changed. Put on one of those dresses and a pair of your new shoes. You're working in the bar tonight." Charlie turned on his heel and was gone.

Siobhan wanted to stay in her room, just looking at all the beautiful clothes laid out on the bed. She chose a pale green dress which emphasised her waistline, and brushed her hair. Dark shiny curls fell onto her shoulders. She stepped lightly down the back stairs to the kitchen. Charlie was waiting for her. He stared in silence for what seemed an age. Siobhan didn't like it. She felt naked. Why was he staring at her like that?

"Stay there," he said, and ran out of the room, up the back staircase. Two minutes later, he was down again. "Lipstick. Put this lipstick on."

She took the small tube to the mirror and did as she was told.

"Good," he said. "Now you look like a barmaid."

Siobhan wasn't sure if this was a compliment or not, but it was what Charlie wanted. She followed him through to the bar.

* * * *

Tom was pulling a pint of Tetley's. He looked at her for the briefest of moments, and then turned his attention back to the beer. There were two men at the bar, and a couple seated at one of the tables near a window.

"Now then, Charlie, who have we got here, then?"

"Siobhan. This is Siobhan." Charlie gestured towards her, indicating he wanted her to come forward. "I'd like you meet Billy Oldroyd and Johnnie Froggett."

If Charlie had had any doubts about Siobhan working behind the bar, they were instantly dispelled. She stepped forward with a grace he had not seen before. Or had he just not noticed? She stretched forward her hand, greeting first Billy, and then Johnnie with a shake of hands.

"Hello, lovely to meet you both." She smiled, and looked each of them in the eye as she spoke. Charlie stood on his board; it made him slightly taller than Siobhan. He convinced himself he had bought flat shoes so she would be more comfortable when she was working. The matter of height was an added bonus.

He showed her how to pull the beer from the pumps. Slowly, slowly, with the spout not quite touching the side of the glass, holding it at just such an angle.

Johnnie and Billy stayed for an unprecedented second pint, pulled by the lovely Siobhan. They smiled and chatted to her, complimenting her on her dress. Siobhan smiled back, graciously thanking them for their compliments. Charlie smiled with an air of pride, while Tom Hicks sulked at the other end of the bar.

At seven o'clock, Siobhan was introduced to Alf Lawrence.

"Alf here is a very important customer, Siobhan."

She smiled at Alf and proffered her hand. He held it for a moment with a firm grip.

"Now, Miss Siobhan, you're a very pretty girl. What you doing working for this old rogue?"

Before she could answer, Charlie intervened. "She's helping out, Alf. She's my housekeeper. All above board. Nothing for you to worry about." Turning to Siobhan, Charlie continued, "Alf's a policeman."

Siobhan retrieved her hand from Alf's grip and, keeping her eyes directly on his, she said, "That's right, Alf. Charlie here has been very kind to me."

"Pleased to hear it, Miss Siobhan. Now, where's that half pint of mine?"

* * * *

Siobhan pulled half a pint of Tetley's bitter. She found the pumps were hard to pull but didn't let it show. Her slender arm ached as she passed the glass over the wide mahogany bar to Alf.

Charlie whispered in her ear. "No charge, unless he stays for a second half, which he won't."

Siobhan turned her head to Charlie and gave him a cheeky, knowing grin.

"So you're the one who has been cleaning and polishing."

Siobhan smiled and inclined her head a little in acknowledgement.

Alf faltered as he placed his empty glass on the bar, pausing with his hand around it. He looked at Charlie, then said, "See you tomorrow," and was gone.

Charlie smiled and shook his head. Turning to Siobhan, he said, "Alf Lawrence…second drink…never… Always pays to keep in with the local bobby."

Siobhan attracted attention all evening.

Charlie insisted she stay behind the bar as Tom collected glasses from the tables, banging them down on the bar. Obviously he thought Siobhan should be doing this, he was the barman, and she was the skivvy.

Siobhan avoided Tom and his scowling face as much as she could. She knew that it would take time to win him over; she wasn't going to rock the boat if she could help it.

By the time the last drinks had been served, Siobhan was exhausted. Her right arm ached with pulling the pints, and yet her eyes still sparkled. Two customers had bought her a port and lemon. She had chatted all evening.

* * * *

Charlie was barely been able to keep his eyes off her. She was remarkable; the customers had really taken to her. This young girl had come into his life from nowhere, not that she was turning his head. Oh, no! Charlie Fletcher knew better than that. It was obvious that most of his customers interpreted 'housekeeper' as 'mistress', but what did he care? They could think what they wanted. Siobhan was good for business. And as for Tom? Well, he could please himself. Charlie knew he could get another barman easily enough. Tom would either get used to the idea or leave.

After closing time, Charlie counted the takings on the kitchen table. Siobhan made a pot of tea. This was the usual routine. The only difference was that tonight Siobhan wore a pretty green dress and smart new shoes.

"You did well tonight, love," he said, as he walked over to his old chair by the range. Siobhan was in her armchair, sipping the hot tea.

"Thank you, Charlie. It was a change. I liked talking to the customers. They're very friendly. I'll get better if you let me work more. I'll get better at pulling the pints." She spoke quickly, the words tumbling out. "I like it here. You're very good to me. I don't care what people think. I know what they think. I can tell by the way they look and talk; the way the women put their hands to their mouths. They speak sideways and quietly while they look at me. They think I'm your, you know…woman."

Charlie finished his tea. He looked straight at her.

Siobhan was instantly on her guard. *Had she said too much?*

He cleared his throat. "There's a big 'do' coming up shortly. The Licensed Victuallers Annual Dinner. I want you to come with me. You will be my guest."

Siobhan was bewildered. She stared back at him, her eyes like saucers.

"What's wrong, Siobhan?" he asked.

"Nothing…nothing… It's just that, well, I don't know what it means. Licensed Victuallers."

"It means publicans, landlords. They have a licence to sell beer and wine and spirits. Every year, we have a dinner. I always went on my own before, but I would like you to come with me this time. What do you say?"

"If it's what you want, Charlie, then I will go with you," was all she could say.

"Good. I'm off out now. Business you know."

Siobhan sat back in her chair for a while. A wry smile came across her face as she thought of her Pa. What would he make of it? His Siobhan going to a big dinner on the arm of a rich man. She was sure he was rich. He was the richest man she knew, anyway.

Charlie bought her a sparkly necklace and an evening dress in a beautiful emerald green silk. He gave her a mink stole which he said had been his mother's. They travelled to the Town Hall in a taxi. She listened to the speeches without understanding much of what was said, but she laughed when Charlie laughed and clapped when everyone else did. Siobhan attracted admiring glances from the men all night. Charlie was elated; the wine had put him, quite literally, in high spirits. Siobhan laughed with a little tinkling bell laugh. She was the 'Belle of the Ball.'

Once they were back at the Threlfalls, Siobhan lifted the kettle to make some tea. Charlie took it from her hand and set it back down. He took her hand and kissed it. Without a word, they walked upstairs, taking the grand staircase. It was a mark of the change in their relationship. The back staircase was not fitting for tonight.

Next morning, as soon as Charlie went into his bathroom, Siobhan changed the sheets. She didn't want Charlie to see what wasn't there.

* * * *

Tom Hicks was far from pleased about Siobhan working behind the bar. He didn't like change, and he didn't like women. Tom acknowledged inwardly that he didn't like very much really. What was Charlie thinking of? There had never been a woman behind the bar of the Threlfalls before. They managed alright, even on busy nights. He just didn't see the point. As far as Tom could see, it would only lead to trouble. This young colleen had wormed her way in somehow, and the boss had lost his marbles. True enough, the place looked a lot better for her cleaning. There had even been one or two comments from the customers about the shiny pumps and clean ashtrays. He felt degraded when Charlie told him she was to work at the best room end of the bar, and that he, Tom, who had worked there for years, was to stay at the tap room end and collect all the glasses.

"Whatever you say, Charlie. You're the boss," was all that Tom could bring himself to say.

It hadn't been too bad when she stayed in the kitchen during opening times. When he took the glasses through for washing she was always smiling. Tom told himself he had nothing against her personally. He had always admired Charlie's business mind, but Tom just couldn't see the sense in this. The boss hadn't seen what was happening with Siobhan. She was different to other women, and the boss had been too close to see his own nose. She had made herself fit in. Her whole character changed when he bought her those clothes. She was captivating, and the boss had been captivated. She was too clever for Charlie, and that was saying something. Tom admired the way Charlie never gave away any secrets, or anything else for that matter, but he sold plenty of stuff. He smiled to himself. The fire escape hadn't been built for any safety reasons. It was the goods in and goods out route. Tom was clever enough to keep up the pretence of not knowing about such goings on. The only time he went in the yard was when the draymen brought the beer.

Now there was a sight worth seeing. He never tired of the draymen's visits, the powerful horses, the smart Tetley livery of red and gold. They clattered into the yard on Tuesdays and Fridays, delivering the heavy wooden barrels, taking away the empties that Tom had stacked in the corner. If he could have any job in the world, he would be a Tetley's drayman. Sitting up high on the seat, leather reins in his gloved hands, acknowledging the admiration of all who saw him. It was all a dream, though; it would never happen. The other goods usually arrived on a Wednesday. Not every week, but it would be shortly after the boss had been to Manchester for the day. Tom likened himself to a brass monkey. See all, hear all, say nowt. The second, lesser known part of the saying applied to him, too, he acknowledged with pride. He liked to say it to himself. If ever tha' does owt fo' nowt, allus do it fo' thissen.

Tom Hicks knew for a fact he would never like Siobhan. He didn't want to like her; he would not be tricked into her web. He could leave, of course, but why should he? At first Tom had thought she wouldn't last, that the boss would wise up, and things would get back to how they were. But there had been a change of atmosphere after he took her to that dinner. Nothing you could put your finger on; it was the way they reacted together. Stood a little closer to each other. Tom had known for some time that she was pregnant. It was Charlie who had the shock when she told him. Tom had arrived for work to see a white faced Charlie standing behind the bar.

"What's up, boss?"

There was a pause before Charlie answered. He was staring straight ahead with his eyes unfocussed.

"It's Siobhan. She's expecting."

Tom grinned.

Charlie stared at him blankly. "Did you know? Did she tell you?"

"Course not, boss, I just guessed."

Charlie was speechless.

Tom hoped Charlie was going to say he would get rid of her and the baby, but he didn't. Charlie's face burst into a huge grin, confirming to Tom that all women were trouble.

The awkward silence lasted only a few seconds.

"Come and have a drink with me, Tom, I'm going to be a dad."

Chapter Three

George Hanson was content with his life. His semi-detached house in a pleasant suburb of Sheffield was all paid for thanks to his parents' will. He had taken it for granted that he would inherit from them and that was exactly what happened. His neat appearance was vital to him. He polished his glasses. He polished his shoes. Beatrice made sure he had a clean white shirt every day, and his trousers were pressed to a knife's edge. He manicured his nails every Saturday morning and was forever washing his hands.

"Cleanliness is next to Godliness" was his mantra. His job in the offices at Sheffield City Council would eventually give him a good pension. His position as churchwarden at St Peter's ensured, in his eyes, that he was regarded as a well-respected member of the community.

He had a pretty wife and a beautiful daughter. The very thought of Beatrice and Pauline made him smile. They were so alike with their red hair and green eyes. Their smiles would melt any heart. It was true that Beatrice complained a lot about her health, but he didn't take much notice. Pauline was sixteen now. Her school uniform made her look younger, but there were obvious changes to her body that had not escaped his eyes. She had a trim little waistline and her gymslip was struggling to contain her growing breasts. The thought caused a stir in his groin. He ignored the feeling and enjoyed it at the same time. He smiled, but didn't know why.

Pauline was doing well at the City High School. She passed the entrance examination and had been awarded a grant, giving her the best of education without it costing George a penny. This was her final year, and he was expecting her to get good grades in her School Certificate.

It was all something of a nuisance when Beatrice started to have women's troubles. He hadn't believed her at first. He had heard about women saying they had such aches and pains when really what they meant was they didn't want sex. But then Beatrice had gone to see Doctor Jenkinson, and he had sent her straight to the hospital.

* * * *

Pauline knew her mother was really ill this time. It wasn't like her to take to her bed during the day. After the second hospital appointment, she heard her parents talking late into the night. Then she heard her mother sobbing. The tone of the voices seemed to change, and the talking became arguing. She had never heard them argue before. Never.

"I can't tell her, George. You must do it. For once in your life, you must do something you don't want to do. I simply can't. Neither of you have ever believed me when I've been ill before."

"For Christ's sake, Beatrice. How can I tell her?"

Pauline had never heard her father swear before either.

That was just two months ago, and now her mother was dead. No one was surprised when Pauline arrived at school in floods of tears. She had been absent the day before, attending her mother's funeral. Two of her classmates put their arms around her shoulders; another stood in front of her and held her hands tightly. Her teacher asked if she would like to go home. Pauline could only shake her head. Her thick red hair tumbled around her shoulders and face. She had not plaited it as she usually did. Her eyes were swollen, hiding their gentle, green beauty. They assumed she was crying because of her bereavement, but they were wrong. Pauline had not shed a tear either before or during the funeral. She had listened to the vicar's platitudes with increasing anger. Sitting at the front of the little church next to her father, Pauline was aware that the pews behind them were full. More people stood at the back.

"Her pain bravely borne," he droned on.

The vicar hadn't lived with her these past two months. It wasn't as if he didn't know her mother. In the end, it was her mother who told her she was dying. She had been a hypochondriac all her life and appeared triumphant when diagnosed with cancer. She had suffered her pain with a martyr's air, saving her vitriol for Pauline and her father. Mrs Beatrice Hanson was cheerful and compliant with the nurses and doctors who attended the house, then, as the door shut behind them, she turned into a screaming harridan.

"A blessed release…" he went on.

Well, that bit was right. It was a release for Pauline and her father. Father, of course, had rose-tinted glasses when it came to mother. He would see no wrong in her, simply because he didn't want to.

Her mother's illness, her death and funeral all seemed distant now, even though it was only yesterday. It was as if all that had happened to someone else.

She wasn't crying from grief at school next day. Pauline was crying because after the funeral her father had raped her. The burning pain inside her navy blue knickers wouldn't go away. The shame gave a physical pain deep in her gut. She felt sick. The one person in the world whom she should have been able to trust had raped her. When he crept into her bed that night, she had thought it was to cuddle and comfort her. He had curved his body around her back. She felt his breath on the nape of her neck. The violence and suddenness of the rape had taken her completely by surprise. He pulled up her nightdress. In a second, the comforting closeness had gone, and he was inside her. Her body went rigid with shock. The overwhelming strength of his grip around her with one arm, the other hand across her mouth, made it impossible for her to escape or even scream. She tried to bite his hand. He thrust himself deeper into her virgin flesh, her struggles ignored by him and unknown by any other.

"Stay there," was all he said as he left her room. Her ordeal left her distraught and disorientated. She was in pain. She heard him go to the bathroom and turn on the bath taps. She heard him washing, the water splashing around as he soaped and rinsed his body. Pauline hated her father in a way she could never have thought possible. She despised the air he breathed. Using the cuff of her nightdress, she rubbed the nape of her neck, trying to take away the now imagined draught of his breath. He came out of the bathroom humming one of the hymns that had been sung at the funeral. Pauline's every muscle was tense with fear.

He opened her bedroom door just enough to put his hand around the frame and turn on the light.

"You can go into the bathroom now if you wish. I'm going to bed. Goodnight."

As she heard his bedroom door shut, Pauline grabbed her dressing gown and ran into the bathroom. She turned on the hot tap of the bath. Wiping the condensation from the mirror over the sink, she cried at her reflection. The tear stained swollen face that looked back at her sobbed uncontrollably. She threw cold water over her face, but the contorted features still looked back.

The bathwater was hot. Too hot. She scrubbed her body with a nailbrush to scrub away the shame. The horror of it all. The burning pain inside her filled her with irrational self-loathing. Her tears fell into the water. When the water cooled she turned on the hot tap to maintain the scalding temperature. Her skin was bright pink; she felt dizzy. She stood up and stumbled, almost in a faint, grabbing the edge of the sink to steady herself. Reaching for a towel, she changed her mind and threw it on the floor. She could not bear to dry herself on the towels her father had used. It was bad enough that she had to use the same bath. She tied her dressing gown around herself tightly and returned to her room. Her virgin blood was on the sheets.

* * * *

Siobhan was delighted when Charlie asked the taxi driver to take them to the front door. She wanted Susan to have a grand entrance, not bustled in past the barrels in the back yard. Siobhan couldn't express her feelings; motherhood had transformed her, she saw the world through different eyes. She felt like a queen as she stepped out onto the pavement, looking up at the grandeur of her home. Charlie paid the taxi driver, and was getting the door keys out of his jacket when he turned and saw the expression on Siobhan's face. He, too, was enjoying the moment. Putting on a grand, deep voice, he said, "Mr and Mrs Charles

Fletcher arrive at the Threlfalls Hotel, Briggate, Leeds, with their baby daughter, Susan Joanne."

With Susan asleep in her arms, Siobhan looked at Charlie and smiled. "There are three of us now, Charlie. We are a family."

Charlie unlocked the door and then locked it again behind them. It was five o'clock. The bar wouldn't be open for an hour, time enough to have a cuppa and get settled in before opening time.

"The regulars are looking forward to seeing you in the bar tonight, love."

"Tonight?" There was a mixture of surprise and fear in her voice. She hadn't thought about work.

Susan stirred.

"She'll be hungry, Charlie. I need to feed her."

"You sit there in your chair, love. I'll make us a pot of tea."

Susan sucked greedily at Siobhan's breast. She was a strong baby, a good weight too, at eight pounds two ounces. Charlie and Siobhan were happy beyond words. Replete with her mother's milk, Susan fell asleep.

"I'll take her upstairs now," Siobhan said.

"I'll come with you, love. I want to show you Susan's nursery. Billy made a right good job of it."

They went up the main staircase and into Siobhan's old room. She looked all around. The room had been transformed into a bright and pretty nursery. Pink and white wallpaper, pink curtains, even a pink carpet. A cot had replaced the old bed. There was a chest of drawers and a nursing chair for Siobhan. Charlie had thought of everything.

She put Susan down in the cot, covering her gently with a blanket. As Siobhan sat down, Charlie came over and kissed her head. They held hands, looking at each other, and then at their daughter, in a comfortable silence.

Charlie checked his watch. "We'll have to get a move on, love. What are you wearing tonight?"

"Charlie, I can't come down and leave Susan here on her own." There was anxiety in her voice.

"B-but why not?" He asked, genuinely puzzled. "She's asleep. What are you worried about?" The quizzical look on his face made Siobhan want to smile, but at the same time she knew it wouldn't be a good idea. Charlie really thought she would leave Susan up here on her own.

"And what if she wakes up and cries?"

"So you're going to sit up here, just in case she cries." His voice was a mixture of annoyance and incredulity. He really hadn't planned on this. Siobhan was just staring at him.

"Billy and Johnny and the others are expecting you," he continued. "I told Tom you would be working tonight. We've been run off our feet behind the bar these last few days."

Siobhan was careful to keep her voice calm. "Billy and Johnny have kids. They will understand, Charlie."

The quiet determination on her face and in her voice told Charlie there was no point in arguing. Not tonight anyway. There was no time. He turned on his heel, slamming the door behind him. As he walked quickly away, he heard Susan cry. The sound caused his step to falter. His cheeks flushed with the knowledge that Siobhan was right, and he was wrong.

Siobhan lifted Susan from the cot. Silent tears fell as she hummed the Irish lullaby of her childhood. Siobhan held her baby tightly to her chest, shifting her weight from one foot to the other in rhythm to her humming. She knew that women sometimes cried after they had a baby, even if there was no reason for it. She had been shaken by Charlie's way of thinking. He had done so much. This little room was proof of how he loved Susan. The chest of drawers was brimming with clothes and nappies for her. Everything was brand new. She thought of the hovel she had lived in in Ireland. The thought of her mother brought fresh tears. How she would love to show Susan to her mother…and to Mrs McMahon…but there are some things you just can't have, she told herself. She dried her tears on the hem of Susan's shawl, saying aloud, "Look around you, Siobhan. See how lucky you are." She sat down in the brand new nursing chair, holding her sleeping baby.

Charlie was still annoyed as he opened the doors of the Threlfalls. It was the first time Siobhan had gone against his wishes. That determined look on her face and his own temper troubled him. He was baffled by the whole thing. He'd spent all this money on kitting out the nursery for Susan. He had done it all for Susan. He pushed the big brass bolts down to anchor the doors open. The sun shone in, the shadows of Johnny and Billy cast across the coconut doormat as Charlie stood up.

"Evenin', Billy. Johnny."

"Evenin', Charlie," they chorused.

Charlie knew they would ask about Siobhan and was dreading it. He would have to tell them she wouldn't be in the bar tonight.

"Where's t'lovely wife o' your'n, Charlie?" Johnny asked.

"Sorry, lads, she won't be down tonight. Settling in and all that. Tomorrow. She'll be here tomorrow. You'll have to wait another day, lads."

"Nay, Charlie." It was Billy who spoke now. "Tha's expectin' a lot o' t'lass."

Charlie pulled their pints without further comment. Siobhan had been right again; they did understand. Better than he did, it seemed. Charlie shifted the conversation to the safer subject of football. He was back in his role as publican. Tom would be in soon, and Alf. They would ask about Siobhan and Susan. He would get the subject out of the way as quickly as possible.

In fact, neither Alf nor Tom asked. In a way, it didn't surprise Charlie. Alf was more of a listener. He had an uncanny way of getting people to chat of their own accord. Whereas Tom never asked anything; he just did his job as if nothing else existed. Charlie told them both that Siobhan would be working tomorrow night. If he hadn't, the subject would have lingered in the air like an unspoken lie. As it turned out, the bar wasn't busy. He could have left it to Tom and gone upstairs to check on Susan and Siobhan. But he didn't, preferring instead to stay in his bar. It gave him the chance to hatch a plan in his mind. He would put the pram in the passageway at the back of the bar. That way Siobhan would be able to work in the bar and listen for Susan at the same time.

Siobhan woke with a start. She'd slept in the nursing chair with Susan in her arms. She stood up stiffly and gently put her baby in the cot. Leaving the door of the nursery open, she crossed the landing into the bedroom. It was only nine o'clock, but she felt so very tired, her legs were like lead weights. She put on her nightdress, checked Susan was asleep, and that the doors were wide open. She would hear Susan if she cried. Siobhan was asleep in seconds.

By the time the last customers had left, Charlie was getting quite excited about his plan to get Siobhan working again. He bounced up the back staircase with the good news, all signs of his earlier irritability gone, only to find his wife and daughter asleep. It would have to wait until morning. He went downstairs and put on his jacket. He didn't mean to bang the door as he went out. It crossed his mind that the noise may have woken Susan.

Siobhan woke at 11:30, a few seconds later, as Susan stirred. Only a mother would hear the tiny cry. Her ears tuned to her baby. Even if Charlie had been there, he wouldn't have heard her. Siobhan fed Susan, changed her nappy and cuddled her. She put her back in the cot, but Susan wouldn't settle. Her little cry pulled at Siobhan's heart. She couldn't bear to hear it, such was her love for her baby. She picked her up and sang to her. She walked up and down the landing, trying to soothe her, but she cried and cried. Half an hour passed; Siobhan was starting to worry when Susan's little body relaxed as she fell asleep. She put her in the beautiful big pram on the landing, rocking it gently. She could hear Charlie was back already; he was in the kitchen. He had only been out for an hour. Siobhan was usually asleep when he came in from his business. She heard his footsteps on the stairs. Siobhan had an idea, and as he came onto the landing, she greeted him with a smile. Charlie was smiling too. They spoke simultaneously.

"I've had an idea." They laughed together.

Siobhan put her finger to her lips. "Shhh." She signalled for them to go to their bedroom. "You first," she said. "You tell your idea first, Charlie."

"Okay," he said. "It's this." Charlie sounded awkward, as if he was suddenly afraid that Siobhan might not like his brilliant idea. He took a deep breath. "If I take the pram downstairs…"

Siobhan interrupted. "I could work in the bar and listen for Susan at the same time."

"Yes…yes, that's it. How did you know what I was going to say?"

"Because I had the same idea, Charlie."

They laughed as they threw their arms around each other. They knew everything was going to be all right.

Chapter Four

Florrie Bell was born and bred in Leeds. A Loiner. One of twelve children, the only one who had never married. She had countless nieces and nephews, and they all had kids too, but it was the young girl next door who had really got to her.

Number 16 Vine Street had been empty for a while when a van pulled up one afternoon. A man in his forties and a teenage girl unloaded a few pieces of furniture and some boxes. There were no smiles between them, and he was gone within half an hour. Curtains twitched, tongues wagged, and fingers pointed.

Florrie put the kettle on and set a tea tray for two with a plate of freshly baked buns. She combed her tightly permed hair and straightened her wraparound apron. Kicking the front door shut behind her, she carried the tray to number 16. The door opened as she approached. Big, tear filled eyes looked at Florrie, then looked up and down the empty street.

"Thought you might like a cuppa, love."

The eyes looked back at her, lips sealed together tightly, controlling the sobs that would escape if she tried to speak.

"I'm Florrie Bell. I live next door." Florrie raised the tea tray up a little, her short, fat arms pushing the sides of her ample bosom, making wrinkles appear right up to her neck. The girl stood to one side and Florrie made her way to the kitchen.

The terraced houses of Vine Street were like thousands of others in Leeds. Like those of any northern industrial town. The staircase was straight ahead of the front door. The parlour to the left and the kitchen behind. The girl followed.

"I'm Pauline...Pauline Hanson...I'm sorry...There is only one chair."

Florrie sat down gratefully on the wooden seat. "Thanks, love. Me legs are older than the rest o' me, I swear they are. 'Ave a bun or two, yer look like yer need feedin'. I made 'em this mornin'. Don't know why I bake so much. Young Doctor Ramsey says me legs are bad 'cos they carry too much o' me about all o' time." Florrie chuckled at her own joke. "You on yer own, love?"

Pauline sipped the tea gratefully. "Yes, I'll be on my own. That was my father who dropped me off. He'll not be back." Pauline's voice trailed away.

"Me, too," said Florrie, chuckling again. "I mean, I'm on me own, like. I'm not meanin' I'll not be back."

Pauline smiled weakly. They ate the buns and drank the tea.

Florrie prattled on. "I was born next door, yer know. One o' twelve. It were a right squash 'til t'older ones started to go. The girls into service an' boys ter war. Our Ernie and Jim never came back, o' course. Our Mam were sad forever after that. T'others all wed, 'cept me, so when Mam an' Dad passed on, well, I were just on me own, like, so that's where I am."

"Miss Bell..." Pauline started.

"Florrie. You must call me Florrie. I want none of that Miss Bell Stuff. I get that from me piano kids. Did I tell you I teach t' piano?" Florrie didn't wait for a reply. "Well, I do. So you'll see t' kids comin' and goin' fo' t' lessons. Now what were you goin' ter say?"

"I was going to ask you where I am…I mean…I don't know. Father says I must live here now."

Florrie Bell wasn't often lost for words. In fact, she couldn't remember ever being lost for words before. It was a full ten seconds before she whispered,

"Dear God, child. Whatever has happened?" As she spoke, Florrie knew the reason. The oldest reason in the world. This girl was expectin'.

Pauline burst into tears that wouldn't stop.

Florrie stood up and put her arms around her. She tried to get her to sit down, but Pauline clung on to her as if her life depended upon it. Leaving the tea things behind, Florrie guided her out of the front door, and they went to number 14 together. Florrie's cosy kitchen with its coal fire was a world apart from the cold bare house next door.

"Sit you down in that rocking chair, love. You'll stay 'ere tonight. You're not sleeping in that cold, damp place in your condition, not while I've got breath in me body."

Pauline's baby was born in Leeds General Infirmary on the 14th of August, 1948. Florrie was the only visitor. The other mothers and the nurses assumed this elderly lady was Pauline's grandmother. No one talked to Pauline much. The lack of a wedding ring erected an invisible social barrier. A young Irish woman in the bed opposite had smiled at her once, but she was too busy with her daughter, or asleep, to talk to anyone. Pauline didn't care. She only had eyes for her baby, with his head of red hair to match her own. It was good to see Florrie. No one else would come. No one else knew she was here, and Florrie always made her want to smile, the way she chattered on.

"A pram's no good ter me. It's as old as t'ills, but better than no pram at all. It belonged ter one o' me nieces. 'Er kids are all grown up now. You have it, love, and you're welcome."

"Thanks so much, Florrie. You're like my Fairy Godmother." The two of them laughed together. "Like I told you, Florrie, I'm going to call him James Ernest, after your brothers who died in the first war." When Pauline first told Florrie she would call her baby Florence Ann if it were a girl, and James Ernest, after Florrie's brothers, if it were a boy, Florrie had been speechless. "It's what I want to do. You have been so kind."

"Why, love? Why would you do that? I mean it's lovely of yer, but what about yer family? Is there no one you want ter name t'babby after?" As she spoke, Florrie realised she was treading on thin ice. Pauline's Dad was alive because he had brought her to Vine Street. As Pauline had predicted, he never came again, nor did anyone else, and she never spoke of anyone else either. Tears filled Pauline's eyes momentarily. Florrie saw them, and saw how quickly Pauline controlled them.

"No, Florrie. There is no one." There was steel in her voice. "He chose to get rid of me. Why would I want to remind myself of him? My baby is my future, not part of the past. All that's gone, and good riddance."

"Are you sure, lass?" Florrie's voice was almost a whisper.

"I'm sure, Florrie. Quite sure."

Three days later, Pauline and her baby took the short bus ride from the infirmary to Vine Street. Curtains twitched up and down the street as she unlocked the door of number

16 and let herself in. Pauline loosened the shawl from the sleeping baby, then tucked it around him as she gently lay him down in the pram. The pram was old, it was true, but it was clean, and as Florrie had said, better than no pram at all. The spare bedroom in Florrie's house had been stacked high with odd pieces of furniture.

"I never like ter throw out good stuff," she had told Pauline. "I put things in 'ere that no one wants, and sooner or later I find a good 'ome forrit." They had spent an afternoon, before Jimmy was born, going through everything. Pauline asked about the door that led from her second bedroom into Florrie's spare room. It was bolted from both sides.

"It was when we were kids. T'old couple as lived in your 'ouse 'ad none, an' we was a bit pushed fer space, there bein' so many on us. Me Dad knocked it through when our Gertie were born. She were number eight if I remember rightly. It's bin locked up many a year now, lass, but I'm happy t'oppen my side if tha likes." They pulled and tugged the bolts on Florrie's side. When they finally gave way, they went round to Pauline's house. The bolts on her side were rusted and unwilling to move. Florrie went home again and returned with a bottle of sewing machine oil. She unscrewed the metal top and carefully poured a little oil on each of the bolts.

"We'll not stick fast at gettin' these ter shift. That we won't. Put t'kettle on lass. By the time we've 'ad a cuppa, this 'ere oil will 'ave loosened 'em up a bit."

Florrie was right. They drank their tea, then, with a bit of pushing and shoving, the door gave way. With a cloud of dust and old paint, the doorway between their houses opened.

"That's better," said Florrie. "Now we can shift this furniture into your place wi'out any nosy pokers seein' what we're doin'."

Pauline loved Florrie for her kindness. She also loved her because she rarely asked any questions. She imagined Florrie giving the neighbours short shrift if they said anything remotely unkind about her being unmarried and expecting. She was sure they would have said something. For her part, she always smiled and said hello if she passed anyone in the street. Most of them didn't reply, and if they did, it was in a way that didn't invite further conversation. There was never any hint that they would stop and chat, no pause in their footsteps.

Florrie was sad, even angry, to think that people could be so cruel. Pauline had been turned out by her family just because she had made a mistake, and her new neighbours judged her harshly. In many ways, Florrie Bell was ahead of her time. Maybe she didn't have much schooling or any of the advantages of the middle and upper classes, but she was a worldly woman for all that. An avid reader, and not just fiction, Florrie loved a good read. It could be a romantic or historical novel, travel books or an autobiography. She read the Yorkshire Post every day, particularly the foreign and political news. The crossword was saved for the evening. Her brothers and sisters had thought her odd. "Too bookish for a girl," they had said. She taught herself to read music and play the piano. A faded photograph of Florrie Bell in her cap and gown hung on the wall above the piano. Her students were mostly family, the children of her nephews and nieces. They didn't pay, but a few pupils from the high school still did. They came once a week and played their scales and simple pieces. One achieved a pass at grade five before giving up.

Pauline felt she had a lot to be happy about. The six weeks since Jimmy's birth had flown by. The tiny, helpless baby she had brought home on the bus was starting to smile and take notice of things around him. She rocked the pram with one hand and shook a rattle with the other. Jimmy turned his head to the sound. He had given her a new outlook on life. A new perspective. She could do anything for Jimmy. Anger and hatred for her father was pushed to the back of her mind. She blotted out the physical horrors of the rape. With a mixture of defiance, hatred and pleasure, she had written to her father and told him she no longer wanted anything from him. He could stop sending his money. She had cut all ties with Sheffield. There had been no response from her father directly.

A large envelope had arrived from a solicitor's office. When she was twenty-one, the house in Vine Street would be transferred into her name; meanwhile, she had no rent to pay. It wouldn't be easy, working nights at the bakery and looking after Jimmy during the day. Without Florrie's help, she wouldn't be able to do it. But then, without Florrie a lot of things would be different. She had given her most of the furniture that had helped turn number 16 into a home for Jimmy.

For her part, Florrie felt young again. She had a genuine affection for Pauline and little Jimmy. There was something about the girl. She was always polite, well mannered, but there was something not right. For all her steel, she was vulnerable somehow. Not surprising really.

But Florrie had a feeling there was more to it. 'None o' my business,' she thought. 'The lass'll tell me if she wants to.'

* * * *

Charmaine Fournier was born in Provence in the summer of 1948. Her parents were quite well off, not rich, but not poor either. They lived in a beautiful old rambling farmhouse. Jeanette and Anton had married in their late thirties; they were keen to have children, but it was four long years, with Jeanette's body clock ticking away, before Charmaine was born. Jeanette loved being pregnant, no morning sickness, no backaches, and a quick easy childbirth.

The midwife almost fainted as she lifted the little baby. She wrapped her in a blanket and handed her to her mother before calling the doctor to the room. Jeanette had wanted her baby to be born at home, but being an older first time mother she was advised to go to the hospital.

There was a lot of fussing and Anton was called in. Jeanette couldn't remember much after that, only that there was a lot of weeping. Jeanette and Anton wept for their daughter; she remembered the weeping going on for a long time. Charmaine was born with her feet turned inwards, almost at right angles to her legs.

They took their beautiful daughter to Paris to see all the paediatricians and orthopaedic specialists they could find. At the Hospital des Infants Malade, a paediatrician recommended Leeds General Infirmary and the wonderful work that was being pioneered there. He told them the surgeons in Leeds were her best chance of correcting her deformed ankles. Jeanette and Anton moved to Leeds with their three year old daughter in 1951. Anton spoke fluent

English and had gained the position of Head of Chemistry at Leeds University. It was a good career move, but that was no more than a coincidence. They moved because it meant their dear, crippled Charmaine would be treated at Leeds General Infirmary. The move wasn't easy for Jeanette; she didn't speak a word of English and, unlike her husband, had never travelled outside of her beloved Provence, except of course to Paris. She expected to be homesick and she was, but it gave Charmaine the best chance and that was all that mattered.

* * * *

Tom was unhappy, even for Tom. He didn't want to leave the Threlfalls. It suited him in every way, or it had before Siobhan came along. As he closed his front door and set off for work, the same question was going round in his head. Should he stay? Or leave?

He kicked a stone. A cloud of dust rose and fell onto his worn shoe. They had been shiny and black when he bought them. It crossed his mind that he ought to polish them to make them last longer. The thought passed. He kicked the stone every few paces as he walked into town.

Why should he, Tom Hicks, be forced out by a woman? If he left, where would he go?

He didn't like change. He only knew bar work, and another landlord would not be so easy going as Charlie. He liked Charlie. Well, not so much liked him as knew him. He was predictable. But then he had married the Irish girl, so maybe he wasn't so predictable after all. The problem was everyone else seemed to like her; she had an air about her. He found himself being left out of the conversations at the bar. She acted like she was interested in whatever the punters were talking about. Even football. She was a quick learner, too. No point denying it.

The solution came to him out of the blue. Tom stopped walking, and a smile spread over his face. It was so simple. He would pretend to like her; it wouldn't cost anything to be polite, and it was in his own interests. The stone rolled into the gutter. His step took on a lighter gait as he started to whistle. He arrived at work dead on time as usual, the way the boss liked it, feeling rather smug with himself.

A cheer went up in the bar, Billy and Johnnie cheering the loudest. Siobhan's smile was as beautiful as ever. Charlie was bursting with pride. All was well in Charlie Fletcher's world. His beautiful daughter was fast asleep in her pram, and his pretty wife was working behind the bar. Her tinkling laugh, which had captivated Charlie, completed his happiness. Tom Hicks tried to look miserable, but the atmosphere was infectious. He felt his lips curl into a smile, then checked himself. He had nothing to be happy about, did he? He hoped no one had noticed.

Siobhan loved the work, the chat, the smiles—the laughter. She was happy to be back. It had been hard during the latter stages of her pregnancy; she'd been worn out, not daring to tell Charlie how tired she felt, not even after they were married. Her first night back at work was wonderful. She had squeezed herself into the pale green dress; it was tight around the waist and a bit painful to her swollen breasts, but it was Charlie's favourite, so was worth a bit of discomfort. She wore lipstick and styled her hair the way Charlie liked it. She shone like a star.

"We keep tellin' 'im, yer know." It was Billy who spoke.

"Telling him what?" said Siobhan, not knowing whether she should ask or not. She had one eye on Charlie, trying to gauge his reaction.

"'Ow lucky 'e is." There were nods and mutterings of agreement from around the bar.

"I don't need you to tell me I've got the prettiest wife in Leeds, Billy Oldroyd." Charlie was smiling.

Siobhan smiled with relief and the laughter lifted the bar, along with the raised glasses.

Customers who had hardly spoken before were smiling and asking about Susan. They asked Siobhan how she was feeling. The compliments poured in. Susan slept. The evening was everything Siobhan hoped it would be. Everything would be all right now.

Susan stirred in her pram as Charlie was counting the bar takings at the kitchen table. Siobhan was washing the last few glasses. Susan's cry was a demand for food, and the noise was a relief to Siobhan. Her breasts were swollen with milk. Damp patches showed on her lovely dress as the milk leaked out. She was pretty sure Charlie hadn't noticed. She hoped not. He wouldn't like it.

Charlie walked over to the pram and lifted her out. She continued to cry as he handed her to Siobhan without a word. He felt a mixture of concern and annoyance. Concern that his daughter was unhappy; annoyed because he had lost count and would have to start again with the cashing up. He simply didn't like the racket. The suddenness of the silence as she took to Siobhan's breast was a liberation.

"Thank God for that." He said with a sigh, returning to the money. He finished counting and wrote the figures in a little black notebook. He stuffed the cash in his inside jacket pocket, the book in his hip pocket; kissed Siobhan on the forehead, put on his coat and hat, and was gone. Half an hour later, Susan was asleep in her cot, replete and warm. Siobhan was asleep as her head hit the pillow.

"Manchester today, love."

Siobhan was clearing away the breakfast dishes. "Oh?"

"What do you mean, 'Oh'?"

"I don't mean anything, Charlie."

"It sounded like a question." His words hung in the air waiting to be answered.

An accusation.

A fear crept over her, she knew it as the fear she still had for her father. Siobhan shuddered at the thought. "Didn't mean it that way. Honest, I didn't. I was just thinking what to cook for dinner, and now you won't be here. That's all, love."

He put his cup down, wiped the corners of his mouth, then stood up and walked towards her. Her head was down, so he didn't see the fear in her eyes as he paused before kissing her cheek.

"See you tonight, then. Tom can manage the lunchtime trade, but he will need your help tonight."

Siobhan sighed with relief as the door closed. Why had she been so scared? Had she imagined the irritation in his voice? Maybe. Maybe not. She knew her place, and the reason she had a place at all was because Charlie liked the way she worked. Even though he had married her, had said more than once that he loved her, and she believed him, she feared, deep down, there was a condition to the love. The condition that she was what Charlie wanted her to be. If she pleased him, he would love her. The more she loved her life, the more she feared losing it.

Siobhan knew about Charlie's visits to Manchester. Of course she did. It was on the train from Manchester that they had met. It didn't take her long to figure out that the Manchester visits were followed by a delivery to the back of the hotel. Siobhan even knew which day the van would come. The day before the delivery, Charlie would check with Tom that he would be able to manage the lunchtime trade alone. Siobhan had offered to help, but for some unknown reason, like an unwritten law, she never worked in the bar at lunchtime.

Charlie would be waiting, ready to take the chain and padlock off the high gates. A battered old brown van would come into the yard at about two o'clock. It was always the same driver, a big, muscular man. He needed to be. Charlie's little fat body wasn't designed to carry heavy boxes up a fire escape. They shook hands, and Charlie gave the man an envelope. As the van drove away, Charlie would shut the gates as quietly as he could, fasten up the chain and padlock, pulling on it twice to make sure it was secure.

Siobhan watched from the window of one of the twelve bedrooms. They were all furnished in that faded way that Siobhan's first room, now Susan's room, had been. The windows had not been cleaned for years, and Siobhan knew that if she stood back a little, she could not be seen from outside.

Charlie looked round the yard, then up at the back of the hotel, and then he would climb the steps of the fire escape, locking the door to the ballroom behind him. He would be in there for the rest of the afternoon, shuffling his boxes about. Siobhan heard all this, but it never entered her head to ask if he needed help. She instinctively knew not to ask. The same way she would not ask what Charlie did every night after closing time. The strange noises had frightened her at first. She thought she was alone in the hotel after Charlie had gone out. Slowly, she had put it together. Charlie's customers came back to the hotel with him to collect their black market goods.

"For Christ's sake, Tom, where is she?"

"Dunno, boss. Upstairs, I think."

Charlie took his coat off and started serving from his step behind the bar. The customers were two deep and getting impatient. There was no time to ask Tom any more. Charlie just had to get on with serving.

"Where's your lovely wife?" It was Billy Oldroyd who asked.

"I'd like to know that myself." Charlie replied. Inside, he was boiling with rage. The customers loved her and Billy was one of her biggest fans. Charlie couldn't say what he would have liked to have said. As he worked, his temper increased. How could she let him down? This was the first time he had been to Manchester since Susan was born and apart from that first night, everything had worked well. Susan had slept in the pram in the passageway and Siobhan had worked in the bar. It was a full hour before it quietened down.

"It was the baby, boss," said Tom. "Just as Alf came in. Siobhan was all dressed up and looking lovely, like she does. Then, when Alf came in, the baby starts up. What with Alf being a copper and all, Siobhan said she had to go. Don't think Alf heard the baby, but you never know with him. Anyway, Siobhan went. I think she took the baby upstairs, but I've not seen her since."

Charlie was puzzled by it all. For a start, Tom seemed happy to talk about Siobhan, and in a kindly way at that. Tom didn't usually talk much at all.

At the first lull in serving, Charlie left the bar and went through to the kitchen, passing the empty pram on the way. He heard the all too familiar crying as he reached the stairs. He winced involuntarily at the noise which increased in volume as he approached Susan's bedroom.

"I don't know what's wrong with her, Charlie. She's been crying for hours." Siobhan looked flustered. She was red in the face, her hair dishevelled. Anyone would think *she* had been crying, Charlie thought. He didn't like what he saw or heard. He turned on his heels and went back to the bar. There was nothing else to be done.

When the back door slammed that night and Siobhan knew Charlie had gone out, she crept downstairs. Susan was sleeping at last and the Threlfalls fell silent. Tom had washed all the glasses. Everything was neat and tidy. Siobhan made her way through the kitchen to the bar. No need to turn on any lights. She took a glass from the overhead rack and poured herself a glass of port. She sipped it slowly, savouring the warmth of the sweet, rich flavour. She washed the glass and silently put it back on the shelf.

Chapter Five

September 1952

Susan had looked forward to her first day at school so much that the reality was going to be a disappointment. No one had told her it was like this. She became increasingly bad tempered. The teacher, Miss Hughes, stood in front of the blackboard. Her brown curly hair had some grey bits at the front; maybe it was all the dust from the chalk that had flown round and settled on her head. Susan decided Miss Hughes was too little to be a teacher, lots smaller than Mummy anyway. She was talking about milk and playtime, and taking turns to ring the bell. They would only be allowed to use pencils, and not ink, in the first year. Susan wasn't interested. Her pencil rested in a little groove next to the inkwell. She picked it up and turned it round and round in her fingers. Mummy and Daddy said school would be fun and she would make lots of friends. How was she supposed to do that? Miss Hughes had made her sit next to a *boy.* She wanted to go home and tell Mummy and Daddy that they were liars, and that school was horrible. She looked round the classroom. The double desks with attached seats were arranged in rows, three across the room and five deep. Susan was right in the middle. Her desk was old and tatty with scratches and ink stains all over it. She wondered how the desks got so inky when they only used pencils. There was a horrible smell too, like mashed potato and plasticine mixed together. Some of the other children had been crying; their faces were all red and puffy. The girl in front of her was shaking as if she was still crying, but wasn't making any noise. She had really pale blonde hair in long, long plaits with red ribbons tied right through them into bows at the bottom. Susan had to lean forward to see the bows because the plaits were so long.

When she dropped her pencil, Susan had to crawl under her desk to retrieve it. That was when she saw the shiny red boots. When she sat down again, her face was bright red with jealousy. Everything Susan wore that day was brand new, from her vest to her gabardine coat hanging in the cloakroom, but what she really wanted right now was some shiny red boots. She wished she had long blonde plaits too, instead of stupid brown curls.

Miss Hughes wrote the numbers one to ten on the blackboard. They had to repeat everything she said, and then were given an exercise book with their names written carefully on the front. They had to copy the numbers from the blackboard. The boy sitting next to Susan did it really quickly and neatly. That annoyed her too. Things were made worse when *he* was chosen to ring the bell, announcing playtime. Susan asked the girl with the plaits and boots if she would play with her, but she didn't answer, she sat at her desk and just stared at her.

"Out you go, Susan. Playtime." Miss Hughes patted Susan on the head. "Come on, Charmaine, let me hold your hand." It was all too much for Susan. She stamped out of the room. Blonde plaits. Red boots. Teacher's favourite, and now a beautiful name. It just wasn't fair. Susan sat on a bench in the playground, tears of rage welling up in her eyes. She saw Miss Hughes open the door as wide as she could while still holding Charmaine's hand. Susan felt a shudder go right through her; there was something wrong with

Charmaine's feet. Her toes pointed inwards and her ankles were sort of floppy.

Susan went over for a closer look.

"Susan," said Miss Hughes. "This is Charmaine. Would you like to hold her other hand?"

Susan was speechless. Charmaine smiled at Susan as she took her hand. Susan smiled back.

"Charmaine is French, Susan. She can't speak any English, and so it's very hard for her."

Susan held Charmaine's hand tightly. Susan had never heard of anyone who couldn't speak English, and she hadn't met a girl who couldn't walk properly either.

"How did it go, Princess?" Charlie held his arms wide as Susan came in the kitchen.

"It was okay." She ignored her daddy's outstretched arms and climbed onto Siobhan's armchair.

"Only okay? Did you make any friends?"

"Sort of."

Charlie looked to Siobhan. It was obvious he had been hoping for a more enthusiastic response.

"She's been telling me on the way home she has a friend called Charmaine, but she's French and doesn't know how to talk or walk. I think she means she can't speak English. Not sure what she means about not walking." Siobhan pursed her lips and shrugged her shoulders, indicating to Charlie that was all she knew.

"That's right, Daddy. She wears shiny red boots that hold her feet on."

Siobhan handed her a plate of jam sandwiches.

"Anything else?" Charlie asked.

Susan thought for a while. "I sit next to a boy called Jimmy. He's clever." Susan didn't want to talk to her parents about school. She was still annoyed with them for telling her it was good fun. "I don't like school. If it wasn't for Charmaine, I wouldn't go again."

"Is that so, missy?" Siobhan smiled as she spoke. "Well, all I can say is thank goodness for Charmaine."

Charlie and Siobhan laughed together. Susan didn't know what they found so funny. They were laughing at her and she hated it. She ate her sandwiches in silence, telling herself she wasn't going to tell Mummy or Daddy anything else about school, ever.

* * * *

"Hurry up. The party starts in half an hour." Susan heard the irritation in her mother's voice, but she would not be hurried. It was the middle of the summer holidays, but the party invitations still kept coming from her school friends. Susan had wanted to have her own party today. After all, it was her birthday, but Mummy and Daddy said they were too busy on Saturdays, so she would have to have her party the next day. She had tantrums, cried and pleaded, but it was no use. Then the invitation to Jimmy Fletcher's party arrived, so she stopped making a fuss and settled for having her fifth birthday party on Sunday. There had been several discussions between mother and daughter over the past week, all related to Susan's clothes. It was a big problem for a five year old. If only she didn't have so many dresses...

"That's the problem, Mummy. I have too many dresses to choose from." Siobhan sighed.

"Did you hear that, Charlie? This is all your fault."

"My fault! Now, how do you make that out?" Charlie was genuinely incredulous.

"Daddy…look at me."

"Okay," said Charlie. "I'm listening. Why is it my fault?"

"You bought me too many dresses, Daddy. If I only had one, there wouldn't be a problem."

As if he could hardly believe what he was hearing, his face flushed with exasperation. "Just put that pink one on, Susan."

Susan turned to her mother. "Which one do *you* like best, Mummy?" Susan asked, even though she knew the answer.

"I like the blue one, Susan, you know I do," Siobhan said with a sigh.

Susan put her right hand under her chin, her left hand supporting her arm at the elbow, in mock thought. "You are both quite wrong. This is the best one." She grabbed the lemon one with the lace trim and pearl buttons.

"Just put it on, then." Siobhan knew she sounded cross, but not nearly so cross as she felt. She struggled to control her anger. If she was angry with Susan, Charlie would be angry with her, saying Susan was only a little girl. If she was late to work in the bar, Charlie would be angry with her. "I'm going to be late back with all this deciding what to wear palaver. Your daddy needs me to work this afternoon. I will have to drop you off at Jimmy's, and pick you up when the party finishes. Have you got the present?"

Charlie left them to it and went to help Tom. Five minutes later, Susan appeared at the back of the bar.

"Look at me." She twirled around and curtseyed for him, smiling her very cutest smile.

"Very pretty, Princess." Charlie smiled and put his hand out to pat her head.

"Mind my hair, Daddy. I spent ages brushing it."

Charlie turned to Siobhan. "Where is the bloody party, anyway?"

"Vine Street. I'll be back as soon as I can." They walked through the bar and out into Briggate. Twenty minutes later, Siobhan was back at The Threlfalls. Charlie's mood was restored to that of the convivial landlord. Tom worked in his usual quiet way. Siobhan had been working Saturday lunchtimes for about a year. Trade was usually brisk due to the nearby market. There had been a crowd in at opening time, but now there were just four people in the bar.

Siobhan smiled at the customers, but behind the smile she felt annoyed. Mrs Hanson had invited her to stay for the party. Siobhan was trying to recall where she could have met Jimmy's mother before. She just couldn't place her, no matter how she tried. How could she forget someone with such remarkable red hair? Mrs Hanson had recognised her though, and no doubt about it.

* * * *

Charlie preferred not to think too much about the way things had turned out. When the bar was quiet like this, he had too much time to ponder. His mind would go wandering of its own accord. Charlie didn't know why, but such thoughts always left him feeling fed up with himself. He had a very pretty wife. She had kept her neat little figure after

Susan was born. She cooked and cleaned, never asking for anything. He was the envy of every man he knew, especially when they went to the Licensed Victuallers Dinner each year. She warmed his bed, no complaints there. He didn't fancy anyone else; he had never so much as looked at another woman. So why was he always waiting for her to put a foot wrong? Was she too good to be true? They argued, of course, but no one ever saw that, so it didn't count.

Siobhan could be very annoying. He looked over towards her. She was smiling as usual. He noticed her face was flushed from rushing back from Vine Street. His thoughts wandered to his daughter. She was five today. The presents had been stacked high in the kitchen that morning. A doll's pram with a porcelain doll had been her big present. Then there were all the doll's clothes, and a doll's baby bath. It didn't seem so long since he had been in Lavells buying all this stuff for Susan.

Five years had passed. Susan had her mother's dark hair and blue eyes; the prettiest little girl he had ever seen. The likeness was there for all to see. Not that he had taken much notice of children before Susan was born. Even now, it was very much a case of 'your own is different'. He didn't like children, as a rule. He didn't know how to talk to them. Susan knew how to talk to him alright. That was a big part of the puzzle. How could a child turn him into such a fool? She was the only one who had ever told him what to do. What was even worse, he did everything she asked of him. He had even cleared out the old ballroom for her party. Siobhan had done all the cleaning, of course, and to be fair, there wasn't that much stuff up there to shift. Not like in the good old days when Charlie had his little schemes and contacts. That was all gone now. Even rationing was finished. The war had been good to him.

Other opportunities had come by, though.

The thought cheered him; an involuntary smile crept across his face just as Siobhan looked at him. She smiled back. *Silly woman thinks I'm smiling at her.*

The goods he dealt with these days didn't take up so much space. Good things come in small packages. That was what Arnold said. Charlie liked to think of Arnold as his supplier. It had a ring to it. Better than 'thief', anyway. Arnold had once called Charlie a facilitator. Charlie didn't know what that meant, so he went to the library and looked it up in a dictionary. It said, 'Somebody enabling something to happen'. He liked that. Better than being a fence, anyway. 'Charlie Fletcher, facilitator.' It had all fitted together very smoothly in the end. When the black market goods had run their day, the Manchester connections had produced Arnold. Funny thing was, Charlie didn't know anything about Arnold. Not even his second name, or whether he was married. It was a mutual thing, strictly business. Arnold didn't know Charlie's second name, or that he was from Leeds. That was the way they both liked it. Charlie once told Arnold he lived north of Manchester somewhere. There was a thread of truth in that, as Leeds was north of Manchester. North and east a bit.

It was good to get out of Leeds every now and again. The trips to Manchester had always been enjoyable. Business first. It was easy to spot Arnold, he being so tall and skinny. It crossed Charlie's mind that it was no accident that Arnold was the skinny one. Charlie would never be able to climb over walls or squeeze through windows. They would meet at the Piccadilly Gardens, so there was no need for Charlie to go out to the docks at Salford Quays anymore. The stuff that came off the barges no longer interested him. He and Arnold would meet at the park gates, then walk to a bench to sit and chat. To the entire world, they looked like a pair of city gents, smartly dressed and each carrying a small attaché case. When no one was about, small packages and envelopes passed between them. Then, business done, they would stand up and shake hands, walk to the gates and go off in opposite directions.

Charlie would take himself to The Railway Hotel for a couple of beers before returning on the 6.15 to Leeds.

Charlie liked his secrets. The fact that Siobhan didn't know what he was up to made it all the more attractive. His business dealings gave him a feeling of power. He had a fair bit of cash stashed up too. His dealers in Leeds couldn't get enough of the jewellery. Nothing was ever said, but he knew they reset the jewels and sold them on. Bullion. That was what they called the goods. Nice word that. Bullion. It had a powerful ring to it.

"Bye, Charlie, won't be long." Siobhan's words woke him from his thoughts. "I'm going to collect Susan from the party."

"Don't be long," the words snapped from his lips. The tone of his own voice irritated him.

Siobhan picked up her handbag and left, turning sharply on her heel as she left the bar. It was as much as she dared to show her resentment. She would like to have given him a piece of her mind. She would like to have asked him what the hell she had done wrong. Why was he so bad tempered with her? Why was he such a pig-headed shit all the time? But she wouldn't ever ask. She knew that. Instead, she walked quickly to dissipate her anger, and as her anger subsided, her pace slackened.

"Come in, come in, lovely to see you again." There were just four children in the front room of the little house. Two girls and two boys. Siobhan quickly noticed that Susan's dress was much prettier than the one the other little girl wore. Certainly more expensive.

Jimmy's Mum was still talking as she knelt down to pick up a jam sandwich that was in danger of being trodden into the rug. "We were on the maternity ward together, Mrs Fletcher. Do you remember? I was in the bed opposite you and Susan." Siobhan had a faint recollection of an unmarried mother being in the ward; a quick look at Jimmy's mother's left hand confirmed this was Miss Hanson, not Mrs.

"Of course. Sorry. I'm usually good at remembering faces." The birth of Susan was all rather a blur. All she could remember was that it was when Charlie had said he loved her.

"Please, call me Pauline. We were so pleased that Susan could come. Not many could make it, as you see. Jimmy was particularly disappointed that Charmaine couldn't make it. She's in France for the summer with her family. Still, we've had lots of fun, haven't we, Florrie?" Pauline turned to the old woman sitting in the corner.

"That we 'ave, love. I never 'eard so much laughing in t'ouse."

There was a knock at the door and the other boy and girl were collected by their mothers.

"Now," said Pauline. "What about that cuppa?"

Florrie stood up with difficulty. "I'll be off back 'ome if yer don't mind. Leave you two ter chat," Florrie chuckled as she spoke. "All t'noise 'as fair worn me out."

Pauline smiled at her. "Thanks for all your help, Florrie. I couldn't have managed without you,"

As Florrie left, Siobhan followed Pauline into the kitchen, leaving Susan and Jimmy playing in the front room. This was the first time she had been in a real house since she left Ireland.

"Florrie is a wonderful neighbour, more like a granny to Jimmy. Don't know what I'd do without her." Pauline filled the kettle as she spoke.

Siobhan looked around the little kitchen. It was tiny compared to that of the Threlfalls. There were children's books on a shelf, crayons and a few toy cars in a box by the fireside. An old radio played jazz from a high shelf at the side of the chimney breast. What the room lacked in size, it made up for in its welcoming atmosphere. It was warm and friendly. The furniture was old and worn; the odd cups and saucers spoke volumes.

Pauline turned the radio off. "Sorry. Jazz isn't everyone's favourite. Florrie says it sounds as if they are all playing a different tune at the same time." She smiled at the thought. "Jimmy told me about a girl in his class having the same birthday. He's looking forward to Susan's party tomorrow. We were glad it wasn't today."

"We thought we'd be too busy in the bar for a Saturday party. Tomorrow should be good, though. Charlie, he's my husband, has been clearing out the old ballroom. The party will be in there. There's a magician coming. I think a lot of the parents will be staying for the party, and you're very welcome."

Pauline hesitated, her lips tightly pursed as she looked down to the floor. There was a pause of no more than five seconds before she looked up. Siobhan saw the sadness in her eyes.

"I'd like that, but I don't know. The other parents look down on me…because I'm not married. I'm convinced that's why not many children came today. People can be funny about it."

"Well, I'd like you to come. I mean that, and I'm sure Jimmy would like it as well." Siobhan had taken an instant liking to her. On impulse, she stepped forward and held Pauline's hands in hers. The two women looked each other in the eye. It was no more than a moment.

"Kettle's boiling." Pauline moved away, obviously glad to have her hands busy. She made the tea, and they sat at the table.

The conversation easily shifted to the children, to school, the teacher Miss Hughes, and to the weather. They had a second cup and finished off the sandwiches and buns. The children came through from the lounge and ate the last of the birthday cake.

Pauline told Siobhan about her job at the bakery. "I've got used to it now. It was hard at first, when Jimmy was a baby. It's honest work. We have our routine, and Florrie makes it all possible. I don't have much, as you can see, but what I have is mine." A comfortable silence followed, each in their thoughts.

Siobhan spoke first, very quietly, but with a firm sincerity in her voice. "I'll never look down on you, Pauline. I have no room to talk. I was seven months gone when Charlie married me. I was lucky he stood by me."

Pauline gave a thin, watery smile and breathed in deeply. She paused, about to speak, but then just released the air from her lungs in a sigh. Tears filled Pauline's eyes, her lips tightly sealed. She leaned back in the chair, her eyes closed. She could never share her story. Not with anyone.

"Good grief, is that really the time? Charlie will wonder where on earth we are. I must dash. You will come tomorrow, won't you?" Siobhan's words came out in a rush as she picked up her bag in one hand and grabbed Susan with the other.

Susan wriggled and pulled at her mother's hand. "I don't want to go home. I want to stay here and play with Jimmy. Pleeeease, Mummy."

"We have to go. Daddy will be cross if I'm not back for opening time. Come on, Susan, don't be so difficult." Siobhan was walking towards the door, dragging a reluctant Susan along. She turned to Pauline as she opened the door. "I would like you to stay for the party, really I would. You could help me hand round the sandwiches. Even better, you could come along earlier and help me make them." Siobhan smiled.

"Okay. You talked me into it. I know Jimmy would like that. Sounds like fun. We don't go out much."

* * * *

As Charlie opened the doors at six o'clock, Johnny and Billy walked in. A sulky faced Susan walked in behind them, followed by a very flustered Siobhan.

"Sorry, Charlie. I lost track of the time." She could see he was livid. His jaw was set tight, a sure sign of rage. He stormed off towards the bar, stepping onto his board with an angry stamp.

Siobhan called to Susan. "Come on, love, you can't stay in here."

Billy and Johnny were making a fuss of her.

"Five years owd t'day. Is that reet, Miss Susan?" Johnny said.

"That's a reet pretty dress tha's got on, Miss Birthday Girl," said Billy.

Susan danced around the room, holding her skirt out to the sides to show off the frills and lace. She sang as she danced. "I am five. I am Susan. I am five. I am Susan," over and over again, to the tune of 'Twinkle, twinkle, little star.'

Siobhan smiled at her daughter, watching her every movement. It meant she could avoid any eye contact with Charlie. As Susan curtsied at the end of her dance, Siobhan spoke briskly. "Upstairs, young lady, quickly now," she said.

Susan pulled a face. "Can I stay a little while, please, Daddy?" Susan put on her cutest smile as she twirled towards the bar.

"Five minutes, no more. If we get busy, you go straight away. Okay?"

Charlie could hardly believe what he was saying. He didn't want Susan in the bar. He only said it to contradict Siobhan. Johnny and Billy had each given her a threepenny bit. More regulars came in. Susan twirled and sang, and was given more birthday money.

"Mind you put it in the Post Office for her, Charlie," said Johnny.

"I will, I will, don't you fret." Charlie replied as he took the coins from Susan. Siobhan was behind the bar now. Tom had arrived and given Susan sixpence. The atmosphere was restored, diffused by Susan and her showing off. Everyone in the bar knew it was Susan's birthday. As customers came in, she told them so. Her confidence was incredible, her laugh infectious.

Siobhan and Charlie were both amused and proud of their daughter.

Charlie whispered in Siobhan's ear, "You'll have to get her out of here before Alf arrives. He'll have something to say about her being in the bar. Could cost me my licence."

Siobhan nodded, and at ten to seven she took Susan by the hand and led her from the bar. "Come on, birthday girl, time for bed."

Susan looked at her father. He nodded and tipped his head in an upward and backwards motion. She turned and waved to the customers. Susan pulled her mother by the hand, out of the bar, and towards the main staircase.

* * * *

"So where the bloody hell were you?" The bar was closed, and Tom had left. Charlie and Siobhan were in the kitchen. He banged the money bag down on the table. He was furious. It was as if someone had flicked a switch. He had played the convivial landlord all evening, walking along his board, laughing and chatting with the customers.

"I'm sorry, Charlie. It was like I said, I just lost track of time."

"That doesn't answer my question, you stupid bitch. I said, where the hell were you?"

"I went to collect Susan from the party, you know I did."

"That doesn't take the best part of three hours. I'll ask you one last time. Where the hell *were you?*" He was shouting now, his face flushed with anger. He spat his words at her. "Do you think I'm stupid?"

Siobhan was frightened. She kept her voice calm, but couldn't disguise the tremor in her voice. "Jimmy's mum invited me to stay for a cup of tea. We got chatting and…"

"You got chatting? Is that the best you can come up with?"

"It's true. Ask Susan, Charlie. I'm sorry." Siobhan stepped towards her husband, her arms outstretched. Charlie turned away. "I never…" she began, but he wouldn't let her finish.

He had put his coat on and banged the back door behind him before she could say any more. Siobhan dropped her arms to her sides and steadied herself with her hands on the edge of the kitchen table. Silent tears fell from her cheeks, wetting the scrubbed boards of the table top, spreading along the grain of the wood in rivulets. She shut her eyes and took several deep breaths before walking back into the bar. She poured herself a large gin, adding a dash of port to the glass. She took a sip, the sweetness of the port sticking to her lips as the liquid warmed her throat, then her stomach. Every night when Charlie went out she had a little drink. Siobhan enjoyed her 'little treat' as she thought of it. Tonight she needed it. Tonight she had a second.

Susan heard the shouting as she lay in bed. She put on her dressing gown and walked to the top of the stairs just in time to hear the back door bang. She knew her daddy had gone out, so there would be nothing else to listen to. Her party tomorrow was going to be the best ever birthday party. She was too excited to even shut her eyes. The street lights filtered through the pink curtains. She called her new doll Angel Face, and Angel Face lay on the pillow beside her. Mummy and Daddy had laughed at the name. She had read it on Mummy's face-powder box. Angel Face was her doll anyway, and they could laugh as much as they wanted. She liked it when they were all together and Mummy and Daddy were happy, even if they were laughing at her. Better than Daddy being cross and Mummy crying. They thought she didn't know, but it was Mummy and Daddy who didn't know. They didn't know about her special place on the kitchen stairs. Sometimes she sat there and listened to them after the bar closed. Then there was her special place on the big stairs where she could sit and listen to all the talking in the bar.

She couldn't always understand everything that was said, and sometimes the voices were too quiet. She liked the different voices and recognised a few of them, like Billy and Johnny and Tom. She wondered what the other people looked like, but always stayed hidden from view. When the bar closed she would run quietly along the long landing, past Mummy's bathroom, to her place on the kitchen stairs. Mummy and Daddy talked about how busy the bar had been. Daddy would tell Mummy off if she had been talking to a man too much. Mummy always said it didn't mean anything. Then Daddy would go out and Mummy would go back in the bar for a little while before coming upstairs.

Mummy always came in her room really quietly and tucked the bedclothes in before kissing her on the forehead. Susan could smell the drinking on her breath; it was horrible. She hadn't been on the stairs tonight, though. She just wanted to stay in her room and look at Angel Face and her new doll's pram and all the other presents. It had been a lovely day. She loved all her new toys, and Jimmy's party had been really good fun. She liked Jimmy, even though he was a boy. Charmaine and Jimmy were her best friends at school. It was a shame she hadn't been at Jimmy's party. Charmaine had gone to France with her mum and dad for the summer holidays, so she wouldn't be at Susan's party either. She liked playing with Charmaine, even though she couldn't skip like the other girls. She spoke quite a lot of English now, and had even taught Susan how to say '*je m'appelle Susan*'.

Jimmy helped Susan with her spellings and times tables. He was very clever with things like that.

After the other children had left the party and Granny Florrie had gone home, Jimmy had taught her how to play 'Patience'. He showed her how to set the cards out. He said it helped to learn to count backwards. 10…9…8…7…6… then she heard Mummy on the stairs, then walking along the landing. That was strange, she thought, Mummy is usually so quiet. The drinking smelled strong as she kissed her, and Mummy stumbled as she left the room. Mummy was drunk.

She woke next morning to find a large box at the side of her bed. It had a gold ribbon tied in a bow, the words 'Happy Birthday, Susan' written on the side in big letters. She didn't understand. Her birthday was yesterday. She crossed the landing to her parents' room.

"Mummy," she said. Her tone demanded attention. Siobhan and Charlie were fast asleep. Susan shook the bedclothes. "Mummy, look at me."

Siobhan stirred.

"Mummy. Why didn't I get that present yesterday?"

"What present is that, love?"

"The one by my bed. The one with the big gold bow."

"Susan, I have no idea what you're talking about," Siobhan whispered. She put her fingers to her lips and tilted her head towards Charlie. The gesture was futile. Susan was already on her way round to her father's side of the bed.

"Daddy. It must have been you, then. *Daddy!*" she shouted. "Look at my face." Susan jumped on the bed, pulling at her father's shoulders.

"Hey, hey there, Princess. What's all this about?"

Siobhan relaxed. He was in a good mood.

"The box. The *box,* Daddy."

"Now what box might that be, then?"

Siobhan knew he was teasing her now. She knew nothing about a box; Charlie must have brought something home last night.

Susan ran from the room, returning seconds later with a large white box tied with a gold ribbon. Siobhan recognised Charlie's handwriting on the side.

Susan threw it onto the bed. "This box!" she shouted, triumph and temper mingling in her voice.

"Oh, *that* box," Charlie said. "I found it on the doorstep last night. You had better open it, Princess."

Susan tugged at the ribbon, and with a little help from her parents, the box was opened. With layers of tissue paper frantically pulled away in a rustle, Susan gazed in wonder at the beautiful party dress. She threw her arms around Charlie's neck and kissed him all round his face and head.

"Hey, Princess, don't suffocate your old dad."

Siobhan and Susan laughed together.

The sound of Siobhan's laugh caught Charlie by surprise. He hadn't heard it for a while. She smiled a lot, yes, especially at the customers. But that laugh. It was a thing of the past. He sat up in bed and watched them together. Susan had her nightdress off and with Siobhan's help was pulling the dress over her head. She twirled and sang around the room. Siobhan sat back on the bed to watch her daughter's happiness.

Charlie put his hand over hers.

She turned to look at him.

"Sorry about last night," he said.

Siobhan was speechless.

"I do love you, Siobhan. You and Susan, you're everything to me, and if…"

"Can I keep it on? Can I? Please." Susan's eyes darted between her parents as she jumped up and down in her excitement.

"What? And get breakfast all over it?" Charlie said. "I don't think so, Princess."

Susan pouted defiantly, but knew her father was right. She would hate herself if she spoiled her new dress before the party.

Chapter Six

Charlie hurried along the platform, attaché case held tightly in his hand. Too tightly. A case of sandwiches would never command such a grip. He gave away more than he knew with his darting eyes and twitching hands. There was the best part of five hundred quid in his little case, and Charlie Fletcher wasn't going to let go of it. Arnold had been busy. Business was good generally. Since Susan's party, a few of the fathers had started coming into the bar after work. All good for trade.

Charlie boarded the train, somehow reassured by the hissing of the engine, the familiar smell of steam and smoke.

A corridor ran the length of the carriage with a sliding door to each compartment. Charlie settled himself comfortably in the first empty one he came to; he wasn't in the mood for company. Sitting by the window with his back to the engine, he gazed blankly at the platform with unfocussed eyes. The familiar noises of the guard's whistle and the banging of the carriage doors barely registered, such was his preoccupation as he settled in the worn brocade seat. A scruffily dressed man rose from a bench on the platform, tucked his newspaper under his arm and boarded the train. The porter had been about to bang the door shut, but held it back. He got a tanner tip for his trouble. It paid to be on the lookout in his job. In this case, it had paid him sixpence.

Shiny shoes. Scruffy as can be with shiny shoes and giving a tip. Could only mean one thing. A copper.

The powerful noise of the engine slowly pulled the carriages from Leeds City Station. As the rhythm of the train increased, and the city gave way to fields, Charlie began to relax. No one else had entered the compartment, so he and his attaché case were safe.

His thoughts wandered to Siobhan and Susan. Part of him didn't understand what had come over him the other morning. The sight of the two of them, and the sound of their laughter, had somehow changed his way of thinking. He knew he had been wrong to shout at Siobhan the night before the birthday party. What on earth did he think she could get up to with a five year old in tow? He had it good, and he knew it. All that was three weeks ago: he and Siobhan had been alright since.

He thought he might keep a nice little piece from Arnold's latest collection as a present for Siobhan on their wedding anniversary, whenever that was. When he got back, he would check the date on the marriage licence. It'd be in the bureau somewhere.

The journey passed quickly. Manchester. Rain like stair rods. Nothing unusual about that. The westerly winds hit the Pennines and dumped the rain. No doubt it would be sunny in Yorkshire. Charlie straightened his trilby hat and pulled up the collar of his coat as he left the railway station. At least his brogues would keep his feet dry on the short walk to Piccadilly Gardens.

Arnold would be at the gates. He trusted Arnold. Never had cause to do anything else. Arnold named his price, and Charlie always got value for money. He couldn't very well ask to look at the goods in a public park, could he? He splashed through the puddles; the rain would keep the meeting short.

If he had been in a pessimistic frame of mind, Charlie would have said things were going too well. Too good to be true. Too good to last. But even the Manchester rain couldn't dampen Charlie Fletcher that day. As he turned the corner and the park gates came into view, he involuntarily tightened his grip on the attaché case. Whether it was because he was unwilling to part with such a large amount of cash, or because he couldn't see Arnold, he couldn't say. He turned into the park. He didn't want to sit on a wet bench in the rain. Not only would he get wet, but it would look strange.

Arnold was never late. Where was the stupid sod? Charlie kept walking. The paths took a circular route around the flower beds, where the floral displays, courtesy of the council, were past their best and battered by the rain. Charlie slowed as he approached the gates again. Still no sign of Arnold. Charlie tried to remember their back up plan. They had discussed it when they first met. "If ever I don't turn up, Charlie," Arnold had said, "I will send…" Who? He couldn't remember. It didn't matter anyway. No one was here. He would just go straight home again. Hang on to his cash.

"Charlie?" A man's voice came from behind. Charlie was immediately on his guard. His knuckles white with the strength of his grip. He wasn't going to give his five hundred quid away to anyone who just happened to know his name. If only he could remember the name of Arnold's back up.

He turned slowly as the man caught up with him.

"Arnold sent me," he said.

Charlie looked up into a face with piercing blue eyes. A thin face with thin lips. Siobhan said he shouldn't judge people by the way they looked, but in Charlie's experience thin lips told lies.

"Arnold who?" He replied. His voice was calm, but his insides were in turmoil. As soon as he uttered the words, Charlie realised it was a stupid thing to say. It implied he knew an Arnold. That he had come to meet an Arnold. Anyway, he didn't know Arnold's surname, so anything this man said would be meaningless.

"Arnold Leverret. I'm Steve."

Charlie had to look up to face him; to look into those blue eyes. It made the rain pour from the brim of Charlie's hat, down the back of his neck. It cooled him as he sweated in fear. He still couldn't remember the name Arnold had given him, but he was pretty sure it wasn't Steve. His voice was steady, though anyone who knew Charlie would know it was a little higher in pitch.

"Sorry, mate," he said. "You've got the wrong bloke. I don't know an Arnold, and I'm not called Charlie." Before any more could be said, Charlie straightened his hat, set his eyes down and walked off briskly, out of the gates. He wanted to get back to Leeds, but intuition, and fear, took him in the opposite direction, away from the railway station.

"Well, bugger me if it isn't Charlie Fletcher."

Charlie leaned against the back of the door. Rain dripping from the hem of his coat, his hat sodden. His breathing was heavy with exhaustion and relief.

"Christ, Gloria. Am I glad to see you. I was afraid you might have moved on."

"Me? Move on? Nah. Not your old Gloria. Where would I go?"

Charlie smiled, slowly regaining his breath. "You haven't changed a bit, you old tart."

Gloria moved forward, extending her fat arms, wrapping them around Charlie, crushing his face into her wrinkly cleavage. She wobbled from side to side as she hugged him, bright red lipstick smudging his wet hat. She released her grip to grab his hand.

"Come on. Upstairs with you. The girls aren't here yet. Plenty of time for some fun. This one's on me, Charlie."

"Gloria, I'm a respectable married man…"

"Charlie Fletcher? Married, maybe, but respectable? Nah. Don't bloody believe it."

He hadn't visited Gloria's place since he met Siobhan; and he hadn't come for sex. He took his coat and hat off slowly, swapping his case from one hand to the other. It gave him a few moments to think. To decide. As he put his coat over his arm, he looked Gloria in the eye. She *had* changed. She was older. He suspected she just ran the place now. Not, as you might say, taking an active role in the business. Dark roots on a blonde was one thing, but grey roots on bright copper? If Gloria had still been working, she wouldn't have grey roots. She had always been so particular in a rough sort of way. When he was eighteen, he had thought her old enough to be his mother, which, biologically, if not legally, she was. The age gap of fifteen years didn't seem so much now.

"How about a cuppa, Gloria?"

"Suit yourself." She seemed disappointed.

Charlie followed her into the kitchen, her high heels and black fishnet stockings an integral part of Gloria.

"I'll say this, Charlie Fletcher. I thought I'd heard it all in this game, but you're the first time a punter has asked for a fucking cup of tea." She laughed a deep chuckling laugh. "Your old man dropped off now you're married then? Let me see, you've been married about seven years at a guess. Getting a bit boring, is it? Can't quite decide whether to pay for a bit of fun?"

"Gloria, I need a favour."

"Is that so, Charlie? You mean you didn't just call in for a cuppa?" She tilted her head back in mock surprise. "Well, I'll be buggered."

"Leave it out, Gloria. I need a change of clothes."

"Ah. Now we're getting somewhere. I have a nice red velvet dress you might like. Getting popular it is, dressing up. It's called trans-something-or-other. Fancy a dabble at that, do you, Charlie?"

"For Christ's sake, Gloria, shut up."

Gloria poured two cups of tea. They sat opposite each other at the kitchen table, the worn Formica top in contrast to the dainty china cups and saucers. The prettiness of the cups reminded him of Siobhan. He smiled. An old chair to the side of an empty grate looked inviting, but he needed to talk face to face. He needed to be on his mettle.

"Tell me something, Gloria. A bloke is dressed all scruffy, but clean, and he has really shiny shoes. What does that tell you?"

"That's easy. Tells me he's a copper trying not to look like a copper."

"That's what I thought."

Gloria leaned forward, grasping the top of his hand. "'Course I can lend you some bloody clothes. You'd be surprised what gets left behind here. Can't make you no taller though. You'll have to watch it."

"Thought I'd catch the mail train, you know, the one that goes at two-thirty in the morning."

"Then you're not so clever as you think, Charlie. That's the one the coppers watch, you silly sod."

"Oh, yes, and how do you know that?" There was sarcasm in his voice.

"Because, believe it or not, Charlie Fletcher, coppers is punters."

He looked at her blankly.

"They say, 'Gotta go, Gloria, gotta catch the mail train.' They think I don't know. Just a stupid old tart. That's me. Take a tip from this stupid old tart, Charlie. Catch the twelve-ten, or stay overnight."

"I'll take the twelve-ten."

"Shame, we could have had a little reunion. Not too late to change your respectable married mind, you know."

"Thanks, but no thanks. What I'd really like is to sit in that chair and have a nap, if that's okay with you."

Gloria sighed.

Charlie pushed his cup to the middle of the table. In two short paces he was in the armchair, shuffling down in the worn cushions, his attaché case tucked underneath.

"I'll go sort those clothes out, then." Gloria felt insulted, rejected even. Turned down in favour of an old chair. She'd get over it.

When she returned to the kitchen, Charlie was fast asleep. By the time he woke up, she had cooked him a dinner, counted his money, found his address on a bill in his coat pocket, and taken the hem up on some trousers. A punter had once told her that education was never wasted. That you could never know too much. He said intelligence and education and knowledge were three different things. Funny bugger he was. Gloria knew a lot of stuff. You never know when you might need to know something. That was her rule, and she educated herself whenever, and however, she could.

* * * *

With Charlie away in Manchester and Susan back at school, Siobhan had the day to herself. She had arranged to meet Pauline in the Merrion Street Gardens at two o'clock, but until then the day was her own. She made the beds and cleaned the bathrooms. She was happy. Since Susan's birthday, things had taken a turn for the better between her and Charlie. He still went out every night, but she didn't mind that. She enjoyed her bit of time to herself, her treats. No harm done. She wandered into bedroom number three. Susan's party dresses were kept in the big wardrobe there. Susan's dresses. Not just kept for parties these days. Since she turned five, her Daddy had allowed her in the bar at opening time, just for half an hour. The customers liked it. She would sing and dance in her little girly-twirly way. Some of them gave her money. Charlie put it in a pot to take to the Post Office. Siobhan touched the dresses one by one, running her fingertips over the fabrics. Feeling their luxury was a tangible joy. She closed the wardrobe silently and left the room, walking along the landing and down the big staircase to the ballroom. The memories of Susan's party flooded back. She could hear the laughter of the children as they made a slide on the dance floor, the remnants of the old wax, polished to a shiny, slippery path by their shoes. Pauline had helped with the sandwiches, and the new friendship grew.

Like the other parents that day, Pauline had been surprised at the size of the ballroom. Siobhan admitted that even she had not been in all the rooms of the Threlfalls hotel. When she had been cleaning up in readiness for the party, she found a door at the back of the stage. The top half was glazed, the glass etched with the word 'PRIVATE'. She had pushed it open and seen a staircase; it went straight to the top floor of the hotel. She had had no time to go any further then, but today she relished the opportunity. It felt like an adventure. The stairs creaked a little as she trod the threadbare carpet, the brass stair rods black with age and neglect. The staircase was wider than the kitchen stairs, but not so grand as the main staircase. Half way up, there was a doorway off to the left. Siobhan opened it towards her, only to find it had been bricked up from the other side. She continued up to the top, to a large square landing with several doors. The ceiling was partly glazed in a pattern of leaded triangles. The sun shone though, blinkered by occasional scudding clouds. A faded circular rug covered most of the once polished floorboards, its muted colours a testament to the years of sunshine that had robbed its former beauty, but its quality was indisputable. A grandfather clock ticked in perfect rhythm at the opposite side of the landing. Siobhan crossed the floor and looked up at the clock face. In the worn brass and in copper plate script she made out the words 'thirty day movement'. She frowned.

"So, Charlie," she said. "You come up here at least once a month."

The first door she tried led to another long, narrow landing. The paint had peeled from the walls and ceiling, falling to the floor and lying undisturbed. No one had walked along here for a long time. The air was stale and the damp smell of mould hung like an invisible veil. The rooms were all small with high dormer windows, tightly shut, with cobwebs layered in the corners. Some rooms had a small iron bedstead, others were empty. A stained mattress, nibbled by mice, sagged against a wall. Siobhan walked to the end of the landing and looked in the last room. Empty boxes were strewn across the floor. Another door with the words 'Fire Escape' painted across the top had been added some time ago. Siobhan dragged a box to the window and stepped onto it. From there, she could just see the yard with its high gates. Stepping down, again she looked around the room.

"Another little store, eh, Charlie? In and out through the fire escape. Very clever, you old fox. Wonder what you kept up here?"

She walked back along the corridor to the square landing, checking the soles of her shoes, brushing away the traces of flaking paint with her hand. She paused in thought. If the little rooms were servants' quarters, then these bigger doors must lead to the owner's rooms. She had plenty of time. There were two bedrooms, a sitting room, a dining room, a bathroom and a small kitchen. The whole area was less than half the size of the ballroom. The ceilings were low and sloped. The high dormer windows made angular shapes in the ceilings as they pushed their way out of the roof. She stood on tiptoe in the sitting room to see the busy street below. All furniture was covered in dust sheets, giving the room a ghostly air, with years of undisturbed dust settled in the folds of the fabric. All except one that was dirty in a grubby, even sort of way. Siobhan lifted a corner of the sheet. Four legs standing on brass feet supported a desk of some sort, a chair on wheels in front of it. She slid the cover off to reveal a marquetry bureau, inlaid with brass. The wood was dry, with its surface crazed, thirsty for polish, but beautiful for all that. Siobhan pulled the handles at the front. The top rolled back noisily, breaking the silence like unexpected thunder on a summer's day. Inside were several little drawers and sections, fashioned by the skill of a craftsman.

"So this is where you keep your secrets, Charlie Fletcher."

The bureau was stuffed with envelopes of different sizes, some bulging with scraps of paper, others quite flat with little or nothing in them. She touched nothing. At one end, she could see a thin beige book, about six inches high and four inches wide. It leaned over slightly. Siobhan turned her head to one side to read 'Post Office Saving Bank' in red letters on the cover. She smiled. He was putting the money away for Susan after all. She had wondered about that, but not dared to ask. She closed the bureau without touching anything, and put the dirty old cover back as she had found it, leaving no trace of having been on the top floor as she stepped lightly back down the stairs and into the ballroom.

Back in the familiar kitchen, she curled up in her armchair, deep in thought. Her adventure had provided some answers, but more questions. The bureau contained the answers, she was sure of that.

* * * *

Pauline sat on one of the benches in the Merrion Gardens. She was early, but she hadn't been quite sure where the gardens were and didn't want to be late. Not that it would have mattered. It was just that she was looking forward to meeting up with Siobhan so much. In reality, the gardens were more of a paved area with seats and a few bushes around the edge. Only a stone's throw from Briggate, it was quiet and calm by comparison to the bustle of the busy street. She closed her eyes to feel the warmth of the sun on her face and was drifting off in a daydream when a soft Irish voice broke her reverie.

"Hello, Pauline."

She opened her eyes and sat up, blinking in the sunlight. That soft Irish accent meant it could only be Siobhan. A casual observer would think they had been friends for life, so warm was their greeting. The relaxed chatter, punctuated by laughter, portrayed an enviable friendship. The children, their likes and dislikes, their teacher, Miss Hughes, and the way they, Susan and Jimmy, had also become friends, were all topics of conversation.

Siobhan talked about Charlie and the Threlfalls, though not much. Pauline told of her work at the bakery. She had friends there, but the friendship stopped at the bakery door. She had never met any of them outside work. Night shift had its advantages, once you got used to it. She was always there to take Jimmy to school and to pick him up at four o'clock. She would do anything for Jimmy. Pauline's only friend, she said, other than Siobhan, was Florrie Bell. Pauline didn't know what she would have done without Florrie.

"She's not a relative, then?" Siobhan asked.

"Oh, no. No…not a relative at all." The pause that followed was comfortable between them; neither saw the other's pain. Siobhan was thinking of her family in Ireland, Pauline of the man whom she hated so much she could not think of him as her father. They looked at one another and smiled. The conversation switched back to the safe subject of the children, polio vaccines and how to learn multiplication tables.

"Come on, Pauline. Time we went to pick up the little darlings." They fell into step on the short walk to school. Since Jimmy and Susan's birthday parties, they had chatted every day as they waited for the children to come tumbling through the door.

Siobhan touched her arm. "Why don't you and Jimmy come back to The Threlfalls for tea?"

"Won't Charlie mind?"

"Charlie won't know. He's away on business today. Anyway, why should he mind?"

Pauline smiled in reply.

Boiled eggs and soldiers were quickly on the table for Susan and Jimmy. Pauline and Siobhan had tea and sandwiches as they chatted away; the two young mothers were never short of conversation. Footsteps running around upstairs reassured them that the children were playing happily, racing up and down the landings.

Tom arrived for work at six o'clock. Pauline and Jimmy left soon afterwards by the back door. Tom worked alone until Siobhan had put Susan to bed. She changed into her 'work' clothes hurriedly, applying lipstick as she dashed downstairs.

Siobhan looked at the clock. Twenty to nine. Only five minutes had passed; it felt like half an hour. Charlie had never been this late before. She pulled another pint, glad to keep her hands busy. Tom worked in his quiet way at the other end of the bar. She was aware he was watching her more than usual. He watched her—she watched the clock. Their eyes met briefly, he gave a quizzical look, shrugging his shoulders as he turned back to his work.

"Where's Charlie, then?" This was the third customer who had asked her.

"Oh, out and about. You know Charlie. He'll be back soon." She smiled.

Siobhan surprised herself. How could she sound so calm? So cheerful? She worked automatically, while her mind raced. There could have been an accident... Unlikely, though. Bad news travels fast. Alf would let her know if anything was wrong. Alf... He had been in and had his half of bitter. He was another one you could set your watch by. When she thought about it, this latest customer was the fourth person to ask where Charlie was, not the third. Alf had asked. This worried her even more, because at that time Charlie wasn't even late. The evening dragged on. She looked at the clock, then looked at the door, half expecting Charlie, half expecting Alf with some awful news. Closing time came. She and Tom cleared the glasses in silence. She took the takings from the till and sat at the kitchen table. Tom came over and put his arm around her. The gesture made her cry. He had never shown any fondness before; friendly enough, but never shown any warmth.

"Where can he be, Tom?" She sobbed, knowing he didn't have an answer. "Why isn't he back?"

"I dunno, love. But he'll be back." Tom wasn't sure if he was saying this to convince himself, or to comfort Siobhan. He had never seen her cry before. He didn't know what to do. The only woman who had done anything right by him was his mother, and that was when she died. She left him a little terraced house in Cross Green, close enough to walk into town and walk home again after the pub had shut and the trams had stopped running. "He's like a homing pigeon, Charlie is. Goes out and about but always comes home. You'll see."

"I hope to God you're right, Tom."

"What about a cuppa? I'll put the kettle on. That's what we do, isn't it? We Brits. Anything goes wrong, we have a cuppa."

Siobhan wiped her eyes on her cuff. She gave a thin, weak smile. "You're right, Tom. Tears never solved a problem, now did they?" She sniffed her tears away as she stood up.

Tom filled the kettle as Siobhan set out two cups and saucers, putting milk in one for Tom. Tom didn't want a cup of tea, he wanted to go home, but felt obliged to stay. He was scared that Charlie might arrive and not like him having a cosy cuppa with his wife, especially with the night's takings sitting on the table. Charlie would think they were up to something.

"What if he's been arrested, Tom?" They were sitting at the table again, Siobhan looking into her teacup as she slowly stirred the steaming black drink.

"Why would he be arrested, love? What makes you say that?"

"Come on, Tom. We both know his dealings, his trips to Manchester are, shall we say, not quite straight."

"Dunno what you mean, love."

"Yes, you do." She looked up as she spoke. "You've known Charlie longer than I have. Has he ever been late before?"

"Never."

"And you and I have never really had a conversation before, have we, Tom? So let's make it an honest one."

"Okay, Siobhan. I think you're right. But I don't know. I don't want to know. That's the way I like it, and that's the way Charlie likes it. If he wanted me or you to know what he was up to, he would have told us, and I do think, for what my opinion is worth, that if he had been arrested, Alf would have told us."

"What if Alf doesn't know? What if Charlie is in trouble in Manchester?"

"Then we'll know in the morning." Tom finished his tea as quickly as he could. "I'll be off now. Try to get some sleep, Siobhan." He put his hand on her shoulder again, as he went towards the back door. "Okay if I go out this way, love?"

"Yes, of course, Tom, I'll come out and lock the gates behind you." Siobhan pushed her chair back from the table. "Thanks for staying, Tom," was all she could say, stifling her tears as best she could.

* * * *

As he turned the corner and out into Briggate, he heard his name shouted out.

"Tom Hicks!"

He turned quickly to see Alf Lawrence just a few paces behind him. "He turned up yet, then?"

"Christ Almighty, Alf. You scared the living daylights out o' me."

"Well, is he back?"

"Who?" Alf was showing too much interest in Charlie's whereabouts for Tom's liking. "You been waitin' for me, Alf?"

"I'm the copper, Tom. I ask the questions. Well? Is that a yes or a no?"

"Nah. No sign of 'im. Siobhan's right upset."

"She deserves a better man than that rogue."

"Do you know where 'e is, Alf?"

"Like I say, Tom, I ask the questions." Alf nodded, confirming his authority to himself. Tom was left staring at the policeman's back as he walked away down Briggate in the direction of the police station. Tom was worried now. Alf knew something. The boss was in trouble, and there was nothing he could do about it.

* * * *

Susan was cold from sitting on the stairs. Cold and frightened. Tom had gone and Mummy was coming straight upstairs. She hadn't gone back into the bar. Susan tried to pretend to be asleep, but just couldn't.

"Where is he, Mummy? Where's Daddy?" She sobbed. Siobhan pushed her daughter's hair back; she could feel the tears on her cheeks. Siobhan took a deep breath, trying to disguise the fear and sadness in her voice.

"He's just out on business, Missy. Why are you crying? Why are you so cold?" Susan was sitting up in bed, hugging her mother, both arms wrapped tightly around her mother's waist.

"No, he isn't. I heard you." The words were barely audible as she sobbed into Siobhan's breasts. "I heard you and Tom talking. I sat on the stairs listening. He's lost, isn't he? He's missing."

"Your daddy is not lost. He's just late, that's all. I expect he missed his train."

Susan lifted her head a little.

"Then why were you crying? What did Tom mean when he said Alf would know?"

"Susan." Siobhan's voice was firm. She needed every ounce of strength to disguise her fear. "Your daddy will be home by morning. Tom said so, and now I say so. You must go to sleep." Susan lay her head back down on the pillow.

"Stay with me, Mummy. Until I go to sleep. Granny Florrie stays with Jimmy every night until he's asleep. He told me so." Siobhan stroked her daughter's hair. She sang to her softly, the only lullaby she knew from her childhood.

Too-ra loo-ra loo-ra loo-la bye bye,
You want the moon to play with,
The stars to run away with,
Hush now, don't you cry...

But it was Siobhan who shed silent tears as her daughter's steady breathing soon whispered of an exhausted sleep. Slowly, almost silently, Siobhan stood up, still humming the tune softly. Susan's breathing was steady as Siobhan left the room and returned to the kitchen. She didn't want to go to bed, and she didn't want one of her treats either. She loved Charlie and wanted him back, right now. He could keep his secrets, she didn't care, just as long as he came back home, safe and sound.

* * * *

Charlie's eyes darted everywhere. He turned to make sure he wasn't being followed—alert, feral. His lack of height the only thing to identify him, he boarded the train at the first door he came to. Gloria had done well. An old tweed jacket, hastily shortened baggy grey trousers, worn out shoes, and a flat cap made him melt into the streets of Manchester. With his cash stuffed in the inside pockets of the jacket, he had skulked through the streets. Only now, as he sat on the worn seat of the third class carriage did he dare to think he might get back to Leeds without being arrested. Gradually, his erratic breathing steadied, and a sigh of relief fell from his chest as the train started to move. So far, so good. He looked down at the shabby shoes. He could understand how a bloke might leave his hat or jacket at Gloria's place, but how the hell did anyone forget their shoes? Or trousers? He smiled at the thought. Even Siobhan might have trouble making these cracked old shoes shine again.

Siobhan. She would be worried sick. If only he had had a telephone put in… his thoughts drifted to The Threlfalls. Customers would've asked where he was. What if Siobhan had reported him missing? Tension knotted in the pit of his stomach. He would have to be on the lookout when he got to Leeds. Charlie tried to convince himself that the Manchester police wouldn't get together with the Leeds coppers. Still, all those free half pints he had given to Alf should stand for something. Alf would make sure he was okay. Arnold must've got caught and grassed on him. Still, Arnold didn't know he came from Leeds, so there was no real danger of a connection. The rhythms, sounds and smells of the train made him relax a little. As long as Siobhan hadn't panicked, he would be safe once he got home. With any luck, she would be fast asleep in bed, and he wouldn't have to explain where his clothes had gone.

* * * *

Siobhan stirred in the armchair, pulling an old blanket around her shoulders. The ticking of the clock broke the silence with its rhythm. The quiet and careful turning of the key in the back door jolted her from sleep. She gripped the chair as she heard the door open and then close. She stood up as Charlie came into the room.

"Charlie! You're back!" She stepped towards him, wanting to hug him. Their eyes met, and Siobhan knew he didn't want her to touch him. He moved away, only the smallest of movements, but Siobhan read the signs.

"Yes, Siobhan. I'm back." There was sarcasm in his voice. He threw the flat cap on the table.

"Your clothes, Charlie. Where are your clothes? Your hat, your brogues? Everything. What has happened, Charlie?"

"Did you tell Alf I was late?" he barked the question at her.

"No, Charlie. Alf was in early, as usual. You weren't late then. I've been worried. Tom said you'd be fine and not to worry, but I couldn't help it." Her voice drifted away. Charlie saw the tears in her eyes, saw her fight them back.

"Sit down, Siobhan. I'm going to get a brandy. I need one."

Siobhan did as she was told and sat in her armchair. A moment later, Charlie was back with his drink and a glass of port for Siobhan. She took the glass from him, gripped the stem, and looked into the deep red liquid.

Charlie sat opposite her in his chair and took a large gulp of brandy before he spoke. "Siobhan, I will tell you what you need to know. No more."

She looked straight at him, but said nothing.

"Don't ask me any questions."

Her blue eyes were wide with fear, not knowing what she was about to hear, but knowing Charlie was in trouble.

"I'm late back because I was delayed on business in Manchester."

Siobhan gave a little nod. Her eyes went to the flat cap on the table. His eyes followed hers. She sipped her port, savouring the flavour and the warmth of the sweet drink. They sat in silence for a while. She turned the glass, holding the stem between her thumb and forefinger. The way she looked at the port, the way she fondled the glass, puzzled Charlie. It was the way of a drinker. He had seen it too many times to be mistaken.

"Just one other thing, Siobhan. You never saw these clothes. Okay?"

"Okay, Charlie," her voice wavered, barely audible. "I never saw those clothes."

Chapter Seven

Ethel Hughes was a spinster, robbed of any potential husband by the battlefields of France. She remembered little of life before the Great War. Being born in 1900 made it easy to remember she was fourteen when the war began and eighteen when it ended. Hers was the first generation of women who found they needed to earn a living. Her love of children made teaching the obvious choice.

She had been at Elder Road Junior School so long, she found herself teaching the offspring of her earlier pupils. Her tiny frame belied her strength of character. Much to her annoyance, she needed reading glasses these days, though her distance vision was perfect. She was glad of that. It meant she could still lip read. A skill she kept secret and often used to her advantage.

She had six tailored suits which were her self-imposed school uniform. Three summer weight and three winter weight. They were worn in strict rotation with a blouse or jumper depending on the weather and the temperamental school boiler.

Her appearance had changed little over the years, a few grey hairs maybe. A few lines around her eyes. Her love of her job and her love of children made Miss Hughes a popular woman. The children confided in her; she had many a secret never to be told. Four weeks into the new school year and Ethel Hughes was getting to know her class of five year olds.

She knew them all by name after the first day; that was the easy part. There were thirty children in her class. Unlike her fellow teachers, Miss Hughes encouraged her pupils to sit with their friends rather than segregate them according to ability. The children preferred it, and it helped her to know them, to study their characters. From her raised desk at the front, with the blackboard behind her, she could, in her words, 'see the whites of their eyes'. The girls usually chose to partner another girl, and the boys with another boy. This year her class had an odd number of boys and girls, so it was fortunate that Susan Fletcher and Jimmy Hanson had become such good friends.

Jimmy was by far the brighter of the two. Susan was a pleasant girl, rather spoilt perhaps, but not academic. Good at heart, too, the way she protected Charmaine Fournier from the taunts of other children. Miss Hughes noticed something strange about their behaviour today. Secretive. Susan was upset about something. Jimmy and Charmaine were trying to comfort her. At playtime, Miss Hughes watched them from the staff room window. Jimmy stayed with the two girls instead of running around with the other boys as he usually did. Jimmy, Susan and Charmaine held hands and walked together in deep conversation. Susan was in the middle and Charmaine appeared to be supporting her friend rather than the other way round. They looked down as they walked, making it impossible to know what they were saying. The bell rang to signal the end of playtime. Jimmy looked up. She caught sight of his face as he said, "You must tell Miss Hughes, Susan. She will listen." They filed back into the classroom.

"Are you alright, Susan?" Miss Hughes asked as Susan passed her.

Susan looked up with wide eyes. Ethel Hughes saw fear there.

"Yes, thank you, Miss Hughes," she said automatically. Ethel Hughes wasn't fooled for a moment by the polite reply. Something was badly wrong.

* * * *

Siobhan was worried about her daughter. She didn't believe it was anything to do with Charlie being late home that night. She had been fine the next day as soon as she saw her daddy was safely home. It had been a couple of days later that Susan suddenly became all quiet and withdrawn. Pauline noticed it too. The two women walked behind Susan and Jimmy on the way to Pauline's house.

"I've asked her what's wrong, but she won't tell me." Siobhan said quietly. "She just shakes her head and says there's nothing wrong."

"Do you think she'd talk to Charlie?"

"No. I suggested that, and she looked even more scared. She doesn't even want to put her party dresses on anymore, and you know how she loves to show off."

When they got to 16 Vine Street, Jimmy asked his mother if they could go to Granny Florrie's house.

"Just for a while. Ask Granny Florrie if she'd like to come round here." The two children scampered off upstairs and through the connecting bedroom door. By the time the kettle had boiled, Florrie had joined Pauline and Siobhan in the kitchen of number sixteen. Rather than go up and down the stairs, she had come to the front door, given a brief knock and let herself in.

"Dear God in heaven, Pauline, let me sit down."

"What is it, Florrie? What's the matter? Where are Susan and Jimmy?" Pauline said.

Florrie was so distressed she was having difficulty breathing. "They're in my kitchen. They're safe enough." She gasped. As Florrie sat down, Pauline handed her a cup of tea.

"Here, have a drink of this, then tell us what's wrong. Have you hurt yourself?"

"No, no. Not me. Jimmy told me summat. Susan daren't say. She thinks she'll be in trouble, poor child. Thinks she's done summat wrong."

Siobhan knelt at the side of the old woman, her voice steady, yet fearful of what she was about to hear. "What is it, Florrie? You must tell me."

There wasn't much to tell, but when Florrie finished speaking, they agreed that Susan should stay at Vine Street while Siobhan went home to tell Charlie. She didn't go straight back to The Threlfalls. Siobhan was so shocked by what Florrie had said she needed a little time to think before she spoke to Charlie. In the Merrion Gardens, some children were playing under the careful eyes of their mothers. Some were skipping, others played 'Jacks' with pebbles. An unsmiling Siobhan watched their innocent play, her thoughts plagued.

* * * *

Two weeks after his disastrous trip to Manchester, and Charlie Fletcher was miserable. He sat in his armchair in the kitchen. No longer grateful for his freedom, he mourned the loss of income. His own fault, of course, putting all his eggs in one basket like that. Bloody Arnold Leverett or whatever he called himself. Siobhan was all of a jitter since that night, too. If she'd gone to bed instead of waiting up for him, he could've hidden those old clothes upstairs and simply told her he'd been delayed.

Tom carried on as normal, never mentioning a thing. Charlie couldn't decide whether that was a good thing or not. Cards close to his chest, that one.

Then there was Susan.

She was behaving like a frightened rabbit. Siobhan told him the next morning that she'd woken up and overheard her talking to Tom. She seemed okay, but then she went all quiet. Didn't want to put her party dresses on or show off in the bar. Siobhan and Susan had gone to that Pauline's house for tea. He didn't like them going there. Didn't know why exactly, except that the kitchen was strangely empty when she was out. It annoyed him when Susan was dashing about all the time making a racket, but just lately, even when she was at home, she had gone all quiet. He missed her noise. He'd get Siobhan to sort her out when they came home.

The clock struck six. Charlie pushed himself out of the old chair with both hands on the worn, threadbare arms. Time to open up. At least he had been right about Alf. Siobhan said he came in for his half pint at seven o'clock as usual that night, and at that time Charlie wouldn't have been back from Manchester anyway. She said he asked where he was but that didn't mean a thing. Alf had no reason to be suspicious.

He was in his usual place behind the bar when Siobhan walked in alone. Tom was there, serving Billy and Johnny. All perfectly normal.

"Where is she? Where's sulky little Susan, then?" Charlie asked. The moment he spoke, Charlie knew there was a problem. He had never seen Siobhan looking so anxious.

"I need to talk to you, Charlie."

"What, now?"

"Yes, right now."

Tom, Billy and Johnny all looked at Siobhan, then at Charlie. Billy had his pint half way to his lips, pausing in disbelief at the way Siobhan had spoken, the determined tone of her voice. She walked through the bar to the kitchen, keeping her eyes straight ahead. Charlie followed.

"What the hell do you think you're doing?"

"Charlie, listen."

"Never mind 'Charlie, listen'. Answer me, Siobhan. What the hell do you mean by speaking to me like that in front of customers?" Charlie's face was crimson with anger.

"I'm sorry. I didn't mean to, but you have to listen."

"Okay. So I'm listening, but it had better be good."

"It's Susan."

Charlie was gripped by fear.

"Where is she? What's happened?" Charlie held Siobhan by her shoulders, shaking her.

"Let go of me, Charlie. She's safe. She's at Pauline's."

"Why? Why have you left her there? What's going on?"

"Charlie! You're hurting me." Siobhan was shouting now. "Listen to me, will you? I know why she has been so upset, so quiet."

Charlie sat on one of the wooden chairs, and spoke quietly and deliberately, his teeth clenched. "And it's so important that you have to come into my bar, make me look a fool in front of Tom and all the customers, all because Susan has a few tears? I thought she had *me* wrapped round her little finger, but this…this is beyond anything."

"Let me tell you what is beyond anything, Charlie. Your precious customers, that's what." There was venom in her words, she spat them at him. "One precious customer in particular, who gives Susan money, has been touching her."

"What do you mean, woman, 'touching her'?"

"He gives her a shilling to sit on his knee." She screamed the words at him. "He puts his hand under her bottom and touches her. Tickles her." Tears streamed down Siobhan's face. Charlie was silent, trying to take in her words. Siobhan was sobbing. Charlie stood up slowly and put his arms around her, stroking her hair.

"Do you believe her?" Charlie spoke quietly, the anger gone from his voice.

Siobhan pulled herself away from him a little. Looking straight at him, she said, "Do you?" Her voice calmed.

"I see everything that goes on in that bar, Siobhan," he replied.

"Well, I believe her. It explains why she doesn't want to put her party dresses on and go in there."

"Maybe it's not so bad, just a bit of fun. She does get a shilling."

"Charlie! How on earth can you say that? This is your daughter we're talking about. She's frightened. Thinks she's done something wrong. It has to stop." Siobhan was incredulous.

"Let's not get this all out of proportion, Siobhan. Go back to Pauline's and bring Susan home. It's too late for her to go into the bar tonight anyway. Alf will be here soon. We'll talk about it later."

Susan and Jimmy were playing upstairs when she returned to Vine Street. Pauline was getting ready for work.

She came downstairs when she heard the front door open. Florrie was still in the kitchen.

"How did he take it?" Pauline asked.

"I'm not sure. I don't think he believes it." Siobhan felt numb, her tone flat. Florrie looked at Pauline, then at Siobhan.

"Ow does 'e think a five year old girl will make this up? It's true alright, or my name isn't Florrie Bell." The three women sat in silence for a few moments, each with their own thoughts.

"I don't know what to do," said Siobhan. "If Charlie's made his mind up, he'll just refuse to believe it, even if he knows, deep down, that Susan is telling the truth."

"Susan mustn't go into the bar again. She has to be kept away from that disgusting, filthy sod." Pauline spat her words out. Siobhan blinked in surprise at the strength of Pauline's words and the hatred in her voice.

"Calm yerself down, Pauline. Gettin' all of a fluster isn't goin' ter 'elp," Florrie said.

"How can you say that, Florrie? A five year old innocent little girl is being touched up by a filthy old man, and you say don't get flustered? Well, I am flustered. I'm more than flustered." Pauline burst into tears. She sat at the table, her head down, her forehead resting on her folded arms. She sobbed and sobbed, her body shaking in anger.

"There, there, love. Don't tek on so," said Florrie, her arthritic fingers grasping Pauline's shoulders. "As my mother used to say, there's more than one way ter skin a cat. Don't you worry, nor you, Siobhan. I'm goin' ter get me 'at an' coat. Young Susan won't be goin' in that bar no more."

"What are you going to do, Florrie? Where are you going?" Siobhan said.

"Never you mind. I might be just an old woman, but this is wrong. I'll be back before yer need ter be off ter work, Pauline."

"You're not going to the police, are you, Florrie? Charlie would kill me if he thought I'd even told you about all this."

"No. I'm not goin' ter t'police. You get yerself off 'ome. Get young Susan tucked up in bed. Like I said, there's more than one way ter skin a cat." Florrie shut the front door behind her with a bang.

"What do you think she's up to?" Siobhan said.

Pauline wiped her eyes on a tea towel. "I don't know, but you can trust Florrie. You get off home like she said. If I get time, I'll call in at The Threlfalls on my way to work. I could tell you what she says when she gets back."

"No! No. Don't do that. Charlie will know something's going on if you do that. I'll see you at school tomorrow. Tell me then."

"Are you afraid of Charlie?" Pauline had regained her self-control.

"No, I wouldn't say I was afraid of him. I don't think he would ever hit me. I worry though. If he decided to kick me out… I don't know. He's daft with Susan. Spoils her."

"You could come here and stay with me. You and Susan."

"You're a good friend, Pauline, but I don't think it will come to that. I'll get off now." She called upstairs to her daughter. "Come on, Susan. Time we were going home."

* * * *

Ethel Hughes was surprised to see the piano teacher on her doorstep.

"Miss Bell, What a lovely surprise. Come in, come in." She stood to one side to allow her guest into the small hallway.

"Sorry ter come round, uninvited like. Can I sit down? Me legs are terrible."

"Of course, of course." Miss Hughes was unaware of the way she repeated herself; her phrases always came out twice, the habit as much a part of her as her head. She showed Florrie into the sitting room. The neatness of the room, with its precisely placed ornaments on dustless surfaces, echoed the character of the school mistress. The spotless fireplace ready with newspapers and kindling, waiting for a match to light it; the coal bucket filled in readiness for a chilly evening.

"I can't stop long. I 'ave to get back to look after young Jimmy Hanson."

"What is it, Miss Bell? What is it? What can I do for you? Would you like a cup of tea?"

"No, thank you kindly. Like I say, I can't stop, but I need yer to do summat. It's Susan Fletcher. She's in your class, isn't she?"

Ethel Hughes listened in horror to Florrie's words. In all her years of teaching, she had never heard anything like it. Had she not observed Susan's demeanour over the last few days, she may have doubted the truth in it. There again, while she didn't know Miss Bell very well, she knew her to be an honest, forthright woman. All her pupils who had visited Miss Bell for their piano lessons said they liked her.

She wrung her hands together in her anguish. "What can *I* do? What can *I* do? Shall I tell the police?"

"Yer know as well as I do if anyone just tells t' police about it, nothing will 'appen. They won't be interested."

Ethel knew that was true. No one believed the children.

"Susan's mam knows about it, but 'er 'usband won't believe it. I reckon she's a bit scared of 'im. Yer know Alf Lawrence, don't yer?"

"Yes, yes, the policeman."

"Well, I knew 'im as a lad. Taught 'im the piano, I did. Well, I reckon if you was ter go an' see Alf' 'e would sort it out."

"Why me? Why me? Why don't you go, Miss Bell?"

"Two reasons. For one, I don't think me legs'll carry me all t'way up ter 'is 'ouse. For two, it'll be better comin' from you. More likely 'e'll sort it out quick. 'E's alright, is Alf. 'E'll know what ter do."

* * * *

Susan heard the familiar sounds in the kitchen from her place at the top of the stairs. The bar had closed, and Daddy was counting the money. She heard her mother fill the kettle. The funny thing was, neither of them said anything. They usually chatted or argued about something that had happened in the bar. Daddy would get cross if Mummy was friendly with the customers. Mummy would say she wasn't being friendly because it was part of the job. Daddy would say she was too friendly, enjoyed it too much. They had the same conversation night after night. At least she hadn't had to go in the bar; that horrible man hadn't been able to touch her. He had a nasty smile, with his horrid crooked teeth and smelly breath. After Jimmy told Granny Florrie about him, she had felt a bit better. Granny Florrie was nice. Her house was nice too, all friendly like Jimmy's house.

She was beginning to get cold. She stood up to go to her room when she heard her daddy say something. She sat down again.

"Susan will go in the bar tomorrow night as usual. I'll watch out for her. I want her to tell me which man does this. If it's true, I want to know who he is."

"How can you say that? She's frightened."

"She will do as I say. We need every penny since my Manchester business fell through."

Siobhan was shocked. It took a few moments for her to summon her courage. "I don't want Susan in the bar ever again."

"Is that so, Siobhan Fletcher?" Sarcasm and anger filled his words. "You would do well to remember who you are. What you were when I found you." He pointed his finger at her, jabbing the air between them. "You will do as I say and Susan will do as I say."

"What you are saying, Charlie, is nothing less than prostitution. Your own daughter being paid for sex." Siobhan was shouting, tears streaming down her face as the words tumbled out. "You say we need the money, well, we don't need it that much. I'd rather starve."

"How do you know anything about money? You don't. You don't know anything. Straight from the bog, ignorant Irish. That's you." He raised his fist.

"Charlie!" Siobhan instinctively dropped to her knees.

Charlie closed his eyes; his hand relaxed, the raised arm dropping to his side. Siobhan didn't move until she heard the door slam. He hadn't been going out after hours since the Manchester incident.

Susan got up from her cold stair and went to bed.

Siobhan went for a drink or two. Charlie had called her 'ignorant Irish'. The words kept spinning in her head. He was right, in a way. She was Irish and had no schooling to speak of. Her mind went back to Ireland. The gypsies and Dublin.

Chapter Eight

The school bell rang out across the playground; the old brass bell with its worn handle shaken enthusiastically by one of the older boys. The kudos of the bell monitor showed in his smile. The children ran to the double doors and formed their lines in order of height. Miss Hughes and her fellow teachers stood with their backs to the school building, each at the head of their class line. Everything was as it always was, as it had been for generations.

Ethel Hughes noted both Susan and Jimmy were present, and then looked towards the school gates to see Mrs Fletcher and Jimmy's mother in deep conversation, their arms linked, as they left the playground. She knew Jimmy's mother wasn't married, that there was no man around. Jimmy had told her. She assumed his father had deserted them. The morning routine continued. Register. Times tables. Sums. Playtime. Milk. More lessons. Dinner time. Then, and to the amazement of her colleagues in the staffroom, Miss Hughes put on her hat and coat.

"I'll be back for afternoon lessons. I have to go somewhere." She could feel their eyes on her back as she walked through the school gates.

The short walk to Alf Lawrence's house gave her time to think through her words. She had been awake most of the night, worrying about poor Susan and rehearsing the words she would use to tell Alf what was happening. She raised her hand to the knocker on the police house door. She was anxious that he may not have faith in her words, or maybe he wasn't home. His wife answered the door.

"Is P.C. Lawrence at home?"

Mrs Lawrence smiled as she turned her head towards the hallway. She knew the school teacher by sight. They were on 'Good Afternoon' terms, as Mrs Lawrence thought of it.

"Alf!" she shouted. "Miss Hughes is here to see you."

Alf came to the door.

"Sorry to bother you at home, P.C. Lawrence. It really is rather urgent. May I have a word with you?"

Mrs Lawrence retreated to the kitchen; police business was none of her business. Alf had never discussed his work with her. At first, she had been offended by his self-imposed silence on the subject, but she realised it had been for her own protection. This was a turn up for the books, though. Whatever could the school mistress want to see him about that couldn't be sorted out at the station? It was rather unusual, to say the least. Alf escorted Miss Hughes into the front parlour. He wore his slippers with his uniform trousers and shirt. Somehow the slippers made him more approachable. Miss Hughes relaxed a little.

"Always a pleasure to see you, Miss Hughes. Please sit down." He gestured towards a chair. They sat opposite each other in the tidy, little-used room. "Now, what can I do for you?"

"It's about Susan Fletcher. Yes, Susan Fletcher."

Alf Lawrence raised his eyebrows in surprise. "Go on."

Ethel looked at her hands; unable to look him in the eye as she spoke of the dreadful thing that was happening to Susan.

Alf's eyes widened as she spoke; he struggled to control his anger. Charlie Fletcher was lucky to have his freedom, but this...

"I have to go now, P.C. Lawrence. I have to go. Miss Bell and I were afraid no one would believe it at the police station. That's why I came straight to you. Yes, straight to you. I hope you don't mind."

"Leave it with me, Miss Hughes. I can assure you that Susan will not be going in that bar again—ever."

They stood up and went into the hallway.

"It's important the father doesn't blame Mrs Fletcher, P.C. Lawrence. Important that he doesn't think she told you. I fear for her, too. I fear for her, too."

"I'll make sure of that, Miss Hughes. You did right to come to me. That you did."

Ethel Hughes walked quickly back to school, relieved to be in her familiar environment. Susan didn't know it, poor child, but her troubles were over.

* * * *

"I can't stop, Pauline." Siobhan was agitated. The two women stood amongst the other mothers waiting for the children in the playground. "Charlie has been in a terrible mood. He says I have to go straight home with Susan as soon as she comes out of school. Says she has to eat her tea, put her best dress on to go into the bar. I'm worried sick, Pauline. What can I do? Last night, I thought he was going to hit me."

"I've told you what you can do. You can come and live with me and Jimmy."

"It's kind of you, more than kind. But I can't."

119

"Why not?"

"It's complicated. Charlie would never stand for it."

"The offer stays open, Siobhan."

"Thanks. I—" Her words were cut off by the school bell. "We'll talk another day, not now."

Susan ran towards her mother, her arms outstretched. Jimmy followed her, his reading books held tightly in his hands.

"Mummy! Mummy!"

"Hey, little missy, you had a good day?"

Susan nodded. "Can we go to Jimmy's house?"

"No, not today. Daddy wants us to go straight home."

"You can come tomorrow, Susan," Pauline assured her.

"Why can't they come today, Mummy?" Jimmy looked at Susan as he spoke to his mother. He could see tears in her eyes. "Susan wants to come today."

"Come on, Jimmy. Let's go." Pauline took Jimmy's books in one hand, holding him tightly with the other. For the life in her, Pauline couldn't understand Siobhan. If it was her and anything like that was happening to Jimmy, she wouldn't stay for a second. What was it that held Siobhan to Charlie and the Threlfalls? Siobhan loved Susan, Pauline had no doubt about that.

Susan ate her tea in silence as she sat at the big table in the kitchen, refusing to speak to her father or her mother. They both asked about her school day, what she had for dinner, what she had learned. Susan gave no reply. She finished her beans on toast and put her knife and fork neatly together on the plate.

"Take her upstairs and get her in that new dress. Now!"

Susan slid from her chair and went upstairs, followed by her mother. Siobhan heard Charlie mutter, "Sulky bitch," as they left the room. She wasn't sure if he meant Susan or herself; she didn't ask.

He shouted after them, "Down here. Six o'clock, prompt." They needed to know who was boss. That was the top and bottom of the problem.

Alf wasn't sure how to deal with this. Florrie Bell and Miss Hughes had been right about not going to the station. His sergeant wouldn't believe a word of it, and even if he did, he wouldn't do anything about it. Alf had told the school teacher he would sort it out, and he would. He just didn't know quite how he would go about it. He straightened his tie and was helped into his jacket by Mrs Lawrence. She brushed his spotless jacket. They had been married for ten years, and she could read him like a book. Alf loved children. It was a great sadness to them that they had not been blessed in that way. The school teacher coming to see him could only mean there was a problem with a child. It couldn't be the usual sort of trouble, truanting or the like. That would be dealt with through the proper channels. This had to be something different for her to come to the house in her lunch time. It was in Alf's face too. He was worried.

He kissed her cheek. "Bye, love." He smiled as he put on his helmet.

Alf liked to vary his route when he was on the beat. No good always being in the same place at the same time in his job. Criminals would soon work out where he was, or rather, where he wasn't. There was an exception to his rule; his routes always took him to the Threlfalls at seven o'clock.

That would have to change. Alf stood in a doorway watching Charlie open the doors and fasten them back with the brass bolts. Three men in working clothes followed him in. Regulars. Alf had seen them many a time. He crossed the road and went into the bar. Charlie was pulling a pint, chatting to his customers. Susan was sitting at one of the tables. Her tear-stained face was all the proof Alf needed. He walked over to her, crouching down in front of her. He spoke quietly.

"What are you doing here, Susan, in your pretty dress?"

"Daddy says I must."

"Susan!" Charlie shouted. "What are you doing? You know you shouldn't be in here. Siobhan!" he shouted. She came through from the kitchen.

"What is it, Charlie?" Siobhan saw Alf as she spoke, and Alf saw the fear and sadness in her face. Further confirmation of Miss Hughes' words. "Get Susan out of here right now. It's time she was in bed."

"Come on, Missy." Siobhan held out her hand.

Susan ran to her mother, jumping up into the safety of her arms. Without a word, Siobhan carried her through to the kitchen and straight up the back staircase.

Alf waited until Charlie had served his customers. Once Tom the barman had arrived, Alf beckoned Charlie to the table where Susan had been sitting. A red faced Charlie sat opposite Alf.

"Sorry about that, Alf. She'd been to a party. Not got changed out of her dress. I told Siobhan to take her straight upstairs, but you know what women are like. Never listen to a bloody word I—"

"Shut up, Charlie. You listen to me. If Susan ever steps foot in this bar again, I will see to it that you lose your licence. I will see to it that you never get another licence. Do you understand?"

"But Alf—"

"Don't 'but Alf' me. And don't lie to me. There has been no party tonight. I know that, and you know that. What are you doing, Charlie? Are you trying to turn your own daughter into a whore? Being paid by drunks to touch her? What are you thinking of?"

Charlie was scared. Very scared. His voice a whisper, he asked, "How did you know?"

"Stupid question, Charlie. I'll tell you this, though, it didn't come from Siobhan. She was just as shocked to see me as you were. I'll tell you something else. You are lucky to have your freedom, let alone a pretty wife and daughter. You had help in Manchester that night. God knows how you got back here without being picked up. You're a lucky man, Charlie Fletcher, but your luck won't hold if you ever let Susan in this bar again."

Charlie's mind raced. Alf knew about Manchester. How much did he know? How did he know about Susan being in the bar? Was there a connection? Had there been a plain clothes copper in the bar?

Charlie stood up. "I'll get you your drink then, Alf."

Alf nodded knowingly. Charlie brought the half of Tetley's to the table, setting it down without a word. He went back to the bar, and from his board he looked towards the policeman. As Alf raised the glass to his lips, Charlie nodded in acknowledgement.

Siobhan helped Susan out of the dress and into her nightie.

"Just going to clean my teeth, Mummy." Susan ran along the landing to the bathroom, her dark curls bouncing on her shoulders.

Siobhan sat on the edge of the bed, twirling her wedding ring on her finger. From now on, her pretty dresses would only be worn at parties. Whether Charlie believed what Susan had said or not didn't matter anymore. The only thing that mattered was that Susan wouldn't have to sit on any dirty old man's knee. Siobhan smoothed the fabric of the dress as she sat on the bed, deep in thought, and then took it to the third bedroom to hang in the wardrobe with the others.

She heard Susan's footsteps returning along the landing; she would tuck her in bed and go to work.

"Sing to me, Mummy. Sing the 'too-ra loo-ra' song."

Siobhan pulled the nursing chair to Susan's bedside and began to sing.

"Mummy?"

"Yes, Missy?" Siobhan could see the tears welling up, bringing tears to her own eyes.

"Will the policeman take Daddy to prison?"

"No, of course not. Whatever made you think that?"

"Daddy lied."

"When? What do you mean?"

"Well, it wasn't a really bad lie, but he shouted at me for being in the bar when it was Daddy who said I had to go and sit there. I don't want Daddy to go to prison."

"Daddy made a mistake, that's all. Nobody is going to prison, and you don't have to go in the bar anymore. Everything will be sorted out now. Just you wait and see. Now, can I finish the song for you?"

Susan snuggled under the bedclothes, holding her mother's hand as tightly as she could. Siobhan sang the lullaby over and over again until Susan's hand relaxed, and Siobhan was certain her daughter was fast asleep. She stood in the doorway for a while, just to be sure. Downstairs, she lit the kitchen fire and washed some dishes, put her lipstick on and checked her hair was tidy, before going through to the bar. Johnny and Billy had gone, everything looked perfectly normal. Cigarette smoke swirled around. Tom and Charlie were serving, the low hum of conversation, punctuated by laughter, giving a friendly atmosphere. Siobhan wanted a drink, but would have to wait for the opportunity.

"You took your time," Charlie said as he turned to the till.

"She was upset, wanted to know if you were going to prison." Siobhan kept her voice low.

Charlie shook his head and glowered at Siobhan.

"What's going on, Charlie?"

"We'll talk later. Get to work. I have to change a barrel."

"Can't Tom do that?"

"Just get to work."

Siobhan turned to the customers, put on her smile, and got to work.

It took fifteen seconds to pour the gin, drink it, polish the glass and put it back on the shelf.

Tom timed her. Siobhan was on the hard stuff.

Fifteen minutes later, Charlie came back.

Siobhan smiled at him. "You took your time," she said.

"What do you mean?" he snapped at her.

125

"I don't mean anything, Charlie. It was a joke. That's what you said to me when I came in."

"Go to the kitchen and clean up, Siobhan." He sounded weary.

"But I left it all clean and tidy."

"Just do as I say, woman."

Siobhan walked through to the kitchen. At first glance everything looked to be just as she had left it; but there was a strange, acrid smell. Her eyes went to the fireplace; there was ash everywhere. She picked up the brush from the side of the range and started to sweep the hearth. Fragments of material, gold ribbons, lace and pearl buttons were amongst the ashes. Charlie had burned all the party dresses.

* * * *

"He said we'd talk about it, but we didn't. He just counted his money and went out." Siobhan and Pauline were watching the children line up in the playground, ready to go into school. Pauline waved; Siobhan expected to see Jimmy wave back, but it was Miss Hughes who waved.

"What's all that about, Pauline?"

"Tell you later. Come on, let's go." The two women walked out of the school gates and down the street together. "You say he just went out. Where to?"

"God knows. He used to go out every night after closing time. I expected a row last night after we finished."

"Tell you what, Siobhan, right now I need to go home and get some sleep. Come round to my house about 3 o'clock, and I'll fill you in on what Florrie said. We'll have a cuppa before we pick Jimmy and Susan up from school."

Once back at the Threlfalls, Siobhan went about her cleaning. With Charlie two floors up, fast asleep in bed, she knew she didn't need to worry about disturbing him; not like her first morning at the Threlfalls when she had crept about like a mouse. She had a set routine, nowadays. Best room first, then the main room. Pumps polished, fireplaces cleaned, everywhere dusted. She vacuumed everywhere, even following the same route around the tables. Her hard work rewarded with a treat, then a little scented sweet to freshen her breath. Part of the routine. Dusters, polish and vacuum were put away; and then she picked up the mail from behind the front doors and placed it neatly on the kitchen table. Charlie had shown her where the paper knife was kept. Since then the knife had been placed at the side of the letters each morning. Time to start Charlie's breakfast.

"Again. You're going there *again*?" He was tucking into his bacon and sausages. Siobhan had learned over the years this was a good time to talk to Charlie. He was more likely to be in a good mood when he was eating his breakfast. She knew he didn't like Pauline. He didn't like her having a friend, someone to talk to.

"Susan likes to go. She and Jimmy like to play together. It's what children do, Charlie, play. You don't seem to like it when they come here."

"What does Pauline do with Jimmy when she goes to work?"

"Her neighbour looks after him. They have a connecting door upstairs. Why do you ask?"

"Because I need you in the bar. Even you can work it out. As Susan gets older, she'll want to stay up later."

"What are you suggesting?"

"I'm not suggesting anything. But something will have to be sorted out. What will you do when she's nine or ten? When she's older?

Siobhan didn't reply straight away. She poured the tea. Pauline had invited her, more than once, to take Susan and live with them. Susan would be welcome to stay any time. Maybe Jimmy would come to stay at the Threlfalls. The two of them upstairs would be safe enough. She didn't like leaving Susan alone upstairs before she was asleep. Not since the Manchester night. Siobhan was sure it wasn't the first time Susan had listened on the stairs. Susan loved her daddy, so she could never leave Charlie; she could never part them like that. It wouldn't be right; Susan came first.

The real reason was completely denied by any conscious thought. The treat reason. Siobhan could never leave the treats.

"I'll ask Pauline this afternoon. Maybe Jimmy could stay here sometimes, to keep Susan company upstairs."

"Better if Susan stays there."

"Like I say, Charlie, I'll ask Pauline. She's not there at night, remember. She would have to ask Florrie, next door."

"See what you can do. Susan can't be down here once we're open. Not now. Not ever." He picked up the pile of letters from the table. He paused at one envelope, tuning it in his hand. The address was hand written in capital letters. He checked the postmark. Manchester. Picking up the paper knife, he carefully slit the envelope to remove the single sheet of lined notepaper. Written in an uneducated hand, his eyes travelled quickly to the bottom of the page. Gloria. He put the letter back in the envelope. He would read it later, when Siobhan wasn't around. He tucked it in his jacket pocket.

Charlie made his way up the long staircase to the attics. The flecks of dried paint on the landing carpet puzzled him for a moment. He hadn't been along this way for a while, preferring the fire escape. Someone had though. He crouched down to look more closely. The footprints were small. "Bloody kids," he muttered to himself. He stood up and walked quickly into the sitting room. Everything looked the same. Furniture undisturbed, all the dustsheets in place. If Susan and Jimmy had been in here, they hadn't touched anything. He would have to lock the bureau in future though. He couldn't very well ask Siobhan to stop them. She didn't even know about this place, not even after all these years. Showed how stupid she was. She had been right about Susan and that dirty bastard though. Susan had been telling the truth. When Siobhan was clearing up the fireplace that night he heard a customer ask Tom about Susan. '*Where's the pretty girl who likes to sit on my knee*?' Charlie had walked over to him, his face burning with anger. With his voice controlled and menacing, he quietly said, '*Get out of my pub and don't ever come back.*' The eye-to-eye contact between Charlie and the perverted bastard who had dared to touch his daughter indelibly printed on Charlie's mind. His filthy teeth as he grinned, his narrowed eyes, were proof enough. Susan had told the truth.

He angrily pulled the dustsheet off the bureau and chair to rid his mind of the memory. The green leather seat of the chair split a little further as he sat down. The bentwood back creaked in protest. He took the little envelope out of the bureau and read it again. He had ignored it at first, but curiosity was getting the better of him. The letter had been tucked in a little drawer for several weeks. His savings were dwindling fast now his bullion business had collapsed. The

Threlfalls didn't make enough to keep them all. He could have managed on his own, but keeping a wife and daughter was expensive. Bloody women.

* * * *

"Which do you like best, Jimmy? When I stay here, or when you stay with me?" Susan asked.

They were in Jimmy's room, getting ready for bed. Two single beds, a bedside table and lamp furnished the little room. A small striped rug covered the gap between the beds. The mantelpiece of a small cast iron fireplace at the side of his bed gave Jimmy a shelf for his toy cars. Jimmy had rearranged the clothes in his chest of drawers so his friend could keep some spare things at his house. He kept some pyjamas at Susan's hotel. No need for Susan to move any of her clothes though. When he stayed there, he and Susan slept in Room Five. The two single beds at the hotel were further apart than the ones at his house because the room was so big. The wardrobe, dressing table and chest of drawers were all empty. Jimmy used the little drawer in the dressing table because it didn't smell damp.

"I like both. I like your hotel because we can have adventures in all the rooms, but my bed here is more comfortable." Charlie had arranged for Billy Oldroyd to bring a bed from The Threlfalls to Vine Street in his van so Susan could stay overnight.

Pauline could hear them talking; she was in the next room, changing into her working clothes. She couldn't stop herself smiling. Jimmy, the five year old pragmatist. She was so proud of him, not just his achievements at school either. He was such a loving child, kind in every way, maybe a bit serious for his age. Susan was good for him. She was on the ball, that one. Nothing escaped Susan.

"Me, too. But this bed feels just the same as my one at home. I like it here because the beds are close together and we can hold hands. Next time you stay, we'll go exploring again. We haven't been in all the rooms yet."

"I thought we had," Jimmy said.

Pauline would have liked to listen longer, but she needed to leave for work. What adventures? Exploring, indeed. It sounded like fun.

Pauline kissed the two children and tucked them in. "I have to go now, Jimmy. You two behave for Florrie, now. She'll be up to read you a story soon."

"Auntie Pauline?"

"Yes, Susan?"

"What's prostitution?"

Pauline was appalled. Where had she heard that word? Why had she asked her and not her mother?

Pauline took a moment to reply. "Well, it's nothing for you to worry about, little girl. It's a grown up word. Not for children."

"It's not swearing, though."

"No, it's not swearing."

"I didn't think so. I heard Mummy say it to Daddy when they were talking in the kitchen one night. Mummy doesn't swear."

Siobhan had told Pauline how Susan sat on the stairs and listened to them.

"I don't do it now. I don't listen now that Jimmy stays. He says it's too cold."

Pauline smiled and kissed her again. She would have a word with Siobhan about it.

"I have to go now. Be good, you two."

They snuggled down, listening to Pauline lock the front door behind her.

Jimmy wanted to know about the other rooms at the hotel.

"Where are these other rooms then, Susan?"

"If you look up from outside, there's another upstairs, on top of the bedrooms."

"How do we get up there? There isn't another staircase."

"There has to be. You know I told you my daddy used to go out every night?"

"Yes. The back way."

"Well, sometimes he doesn't really go anywhere. He goes out of the back door and then up the fire escape to the very top."

Jimmy's eyes grew wide with excitement. "How do you know, Susan?"

"I've seen him. If I stand on a chair in the ballroom, I can see the fire escape."

"But where's the inside staircase, then?"

"Don't know. At the end of the landing there's a door frame that has no door. It's been made into part of the wall. That might have been it, but there must be another. That will be our next adventure."

"Shh. Quiet. Granny Florrie's coming."

* * * *

Siobhan and Pauline sat side by side in the Merrion Gardens. School wasn't out for half an hour yet. The two friends cherished the time they were able to spend together.

Conversations centred around the children, school, and organising sleeping arrangements.

Siobhan had been horrified when Pauline told her of Susan's question about prostitution.

"When we had all that trouble, I told Charlie if he made her go into the bar again, it was like prostitution. It confirms what I thought at the time. The little minx had been listening on the stairs for some time, on the main stairs, too, when the bar was open. She told me she knew Alf's voice. That he was the man who came in at seven o'clock, but she didn't know he was a policeman until he spoke to her that night. I'm grateful to you, Pauline, for sorting it all out, including telling her it was a grown up word. She must've caught you by surprise with that one."

"It's what friends are for, Siobhan, that's all." Pauline smiled. Slowly, her expression changed, and a frown crept across her face.

"What is it?" Siobhan asked.

"Whatever would I do without Florrie, Siobhan? It worries me. What if Florrie fell ill and couldn't look after the children? Or worse?"

Siobhan had her own reasons to be grateful for Florrie. Charlie had never made the connections between Florrie, Miss Hughes and Alf.

"I never much like to say 'what if'. There's no point. Think about it, Pauline. You have your house, and your job, and Florrie. That's three things more than I have."

"But you have a husband, Siobhan."

"You have your independence."

"What if I lose my job?"

"You're doing it again, Pauline, with your 'what if'." Siobhan laughed, trying to lighten her friend's mood.

Pauline smiled. They sat in silence for a while. "Do you still have nightmares, Siobhan?"

"Just that same one. It started the night I thought Charlie was going to hit me."

"Has he ever hurt you?"

"No, never again, not even threatened. The nightmare won't stop, though. It's always the same. The fist comes down and I wake up just before it hits me. I wake up with a start, sitting up in bed." They sat in silence for a while. Siobhan took a deep breath. "The thing I hate about it most is that as the fist comes down, it changes from Charlie's fist into my Pa's fist. Then I'm just so relieved to wake up, and know I'm safe at home." Siobhan had never spoken of her own childhood before. Not to anyone.

"Does he know where you are, your Pa?"

"No. No one does."

"Best way. Keep it like that, Siobhan. You don't have to fear him turning up. The nightmare is just that – a nightmare."

"Does anyone know where you are, Pauline?"

"No. My mother is dead. I never see anyone." Pauline shuddered as she spoke, unable to say the word 'father'. "That's the way I like it."

"My Ma would love to see Susan. My brothers and sisters would, too."

"Will you ever go back?"

"No, never."

"You could write to tell them you're okay."

"Yes, I could," Siobhan said in monotone.

"But you won't."

"No. If I wrote, Pa would find out, and they would all get a beating. The only person I could ever have written to was Mrs McMahon, and she's probably dead now. It's not worth the risk, Pauline. Best left as it is. Come on, time to go to school and collect our little darlings."

Chapter Nine

June 1964

Charlie stood in front of the bathroom mirror. Leaning forward, he peered at his scalp under the thinning hair. The pomade made the first signs of baldness more obvious. He threw the red and white pot in the waste paper basket. Siobhan and Susan were chattering away in the next room. He glanced at his watch; five to six. As he passed the bedroom door, he saw Siobhan sitting in front of the dressing table. Susan was combing her mother's hair.

"Nearly opening time, Siobhan. Don't be long."

Susan scowled. Charlie didn't see it. He was already at the top of the stairs.

"Okay, Charlie, we won't be long." Siobhan looked at her daughter through the reflection of the mirror. "Have to hurry up, Missy."

"Oh, Mum. I wanted to paint your nails for you." Susan clipped an imitation diamond slide in Siobhan's hair, glowering at the mirror.

Siobhan winced as the slide touched her head. "Careful." She put her hand to the back of her head in an effort to ease the pain. "Tomorrow, Susan. We'll make time tomorrow. I have to go." Siobhan stood up.

"Does your head hurt today, Mum?"

"Not too bad." Siobhan smiled at her daughter. She was nearly sixteen and would be leaving school in a few weeks. The same age she had been when she left Ireland.

She knew her daughter wasn't the cleverest girl in the class, but she was pretty and bright in every other way. Kind, too.

"You're daft the way you jump to his every order. It won't be that busy down there at this time. He just wants you under his eye."

"Your dad likes me to be there. The customers expect it. I like working in the bar, Susan."

"Have you had anything to eat, Mum?"

"No, I'll get something later. There's plenty of food in the fridge if you want anything."

"Will you be having a drink?"

Siobhan was stung by the question. A sadness crept over her face. "Well, now. Sometimes a customer might offer to buy me a drink."

"And do you ever say, 'No, thanks'?"

"Now, that would be rude, wouldn't it?"

Susan's shoulders sagged. She hated the way her mother drank and blamed her father for letting it happen. Susan knew her mother drank more than she ate these days.

"Why don't you go round to see Charmaine?" Siobhan picked up a packet of scented sweets from the dressing table. She peeled back the paper wrapper and offered one to Susan.

"No, thanks, and it's Chaz."

"What's Chaz?" Siobhan asked.

"Charmaine. She likes to be called Chaz."

Susan turned her back on her mother and went to her own room across the landing. The number '2' on the door had been replaced by a pretty plaque with her name written in flowers. She slammed the door behind her and threw herself on the bed. Tears of anger burned her eyes, blurring her focus. Susan knew the sweets were to mask the alcohol, even if her mother didn't admit it. She wiped her eyes on her pillow. Turning to one side, supporting her head with one hand, her elbow sank into the soft bed.

She looked around the room. Angel Face sat in one corner, her unblinking cold eyes staring back. Susan had put a bonnet on her to hide her bald head. Mum had told her she could comb her doll's hair, so she thought she would cut it, too. Nobody had told her that it wouldn't grow again. That was years ago. The doll's pram and her other toys were stored in one of the other bedrooms, with the big pram.

She reached out to her bedside table and switched on a transistor radio. Boring old fashioned music. Big band sound, Mum called it. She turned the knobs for a while, trying to find Radio Luxembourg, or even jazz. Auntie Pauline liked jazz. She switched it off, lazily walking across the room to her record player. She selected her new Beatles L.P. 'With the Beatles.' She took it from its sleeve, pausing to look at the black and white photograph of the Fab Four. The Dansette record player had been a Christmas present two years ago, and since then, Dad had bought her all the records she asked for.

Susan brushed her hair and tidied her dressing table, putting her nail varnishes in a row. She wasn't allowed to wear it for school. Looking around at the faded curtains and wallpaper, she decided to tell her dad to get this room decorated. It was too babyish. She was leaving school at the end of next month, so would be able to wear nail varnish every day. That was the main reason she didn't want to work in the bakery with Pauline. The workers weren't allowed to wear any makeup at all. What she really wanted was a job on the cosmetic counter at Lavells. She lay on her bed for a while listening to the music and then wandered downstairs to the kitchen and put the television on. The News. Boring. She turned it off. Opening a drawer, she took out a pencil and paper, then scrawled across it, 'Gone to Jimmy's'.

* * * *

"Can I have a word, boss?" Tom asked nervously. Siobhan was chatting to a customer at the best room end of the bar. A couple sat at one of the tables; Billy and Johnny had just left.

"What is it, Tom?" Charlie frowned. Tom never chatted, as a rule.

"It's about Siobhan."

"What about Siobhan?" Charlie was defensive. Whatever Tom had to say wasn't going to be welcome news.

"I'm worried about her. You know she drinks and has headaches?" Tom kept his voice low.

"Of course I know. Anyone who drank that much would get headaches." Charlie was irritated that Tom, of all people, should even think to raise the subject with him. "I've known for years. The only surprising thing about it is she thinks I don't know."

"I like Siobhan, boss." Charlie looked puzzled. "Not like that, boss. I mean I think she's a decent sort." Tom knew he shouldn't have started the conversation.

Charlie looked annoyed. "Go on."

"Well, I admit I didn't want her here at first, but I…"

"What's brought all this on, Tom?"

"I just needed to tell you, in case you didn't know. I should've known better. Anyway, I needed to tell you because I'm leaving."

"Leaving? Leaving what?"

"Here. The Threlfalls. I've got another job."

"Where? Why?" Charlie couldn't believe his ears.

"I've been working mornings down at the stables for nothing, grooming and cleaning tack. I like working with the horses, and they've offered me a full time job."

"Horses?"

"The Tetley horses. I might even get a job on the drays."

"Christ almighty, Tom. Are you sure? When will you be leaving?"

"End of the week, boss. They want me to start Monday."

A crowd of men walked in, laughing and talking, putting an end to the conversation.

"Pints all round, landlord. I've been lucky on the horses."

"Horses. I've heard all I want to hear about horses for one night," Charlie muttered under his breath as he and Tom started to pull the pints. Siobhan stayed at the best room end of the bar; she could sense something was wrong. There was no banter between Charlie and Tom and the customers. They spoke only to ask for payment for the beer.

Suddenly, everything was swimming around her. She grasped the worn edge of the bar, unable to focus. Charlie saw her stagger; Tom had seen it too. The two men exchanged a look that, ten minutes ago, they couldn't have shared. She was drunk. As Tom stepped towards her, she put her right hand up in protest to show she didn't want any help. Her left hand grasped the door knob to steady her as she left the bar. Once in the kitchen, she took a deep breath, the pains in her side and in her head bending her body forward, her hand moving automatically to the back of her head. She grabbed the edge of the table, focusing briefly on

Susan's note. The pain in her side lessened momentarily, allowing her to walk carefully up the back stairs to her bathroom. She knelt at the toilet and vomited. Blood. She retched violently. Dark blood. Her only fear was that Tom would tell Charlie she had been drinking. The pain in her head blocked coherent thought.

* * * *

Pauline Hanson had worked at the bakery for fifteen years. If she had been a man, she would have been supervisor years ago. It didn't worry her. She fed and clothed herself and her son, and that was all she cared about. It had been a struggle, especially when Jimmy passed his Eleven Plus and won a scholarship to Leeds City Grammar School. The uniform had been a big expense, and the way he was growing meant it wasn't long before she was back at Rawcliffes buying the next size. He was in the middle of his 'O' level exams and was expected to do well. In September, he would start in the sixth form and study for 'A' levels. He was a good lad. When he was younger, he had been teased at school about his red hair but had coped with it as he coped with the fact that most of his classmates were from quite well-off families. Jimmy took things in his stride.

Pauline was making sandwiches and tea before she left for work. Jimmy had his books spread out on Florrie's kitchen table. Florrie sat in her comfortable fireside chair. Even in June, she felt the cold. Her bed had been in the little front room for a couple of years now. She was eighty four years old, and her legs wouldn't take her up the stairs. There had been a gradual role reversal, with Jimmy looking after Florrie in the evenings, preferring to study in her house where he could hear her if she needed him. It was one more reason for Pauline to be proud of her son.

"Anyone at home?"

The footsteps running down the stairs could only be Susan. She had a key to Pauline's house and used the connecting door in the bedrooms to make her way through. She knew where Pauline and Jimmy would be.

"In t'kitchen, love," Florrie shouted back. Her wrinkled face lit up at the sound of Susan's voice. Jimmy put his pen down and closed his book.

"Fancy coming out for a walk, Jimmy?"

"Sorry, Susan. I've got two exams tomorrow. Maths in the morning and geography in the afternoon. I'll need an early night."

Susan pouted. "You'd come and walk with me if you could, wouldn't you, Granny Florrie?" Susan sat on the rug next to the old lady.

"I would that, love, but Jimmy 'ere wants ter study. Sometimes, I think t'lad'll get brain fever, 'e studies that much."

"Two more weeks of exams, Granny Florrie, then I'm free of school until September."

"You want a sandwich, Susan?" Pauline said as she handed a plate to Florrie.

"Yes, please, if there's any spare."

"That's the one advantage of working in a bakery, Susan. There's always bread to eat."

Pauline liked Susan. She and Jimmy had remained friends, despite the fact they went to different schools. They were like brother and sister, spending time together in the holidays and at weekends. Susan still stayed overnight sometimes, but Jimmy didn't go to The Threlfalls anymore. He preferred to stay at home.

"You can walk to work with me if you like."

Half an hour later, Pauline and Susan walked along Vine Street toward the bakery.

"How's your mum, Susan?" Pauline asked. "I don't see her much these days."

"You want the honest answer?"

"Of course I do. What else?"

"I'm worried about her. You know she drinks?"

"Yes. I know. Well, I guessed it, so I'm not surprised. Does your dad know?"

"He doesn't care. As long as she cooks and cleans and looks nice, he pretends it's not happening." They walked on in silence. Pauline knew Charlie had never liked her and didn't want to make matters worse for Siobhan, so she kept away.

"Shall I come to see her?" Pauline asked. "I could come tomorrow afternoon."

"She usually sleeps in the daytime, after she's done the cleaning. She gets terrible headaches and goes to bed."

"What does your dad say about that?"

"Nothing much. He goes out a lot."

"I'll come round tomorrow about twelve o'clock. Maybe she'll walk to the Merrion Gardens with me like we used to."

"Did she ever talk to you about Ireland?"

"A bit. Why do you ask?"

"Just curious, I suppose. What did she tell you?"

"Just that she would never go back. You should ask her, Susan. It's not for me to say."

"But you do know more?"

"Some, but—"

"Hi, Pauline." One of Pauline's workmates joined them as they neared the bakery gates. Susan wanted to ask more about her mum, but the moment was lost.

"See you tomorrow, Auntie Pauline."

"Okay, love."

Susan walked slowly back to the Threlfalls. She was bored. The summer evening sun on her back made her feel sleepy in a fed-up sort of way. She went in the front door of The Threlfalls. She couldn't be bothered walking around the back. It would annoy her dad, but she didn't care. If he wasn't talking to customers, she would tell him she wanted her room decorated.

"What are you doing coming in this way?" Charlie demanded when he spotted her.

Susan looked at him in an uninterested way. She saw he was serving Alf, the policeman. He wasn't wearing his uniform. She liked Alf. It explained why her dad sounded so cross.

"Hi, Mr Lawrence. Where's your uniform?"

"Hello, Susan. It's my night off, just called in for a half…"

"Go upstairs, will you, Susan, see what your mother's up to?"

Without replying, Susan walked through to the kitchen. Her note was still on the big pine table. She picked it up and threw it on the fire grate; Siobhan had laid it ready to be lit if it was chilly later on.

"Mum," she shouted up the staircase. There was no reply. "Mu-um," louder this time. Susan returned to the kitchen and turned on the television. She watched a quiz show for a while before shouting for her mother again. Still no reply. This time she went up the stairs to find her. The bathroom door was open; a tap had been left running. As she turned it off, she saw blood on a towel. Turning quickly, she ran along the landing to her parents' bedroom. Siobhan lay motionless on the bed, clutching her head in both hands. There was blood on the pillow. Susan let out an ear piercing shriek of terror. She ran from the room to her father's bathroom and was violently sick in one of the basins. Grabbing a towel, she wiped her face and went back to the bedroom. Ignoring the blood and the vomit, she grasped her mother's shoulders, shaking her body.

"Wake up, Mum. Wake up." She let go, and the lifeless body fell back on the bed. Susan ran down the main staircase to the bar.

"Susan! How many times do you have to be told? Get out!"

"Listen to me, Dad."

He ignored the panic in her voice. If Charlie had looked up from pulling a pint, he would have seen Susan's terror-stricken face. He might even have noticed the blood on her hands. He had heard her tantrums too many times.

"Get out, Susan, or I'll—"

"Mum's dead!" she screamed at him, tears streaming down her face. A stunned silence followed her words throughout the bar and the best room. Charlie dropped the glass he was holding. He looked to Tom, then across to Alf before running up the main stairs, Susan close behind him. Low, shocked conversations slowly filled the bar, heads turning in disbelief. Alf's voice was heard above the noise.

"Phone for an ambulance, Tom. Dial 999."

Tom picked up the phone at the side of the till and dialled the emergency number. Alf ran up the two flights of stairs to the private rooms of the Threlfalls. He got to the top just as Charlie was coming out of the first bedroom. The expression on his face told Alf that Susan was right. Siobhan was dead. Susan's keening wail came from the room as she cried for her mother, begging her to wake up. Charlie followed Alf back into the room. He knelt at the bedside, stroking Siobhan's hair, unable to take his eyes away from her face. Susan stopped crying aloud. Silent tears fell from her swollen eyes.

Alf put his hand on Charlie's shoulder. "The ambulance will be here soon, Charlie. Take Susan downstairs."

The hopeless, stunned silence was tangible, filling the room with emptiness. Alf Lawrence had seen some tragic things in his years as a policeman, but he couldn't remember ever seeing such conspicuous shock. Charlie Fletcher was a foolish man in many ways, but right now, Alf felt sorry for him. He stepped back as Susan walked towards Charlie. She knelt at her father's side. Leaning forward, she turned her head in front of Charlie's face to make him look at her.

"Dad, come downstairs with me. There's nothing we can do here. Not now."

Charlie looked at his daughter as if she were a stranger, his expression blank. She stood up and helped him to his feet. They walked out of the room together, Susan's arm under his. Charlie looked over his shoulder, transfixed by the unreal image before his eyes. She guided him down the back staircase to the kitchen, to his battered old chair at the fireside. She turned the volume down on the television.

Charlie stared straight ahead at Siobhan's empty chair. "I did love her, you know," he whispered. "I should have stopped her. Stopped her drinking."

Susan leant against a cupboard. A physical pain twisted her stomach. She couldn't speak, and anyway, she didn't know what to say. Unconsciously, she started to do the things her mother would have done, putting the kettle on, striking a match to light the fire that Siobhan had laid. The kettle made familiar low noises as it began to boil. Charlie leaned forward, his head in his hands; he couldn't bear to look at Siobhan's empty chair.

Susan put her hand on his shoulder. As he sat up, she handed him a cup of tea.

Alf came into the room. "The ambulance men have left for now, Charlie. A doctor will call later on, and she will be taken to hospital after closing time. No need to bring her downstairs when the place is full."

"Hospital? What for?"

"There will have to be a post mortem, Charlie."

Charlie put his hand to his forehead, rubbing it vigorously, trying to make sense of it all.

"Why?" It was Susan who asked. "Everyone knows Mum drank too much."

Alf sighed deeply. "I'm sorry, Susan, but these things have to be done. I expect your mum hadn't seen a doctor for a long time, so no one can be sure."

Susan turned the television off. A hum of voices drifted through from the bar.

"I have to go. Mrs Lawrence will wonder where I am. I'll come back later, after closing."

Charlie stood up. "Thanks. Alf. Thanks for staying. I'll see you through to the bar."

The two men left the kitchen. Susan put on a coat and went out of the back door, banging it behind her. She ran all the way to Chaz's house. The Fourniers were about to go to bed when Susan's banging on the door broke the routine of the household. Susan could barely speak through her tears.

"Come in, Susan. Sit down, *ma petite. Qu'est ce que c'est?*" Madame Fournier ushered Susan into the comfortable sitting room as she spoke in her half-English, half-French way. Chaz came through from the kitchen as quickly as she could, holding on to the strategically placed furniture which enabled her to move around her home unaided on her twisted ankles.

"Susan! What is it? What's wrong?"

"Mum told me to come," she sobbed, her words almost incoherent. Monsieur Fournier brought her a glass of water. Slowly, Susan told the Fourniers what had happened, and how the last thing her mother had said to her was, 'Why don't you go round to see Charmaine'. The two teenagers hugged each other and cried together. Madame Fournier made coffee, and they ate home-made almond biscuits. Monsieur Fournier telephoned the Threlfalls and left a message with the barman to say Susan was staying with them tonight, and to pass on his condolences to Monsieur Fletcher.

* * * *

Two weeks later, on Thursday 2nd July, 1964, Siobhan Fletcher's coffin was carried into Leeds Parish Church by her friends Tom, Alf, Johnny and Billy. Charlie and Susan walked behind, side by side, but not touching each other. Pauline and Jimmy helped Florrie to her seat. The Fourniers were in the pew behind them. A dozen or so customers from The Threlfalls filed in at the back, along with some fellow publicans and their wives. The post mortem had delayed things. Charlie just wanted to get today over with. The shock of her death had barely registered with Charlie when the result of the post mortem hit him like a sledge hammer. He couldn't rid his mind of the carefully written words on the death certificate. *'Carcinoma cerebellum. Medulloblastoma.'* Charlie had expected to see the words *'Cirrhosis of the liver'.* He asked the doctor what it meant and was told Siobhan had died of a brain tumour.

The vicar said something. They all sat down, then they stood up and a hymn was sung. Then they sat down, the vicar spoke again, and they all filed out. None of it meant a thing to Charlie. Pictures of Siobhan flashed through his mind. The frightened girl he met on the train. The young mother in Leeds General Infirmary with a tiny baby at her breast. The beautiful woman at his side at the Licensed Victuallers Dinner. Every image tortured him, each followed by a picture of her dead eyes staring at him from her pillow, then those carefully written words. *'Carcinoma cerebellum, Medulloblastoma.'* The doctor also told him she had stomach ulcers, and there had been some damage to her liver, but not enough to kill her.

Pauline put her arm around Susan as they stood at the graveside. Charlie stood on the opposite side of the gaping hole that was Siobhan's grave. It was a mirror of their relationship. Pauline was devastated. Everything had changed since that morning when Susan came round just after Jimmy left for school. Pauline felt it said a lot about Susan, that she had waited until she knew he was gone, not wanting to upset him when he had important exams. They went upstairs and through to Florrie's house, and Susan told her the sad news. Florrie and Pauline and Susan cried together, holding hands in mutual support. The two women wept for the loss of their friend, and they wept for Susan, a girl without a mother. Susan was inconsolable, still sobbing as she left the house. Florrie and Pauline wanted her to stay, but she said she wanted to be alone.

As days passed, Susan's sadness gave way to anger; she blamed her father for everything. He had bullied her to death. Even after the results of the post mortem were known and after the funeral, she blamed him. She couldn't speak to him; she didn't want to speak to anyone. She felt friendless, walking for hours around the city streets, alone in the crowds. She resented Jimmy and Chaz for having a mother, she resented Pauline and Florrie for crying so much. Pauline kept telling her she was a good, kind person, but Susan didn't feel good or kind. She felt hatred for everyone and everything. Eventually, she felt hatred towards her mother. How could she die and leave her all alone? She shouldn't have. It wasn't fair.

* * * *

Susan had her head down, looking at the kitchen floor of 16 Vine Street. "Why didn't she go to the doctor about her headaches? I'll tell you why. She was too busy cleaning fireplaces and polishing beer pumps, that's why."

Jimmy and Pauline looked at each other as Susan spat out the words. Pauline was worried about her. Since that first day when she came to tell them her mother had died, Susan had hardly cried at all.

"Susan." Pauline put her hand under Susan's chin, making her look her in the eye. "You have to go home and talk to your father."

Susan looked towards Jimmy.

"Don't look at me, Susan. I have no father."

His words stung them both. Jimmy went upstairs to his room. Pauline closed her eyes. In trying to help Susan, she had opened the greatest wound of all. Susan left quietly and went home. Pauline slumped forward on the table, resting her head on folded arms. Slowly, the tears started to fall, wetting her eyelashes, then her sleeve. Jimmy had never asked about his father. She had rehearsed her reply in her head many times. She would tell him he had left her, which in a way was true. But he never asked. There had never been a moment that was right for her to raise the subject. She hoped it would never surface. Well, it had surfaced, and she would have to talk to Jimmy about it, but not now. If she tried to talk to him now, she would make a mess of it. She would cry and upset Jimmy. She would talk to him when she felt stronger.

Pauline took her coat from the hook in the hallway and shouted up the stairs. "Off to work, love," her voice quavered. "See you in the morning."

Jimmy lay on his bed, staring at the ceiling. He heard the sadness in his mother's voice. She had never gone to work without making supper for him and for Granny Florrie before she left.

* * * *

Charlie Fletcher was unhappy and worried in equal measures. From the moment Tom said he was leaving, everything had gone wrong. With all the commotion of Siobhan's death, he had forgotten Tom was leaving until the Sunday night when he said goodbye. It seemed whichever path his thoughts took, there was something to worry about. The new bar staff, Adam and Dave, were students at the university. Unreliable. Never on time; sometimes they didn't turn up at all.

It had been easy enough to find a cleaner. Mrs Roberts had a key and let herself in each morning to clean the bars. She didn't clean it like Siobhan, though, and there was no breakfast waiting for him when he got up. No shirts perfectly ironed and hanging in the wardrobe. Now there was Susan waiting in the kitchen. Said she wanted a chat.

He was worried sick about Susan. Didn't know what to say to her, how to talk to her. Charlie had the feeling she blamed him for Siobhan's death. He hoped she wouldn't want to talk for too long. He needed to be in the bar keeping an eye on things, and, after closing, he had to go out. At least that side of things was ticking over nicely.

The way Pauline said *'You have to go home and talk to your father'* convinced Susan he had something to say. She waited for him in the kitchen and waited for the kettle to boil. Mum had been forever making cups of tea. The kitchen was empty without her. Susan sat in Siobhan's chair, stroking the arm. She pulled up her knees, her feet hanging over the edge of the seat with her arms wrapped around her legs. She curled up to one side, nestling in the comfortable chair that still smelled of her mother's perfume. As Charlie came into the kitchen, he could only see the back of her head. For a split second, he thought she was Siobhan. His hands shook as he poured the tea, the cup rattled in the saucer as he handed the hot drink to Susan.

"Did you ever make Mum a cup of tea?"

"I don't think I ever did. No. Maybe when you were a baby I might have."

"Tell me about Mum," Susan said, almost in a whisper.

Charlie sat in his chair, opposite his daughter. "What do you mean? What's there to tell? She was your mum."

"I wish she hadn't died. I wish she was still here." Involuntary tears filled Susan's eyes.

"We all do. Everyone who knew her." Charlie looked directly at her.

She sniffed, forcing back the tears. "Why didn't you tell her to go to the doctor about her headaches?"

It was a question Charlie had asked himself countless times. "I wish I had. The doctor would've given her something for the pain. He couldn't have saved her though, Susan."

"How can you be sure? How can you say that?" Anger rose in her voice. She wanted her mother's death to be Charlie's fault.

"It's what the doctor told me." A silence fell between them. Charlie stood up. "Listen, love, I have to go back in the bar. I don't trust those two lads as far as I could throw them. We can talk again another time if you like."

"Where do you go after closing time?"

"I…I have to go out…on business." Charlie was stunned. He hadn't expected her to ask that.

"What business?"

He was irritated by the question. "Business that doesn't concern you. Except, perhaps, that you are the reason I need to have other business."

"What do you mean?" It was Susan's turn to be shocked. The question sounded like an accusation to Charlie.

"How do you think I pay for all your records, all your clothes, all of this?" He gestured with his arm in a semi-circle around the room. Charlie was losing his temper, his voice raised. He hated anyone asking about his dealings, and Susan was no exception. "The bar takings don't cover it all, that's for sure. Your mother knew not to ask questions, and I suggest you would do well to take a leaf out of her book." He jabbed the air with his forefinger, pointing it at Susan, turned quickly on his heel and marched out of the kitchen. As he stepped up onto his board, he heard the back door bang. She had gone out. He gritted his teeth, feeling the temper hot under his skin as he ignored the wary looks from Adam and Dave.

Charlie tried to concentrate on his customers, but he couldn't get Susan out of his mind. His head was working on two levels. Outwardly, he smiled and chatted while inwardly he was in turmoil. It annoyed him that he was annoyed. That girl could turn him on his head in seconds. He, Charlie Fletcher, was a fool to no one – except Susan.

* * * *

Pauline looked at the pavement as she walked to work, only lifting her head when she crossed a road. Lost in thoughts and oblivious to others around her, she only heard the sound of her own footsteps. Jimmy meant everything to her. Should she tell him the truth? Part of the truth? He must have wondered why they had no family at all. She wished Siobhan was here. She could have talked it over with her. The thought of her old friend made her despondent. The only person she could have talked to was dead at the age of thirty one. Siobhan was the only person she had told about

Jimmy's father; she couldn't remember now how they came to talk about it. It had been one afternoon when Charlie was in Manchester, and they were in the Merrion Gardens. Siobhan confided in her all about Ireland, and she, in turn, had spoken of her past. A moment shared that deepened the friendship. There was Florrie, of course, but it wasn't the same as talking to Siobhan; she couldn't tell Florrie. She wished she had spent more time with Siobhan over the last couple of years, but she hadn't, and now it was too late. She knew Florrie was in a bad way; her lips turned blue at the slightest effort. Jimmy would miss his Granny Florrie when she was gone. Then they really would be on their own. Pauline shuddered at the thought.

Lost in grief for the past and fear for the future, Pauline walked straight past the bakery gates and on to the town centre and the Merrion Gardens. She wanted to sit on the seat she and Siobhan had occupied before collecting Jimmy and Susan from school. She turned the corner and looked up. The sight before her was awful. The gardens were gone, ripped up, part of the building site that was to be a new shopping centre. She couldn't even work out where the gardens had been. The sight of the muddy chaos saddened her. Pauline had come here to be close to Siobhan. The lost gardens echoed the loss of her friend.

"Oh, Siobhan," she said out loud. "They've taken our seat away."

She stared at the confusion of the building site, then turned back onto Briggate, crossing over rather than walking past the doors of the Threlfalls Hotel. Buses filled the air with diesel fumes.

"What should I do, Siobhan? Should I tell Jimmy everything?" she asked out loud. Siobhan's voice answered clearly in Pauline's head. *'I'll never look down on you, Pauline.'*

She walked on, turning down The Headrow; taking a seat in the bus station, she stared at the grey walls of Quarry Hill Flats. Her thoughts were in the past. The long ago past of Sheffield surfaced in her mind. She pushed them away with a shudder, asking herself what would happen if she told Jimmy the truth of his father. How would it affect her quiet, thoughtful, clever boy? There were no answers. The more recent past was hard enough. What if Siobhan and Susan had come to live with her and Jimmy as she had asked? She heard Siobhan's lovely laugh, *'what if...'* Siobhan was right, there's no point in 'what if'.

The bus station was quiet. Pauline looked around. The last bus had left. The clock showed ten past eleven.

Pauline walked miles that night, hands thrust deep in her pockets, down streets she hadn't walked before. She barely noticed when it started to rain. With her hair stuck to her cheeks, and her feet soaking wet, the sound of jazz unexpectedly caught her attention. Whoever was playing was good. She crossed the road, walking towards the sound. Orange neon lights flashed the words 'The Orange Club'. Pauline pushed the door; passing an empty desk, she went into the club. The chairs and tablecloths were orange. The sparkling backcloth to the little stage was orange. A baby grand piano took up more than half the space; a saxophonist and a drummer made up the trio. Pauline sat at the nearest table, her eyes stinging from the thick smoky atmosphere. A waitress approached her. She wore an orange mini skirt, a white blouse, and fishnet tights, her blonde hair tied up in a French plait.

"Yes?" Pauline lip read. The volume of the music made it difficult to hear anything that was said.

"Water, please." The waitress shook her head. "Bitter lemon?" Pauline asked. The waitress looked around, as if looking for someone to explain. She said something else but Pauline couldn't understand her.

"Pardon?"

"Did you pay to come in?" she shouted.

"No, there was no one there."

"Wait here."

Pauline waited. She knew she would probably get chucked out but was happy to sit and listen to the trio; the three musicians were playing together now. She knew the piece well. 'Waltz for Debbie'. A Bill Evans number. Her feet moved to the hypnotizing sound. She loved jazz.

Chapter Ten

Maggie Marks was a prostitute. It didn't matter to her, and it didn't matter to anyone else. She had her freedom and independence, and that was all she cared about. The Matron at Holbeck Children's Home told her she was left on the doorstep as a baby. Unwanted. Not an orphan. That would have been easier to accept. She could have made up stories about her tragic parents if she had been an orphan.

In their self-righteous, God fearing way, the Council named the unwanted children after a Saint. In her case, it was Saint Margaret's turn to be awarded a namesake. The surname was given as one of the apostles, with an 'S' added to make it sound more—well—more like a surname. It could have been worse. She could have been Bertha Bartholomews. Maggie smiled at the thought.

If Leeds City Council had had its way, she would have been in Australia four years ago. Packed off like cargo with promises of a better life. She would have fallen for it, too, if her friend hadn't written to her and told her the truth of it all. Maggie still had the letter. She didn't need to look at it; she knew its crumpled contents by heart. It was the only letter she'd ever received, and a stroke of luck that she received it at all. It had been her duty week to take the mail to Matron. She collected all the letters and put them on a heavy wooden tray with the big envelopes at the bottom so they didn't fall off. Only then did she notice the strange stamp. Her curiosity made her look again, and she saw her name on the envelope. She quickly stuffed it in her gymslip pocket before picking up the tray and carrying it to Matron's office. As soon as her chores were finished, she went to the toilet and carefully opened the envelope.

Dear Margaret,

Don't let them send you here. It is horrible. I am in a place called The Outback. I have to work on a farm all day, and it's so hot you can't breathe. There are no toilets, just a hole in the ground. It stinks. The farmer hits me if I don't work hard enough. He comes to my bed at night and does horrible things to me. He hurts me a lot. I am terrified. I will give this to one of the sheep shearers who talks to me. I hope you get it. Tell the others.

From your friend,

Helen.

Margaret Marks didn't tell anyone. She was due to leave for Australia in two weeks and had been excited about it until she got Helen's letter. Now she had to make a plan. She had no money and no possessions. Matron and all the others who had told her about Australia were liars. In her fifteen year old head, Maggie worked it out that if the adults had lied to her about Australia, then she didn't believe anything they had ever said to her. Maybe she did have parents somewhere. The problem was, she had no way of finding out. There had to be another way. She knew stealing was wrong, but she didn't believe all that stuff about God punishing people. That was Matron's way of scaring everyone. For the next week, Margaret hardly slept. Her head whirled round and round. Matron kept petty cash money in her desk, locked in a drawer. The staff wages were paid on Fridays. Maybe she could steal one of the wage packets. In the end, the decision was made for her. On Thursday, 5th May, 1960, Matron called her to her office.

"Margaret, I have some good news for you. Your leaving date for Australia has been brought forward. You will go to London tomorrow on the train. From there you will go to Southampton and board a ship."

"Thank you, Matron." Margaret couldn't think of anything else to say. She turned and left the room.

As she closed the door, matron returned to her papers, shaking her head. "That's gratitude for you. I sometimes wonder why I bother."

After cocoa that night, Margaret took her coat and shoes from her locker and put them under her bed. She made sure the window was slightly open and put her clothes under her pillow. When she was sure the other girls were asleep, she wriggled into her clothes as quietly as she could before slowly pushing back the grey blanket. With her coat and shoes under her arm, she pushed the window open and jumped down onto the grass. She had worked it out that if she was caught, she would be sent back to The Children's Home. She would be caned and told she was an ungrateful girl. Then she would be sent to Australia. In other words, she had nothing to lose. She put on her shoes and coat and ran.

* * * *

"Does your dad mind you staying here all the time?"

Susan looked at Jimmy with a frown. They were in Granny Florrie's kitchen. Pauline had gone to work, and Florrie was in bed.

"Mind? Why would he mind? Anyway, I don't stay here all the time. Sometimes I stay with Chaz." Susan sounded annoyed. She didn't like be asked about her movements, not even by Jimmy.

"There's no need to be so defensive. He might worry about you."

"What's there to worry about? He usually goes out after closing time, and I don't like being there on my own. He's just glad I'm out of the way." Jimmy wasn't convinced, but there was no point arguing with Susan. "Do you fancy going for a walk, Jimmy?"

"It's ten o'clock, Susan."

"I know. I didn't ask you the time, I asked if you fancy going for a walk."

"What about Grannie Florrie?"

"She's fast asleep, Jimmy. She'll be alright. We won't be long. It'll be fun."

Susan and Jimmy walked arm in arm to the city centre. Then up past the tall white university building. Heads turned. They were too young to be out at this time of night on their own. Nobody spoke to them. Susan was amused by the reactions. Jimmy was embarrassed.

"Will you go to this university, Jimmy?"

"Give me a chance. I don't know if I've passed my 'O' levels yet." He laughed as he spoke.

"Of course you've passed them! And I bet you get good grades too. You're really brainy, Jimmy."

"Anyway, I'm not sure Mum can afford for me to go to university."

"What's your best subject? What would you like to do?"

"Oh, that's easy. I like maths best. If my grades are good enough, I want to do 'A' level maths, physics and chemistry."

"See. You must be brainy to want to do those things."

"What do you want to do, Susan?"

She shrugged, enjoying the quiet cool of the night and the rhythmic sound of their feet on the stone pavement. They were almost at the park, and there weren't so many street lights. Jimmy would've suggested they turn back, but wanted to hear her answer.

"Dunno. Since Mum died, I sort of lost interest in anything. I wanted to work at Lavells on the makeup counter, but I've changed my mind. If I was older I could work in the bar with Dad, but we probably wouldn't get on. Maybe your mum could get me a job at the bakery."

"Oi! You two!"

Susan and Jimmy turned to see a tall woman waving at them. It was dark; they weren't sure who she was shouting at.

"Yes, you two, come 'ere."

They walked back to her. She wore high heels and a short leopard-print skirt, her low-cut red blouse almost covered by long blonde hair. Her legs were bare. She wore cheap beads and earrings.

"You wanna earn two bob?"

Susan said "yes". Simultaneously, Jimmy said "no".

"Well, do you or don't you?"

"What do we have to do?" Susan asked.

"Can you whistle real loud?"

Again, Susan said "yes", and Jimmy said "no".

"Just stand here, and if a copper comes, you whistle real loud. Got that?"

Before they could answer, she was gone. Running as fast as her heels would allow, towards a man who was waiting down an alley.

"No looking," she shouted as she ran.

Susan giggled. "No prizes for guessing what's going on there."

Jimmy wasn't amused. "We must get back. We've been out too long."

"Wait, Jimmy. She won't be long, and we'll get two bob."

"I'm going *now*, Susan. I don't want her two bob."

"Oh, Jimmy…"

He walked away and Susan was left alone. A few minutes later, the woman emerged from the alleyway. She looked up and down the road.

"No coppers about, then?"

"No," Susan replied.

"Where's your friend?"

"He ran off."

"Typical. Here's your cut." She pressed two shillings into Susan's hand. "My lookout's useless. Hardly ever turns up these days. See you tomorrow if you wanna earn a bit more. My name's Maggie, by the way."

"I'm Susan." There was a pause as each scrutinized the other. "See you tomorrow, then, Maggie."

As Susan walked back towards the university buildings, she saw Jimmy running towards her.

"Susan. I'm sorry. I shouldn't have left you there."

"No, you shouldn't, but I got my two bob. Look." She opened her hand to reveal the silver coins. A memory from long ago flashed in her head. Her hand was small. The money in her hand pressed there by an old man. The smell of bad breath and beer and cigarette smoke filled her nostrils.

"It's wrong, Susan."

"I know it is, but that's how it is. That's how life is. Come on." She wiped her eyes with the back of her hand, forcing away the memory. "Let's get back to your house."

Susan was still awake when Pauline came home. She put her dressing gown on and went downstairs. Pauline was in the kitchen. She was sitting down, kicking her shoes off. Susan pulled a chair from the table and sat next to her. She gently rested her hand on Pauline's arm.

"You don't work at the bakery anymore, do you?"

"How do you know?" The sigh slid out in a soundless whisper. She was tired; she just wanted to go to bed.

"You're wearing nail varnish and lipstick."

"Nothing ever escapes you, does it, Susan?"

"No. Not much. Anyway, where *are* you working?"

"At a jazz club. I like it there. You know I've always listened to jazz on the radio."

"What do you do?" Susan was enthralled and excited.

"I'm the receptionist. I check membership cards and take the money at the door. It's not very exciting work, but I can hear the music and the pay is better than the bakery. I get to keep the tips."

"Does Jimmy know?" Susan knew the answer. Jimmy would have told her if he had known.

"I didn't want to worry him. It's on Chapeltown Road, and before you say anything, I know it's a bad area. The club is good though, brilliant jazz. It's called The Orange Club."

"You didn't talk to him about his dad, either, did you?"

"No, I didn't. His dad was a bad person."

"Then you should tell him that. He won't ask you, but he wants to know." Susan felt anger inside, as she heard her own voice rising. She didn't want to shout at Pauline.

"You're right, Susan. I'll try to talk to him sometime." Pauline was weary of all the questions; she hadn't the energy to argue.

"You see, me and Jimmy, we talk a lot." Susan forced her anger down. "He just has you, and I just have my dad. Everyone else at school has lots of people. Grannies and granddads, brothers and sisters and cousins. It's not fair that we don't know anything." Susan was getting agitated. "I bet my mum had family in Ireland. Maybe I should go there and find them."

"No!" Pauline said quickly. Too quickly.

"You know something about Ireland, don't you, Auntie Pauline?"

"We didn't talk about the past much, Susan. Maybe that's why we got on so well." Pauline looked distant, memories flashing before her eyes.

"But she did tell you something, didn't she?"

"She told me she ran away from home because her father was violent. She travelled to Dublin with some gypsies. She got a job in Dublin 'til she had enough money for the ferry to Liverpool."

"How old was she?" Susan was spellbound by the scrap of knowledge.

"We had a laugh about that." Pauline smiled. "When she met your dad on the train from Liverpool to Leeds, she told him she was nineteen."

"How old was she really?"

"Sixteen. Just turned sixteen."

"Like me, then. I'm just sixteen now."

They sat in silence for a while. Finally, Pauline dragged her thoughts out of the past.

"Your mum was a good friend to me. She was a good friend to everyone. Her going so suddenly has been hard for us all, especially you. Don't be too hard on your dad, though. He isn't a bad man. He has his faults, the same as the rest of us, but I'm sure he loves you in his own way. He loved your mum too, in his own way."

"You mean he isn't bad like your dad was bad."

"Something like that."

Auntie Pauline was wrong about her dad. He had too many secrets, and they were locked in that big desk on the top floor. She tried to pick the lock once, making sure she replaced the dust sheet exactly as she found it. The fact that he locked it proved to Susan that it held secrets. Secrets he had kept from her mother. Pauline meant to be reassuring, but her words made Susan feel more confused than ever. She changed the subject.

"When did you leave the bakery?"

"Only two weeks ago. The night Jimmy said he didn't have a father I just didn't go to work. I walked around a bit and went in this jazz club. I walked in without paying; there was no one at the desk. The waitress called the manager over, and I thought I was going to get chucked out. I think he must have fancied me. We got chatting about the music. You know how I always listen to jazz on the radio. Next thing I know, he's offering me a job as receptionist. I gave my notice at the bakery next day. They owed me some holidays, so I never went back."

"You will talk to Jimmy about his dad, won't you?"

"I will. I promise. I'm off to bed, Susan. You must, too."

"And you must tell him about The Orange Club. What if Granny Florrie was poorly and Jimmy went to the bakery to find you?"

"You're right again. Your mum used to tell me off for saying 'what if', but you're right."

* * * *

Charlie climbed the long staircase to the top floor. He seldom used the fire escape these days. Susan stayed either at Vine Street or at the Fournier's house, so there was no need to pretend he was going out every night. He couldn't remember why he started it, except that it meant he didn't have to tell Siobhan what he was doing; whether he would be in or out. He missed Siobhan. Not just the clean shirts and breakfasts. He hadn't known he loved her until she was gone. After she died, he started wearing a wedding ring. He turned it between his finger and thumb. Susan didn't understand, but maybe she would one day. He didn't understand it himself, really. Charlie turned the key in the bureau and then settled himself in the worn leather chair. Most of the paperwork was to do with the Threlfalls. His other affairs didn't involve paperwork very much. The deeds for the houses were in the bottom drawer, along with the letter from Gloria. He liked to read it occasionally. It made him smile.

Dear Charlie,

I have been in business in Manchester for a long time now and I want to come to Leeds. It is better that I am not here now and I think you will like to help me. I need a house and we can share the profits. I can set it up if I have a house. Come and see me soon.

From your friend,
Gloria.

He'd ignored the letter for long enough, several weeks, maybe months. He couldn't really remember. He hadn't wanted another woman in his life. A wife and daughter were enough. He certainly hadn't wanted to go into business with one. Money had become a problem, though, what with Alf knowing more than Charlie would have liked, and he had been in a tight corner. Against his better judgement, he'd gone to Manchester. Gloria had been delighted to see him in a Gloria sort of way.

"Charlie! There you are! I thought you must be fucking dead."

"Here I am, Gloria."

They had laughed at the ridiculous greeting. This time, she showed him straight through to the back of the house. They talked together for a couple of hours that day. Charlie saw a different side to Gloria. The thought amused him; he had seen all of Gloria many times in the past. That day, he had to concede she had a good business head. She explained her problem. Gangs of pimps had moved into the area; they were threatening her and her girls.

"Now, Charlie," she had said, "you are a businessman with a bit of cash you might like to invest."

"What makes you think I've got a bit of cash?" he asked, trying to sound puzzled.

Gloria didn't answer straight away. She had a decision to make. It only took a few seconds. "I've decided to be honest with you."

"Good," Charlie interrupted. "If we're going to be in business, that's the first thing we need to establish."

"Shut up, Charlie." Gloria looked down at her wrinkled hands, picking at her chipped nail polish. "When you were here that time, I looked in your case. I saw all that money."

"You did what?"

"You heard me. Now, are we going to be in business or what?"

Within two months of that meeting, Charlie had moved Gloria and three girls into a house in John Street, behind the new Merrion Centre. Ten minute's walk from The Threlfalls, it was an anonymous sort of house in an anonymous sort of street, semi-detached with an old couple next door. Charlie went round to see them when he first saw the 'For Sale' sign. They didn't answer the door until he really banged on it. They were both as deaf as posts. Perfect. Gloria's ill written letter had started his new business. That was nearly ten years ago. The old couple next door were both dead, and their house was up for sale. Charlie was now deciding whether to expand the business.

Gloria was all for it. Well, she would be, wouldn't she? She took a percentage of the profits without having to think about overheads. They had worked it that way right from the start, and she'd always been straight with him. Gloria had a roof over her head, and all the bills were paid by Charlie. She made the appointments; pairing up the girls and the punters was her special talent. More girls meant more profits meant more money for Gloria.

"I can do it with me eyes shut, Charlie."

"I know you can, Gloria. But if we expand the business, we'll need more staff. I don't just mean more girls; that's the easy bit. We'll have to protect the business, make sure we keep the market, you might say."

"Satisfied customers, that's what we want. I can tell soon as they walk in the door which of my girls is right."

"Gloria, you're not listening. If I buy that house, you'll have to organise some protection to keep the girls safe. We have five in here now. If there's another five next door, we'll attract the attention of drug gangs, pimps. Now, I might not be perfect, but I don't hold with drugs. You don't want to have to move on again, do you?"

"What you're saying, Charlie, is that ten girls instead of five doesn't add up to twice the profits."

"Well done. You got it!" Charlie clapped his hands slowly.

"Are you taking the piss, Charlie Fletcher?"

"Who? Me?" Charlie pointed at his chest in mock surprise. "No, Gloria. Now don't get all uppity with me. We just need to think this through."

"Why don't we set up above your pub? No overheads there, and plenty of room."

"Nah. Wouldn't work."

"Who's not thinking things through now, then?"

"You're not. That's who. I live there, remember."

"And I live here." Gloria spread out her wobbly fat arms, the palms of her hands facing upwards. "I could move in to your place with the girls. What's the problem?"

"No, you couldn't. I'd lose my licence. Alf Lawrence has eyes in his backside."

Gloria sighed deeply, folding her arms under her ample bosom. "What about all the coppers we have as customers, then?"

"No, Gloria. You have free rein here, but there is no chance of you bringing the business to The Threlfalls. I have a daughter, remember? She might not stay at home much, but she is my daughter. She's sixteen and the Threlfalls is her home."

"Okay, you win. I'll ask around for a couple of handy boys. Find out what we can get, and for how much."

Charlie tilted his head to one side, nodding slightly. "Now you're thinking."

* * * *

"You say he goes out every night?" Maggie asked. They were standing near a fish and chip shop. Susan liked Maggie. She liked working with her, and she liked the fact that no one knew what she was doing. Jimmy and Auntie Pauline thought she had gone back to live with her dad, which she had, in a way. Her dad thought she was staying with Jimmy and Auntie Pauline or with Chaz. After they finished work, she went back to Maggie's place until it got light. Maggie said it was too dangerous for Susan to walk home alone in the dark, and if Maggie said it was dangerous, Susan didn't argue.

"No, he doesn't go out *every* night. Most nights, though. He used to pretend he was going out even when he didn't. He'd come back in, up the fire escape and in the top floor. Mum never knew. At least, I don't think she did."

"And you've no idea what he gets up to?"

"Nope. When I get home, he's in bed. He stays in bed until late morning. Always has."

"Well, it's my guess there's another woman."

Susan was stunned by the simplicity of it. Why on earth hadn't she thought of that?

"He always says it's business, that he has to make more money than the pub brings in."

Maggie shrugged. "Big place like your dad's pub must make a fair bit."

"He says it's for me, but I'm not even there that much. Not since Mum died. It doesn't feel like home anymore."

They stood in silence for a while. Maggie looked up and down the street for slowing cars; Susan tried to imagine her dad with another woman. It made her feel sick.

"Come on, Susan. It's quiet tonight. Let's go back to my place. We'll come out again later." Susan walked beside Maggie the short distance to the bedsit above a launderette. She made coffee for herself and Susan. The single bed, covered by a bedspread of knitted squares, doubled as a sofa. There was nowhere else to sit in the little room. A sink unit in one corner served to wash dishes and as Maggie's wash basin. A bottle of cheap shampoo was next to the washing up liquid on the windowsill. Two electric rings with a grill completed her kitchen. An electricity meter under the windowsill gobbled up shilling coins and a single bar electric fire was the only source of heat. The toilet down the passageway was shared with other tenants. The walls were stained with the damp and dirt of neglect by disinterested landlords, the paintwork on the doors and skirting boards chipped to bare wood.

"I could follow him one night. Find out where he goes, or where she lives."

"Are you sure you want to? What good would it do? You've looked out for me enough times to know what men are like."

"This is my dad, Maggie."

"So what?" Maggie saw the confused look on Susan's face. "Kids never think of their parents as wanting sex."

"I'm not a kid!" Susan snapped.

"Okay, okay! Keep your hair on. But I'm right, aren't I?"

Susan didn't answer. She sipped her coffee, wrapping both hands around the hot mug.

"Do you and Jimmy have sex?"

"No, course not. He's my friend. My best friend, along with you." Susan didn't look up, her eyes focussed on the contents of the mug. She thought about Auntie Pauline. She was her friend, too, but she found it easier to talk to Maggie. Maggie didn't tell her what to do.

"Are you a virgin?"

"What's that to do with anything?"

"You must have had boyfriends at school."

"Why must I?" Susan looked up. Maggie was sitting sideways on the bed, looking straight at her.

"You're pretty. Streetwise for your age."

"I'm sixteen, Maggie. There are girls out there my age working the streets like you. I'm just the lookout. I don't want a boyfriend. My mum had me when she was only a bit older than I am now, and Auntie Pauline had Jimmy when she was sixteen. Men mess you about."

Maggie laughed. The thought of this pretty young girl telling her that 'men mess you about' was the funniest thing she had heard for a long time.

Susan realised what she had said and started to laugh with Maggie. It felt strange; laughing at herself. She liked Maggie though. Maggie was good fun. They finished their coffee and walked back to the chip shop.

"You reckon your mate Jimmy won't come out with us to earn a bit of cash, then?" There had been two punters since the coffee break. The 'outdoor types', Maggie called them. A quick shag up the alley and they were gone. Less than ten minutes.

"No, not Jimmy. He doesn't even know I come out with you. He thinks I go home when his mum leaves for work."

"We need a lad as bait for the queers. All he would have to do is stand here by the chippy."

"Then what?"

"Then a queer would buy him some chips and ask him to go to the park with him."

"Jimmy wouldn't do that. Never."

"He wouldn't get that far. I'd have a couple of lads waiting, and they'd roll the dirty bastard for his cash. We'd split it. Easy money, Susan."

Susan laughed at the thought of Jimmy being queer bait. There was no chance.

"What's so funny?"

"Nothing. But if you knew Jimmy, you'd know why it's so funny. Tell you what, though, why don't I dress up like a lad? I could do it."

It was Maggie's turn to laugh, but only briefly. Her smile turned to a frown.

"You might have something there. They like the lads who look a bit girly."

A car pulled up. Susan recognised the big dark green Rover. Maggie got in the car; Susan went into the chippy and bought a bag of chips. She would stay in the warm shop 'til Maggie got back. She would be about half an hour.

Chapter Eleven

Jimmy slung his school bag over his shoulder as he got off the bus. The books were heavy, but he needed them for his homework. He had been at Leeds Grammar School for Boys on Harrogate Road since he passed his Eleven Plus. He pulled his cap from his blazer pocket and put it on the back of his head. He hated it, but uniform was strictly applied. If a teacher or prefect saw him without it, he would get a detention. He would stuff it back in his pocket when he was nearer home. He would be safe to take it off then.

He liked the grammar school. It had taken a bit of getting used to after Elder Road Juniors. Slowly, he made friends with boys who, like him, were interested in science and maths. Some of them thought he was a nerd, but Jimmy didn't care. Susan didn't think he was a nerd, and she knew him better than anyone. Better than he knew himself, really. She worried him though. She didn't stay at their house anymore, and Chaz said she didn't stay with her either. He was sure she was working as lookout for that prostitute. He didn't ask; he wasn't sure he wanted to know.

It had been Susan who told him about his father being a bad man. Susan had even coaxed it out of his mum that she was from Sheffield and that her father had bought the house in Vine Street. At least it meant Mum didn't have to worry about paying rent. It had been different about the job, though. Susan worked it out that Mum wasn't working at the bakery. So much for him being the brainy one. Susan was on the ball when it came to people. He never noticed stuff like nail varnish. Maybe he was a nerd after all. He was studying for three 'A' levels but didn't notice his mum's nails. When he asked about her new job, she had been so enthusiastic he was happy for her. Jazz was the only thing she had ever shown any interest in, apart from cooking and looking after Granny Florrie. He turned into Vine Street and took off his cap. Susan would be there, talking to his mum. They'd be in Granny Florrie's kitchen. After tea, he and Susan would go upstairs to talk.

Susan talked about her mum a lot, and went on and on about not having a job, but made no attempt to get one. She always had plenty of money; Jimmy didn't ask where she got it from. It had to be her dad, or that prostitute. Mum would check Granny Florrie was okay and have a cup of tea with her. Mum left sandwiches for supper, then she and Susan left. Mum went to work, and she thought Susan went home to her dad. Maybe she did, but deep down Jimmy knew she didn't. Susan had told him ages ago she didn't like being at home on her own. She was always going on about how her dad had secrets, but Jimmy reckoned Susan was just as bad.

Jimmy liked his mum to make his breakfast. She wore her old dressing gown, the one with flowers on, and the pink fluffy slippers he bought her for Christmas. They talked about his school work mostly. She seemed really interested, like she wanted to learn it with him. He sometimes wondered what she would have done if she hadn't got pregnant; if she had gone to sixth form and taken 'A' levels.

He left the house at eight o'clock to catch the bus. Mum went to make Granny Florrie a cup of tea, and then she would go back to bed. Saturdays and Sundays and school holidays were different. Mum stayed in bed and Jimmy made the tea. As he waited for the kettle to boil, he looked out of the window, watching the January rain fall in the back yard. He would light the fires when he had given Granny Florrie her first cuppa. She would be sitting up in bed, her ready smile greeting him. She liked her tea in a china cup with a saucer, not a mug. He pushed the door with his foot, his eyes on the hot drink.

Jimmy didn't know why, but even before he looked up, he sensed something was wrong. Granny Florrie was trying to get out of bed, but her face looked all wrong. Jimmy quickly put the cup and saucer down on the bedside table.

"Granny Florrie? What's wrong?"

Jimmy tried to push her legs back onto the bed. Florrie tried to speak, but no words came from her twisted mouth.

"Stay there. Don't try to get up. I'll get Mum."

Jimmy ran from the room, up the stairs two at a time, shouting for his mother as he ran.

"Whatever is it, Jimmy?" Pauline was turning in her bed as he ran into her bedroom, her speech sleepy.

"You must come...*now,* Mum!" he shouted as he grabbed Pauline's dressing gown from the back of the door and held it out to her. "It's Granny Florrie. Something's wrong with her."

Pauline was out of bed and wide awake in a second, pushing her arms through the sleeves of her dressing gown as she ran down the stairs and into Florrie's room. Pauline was shaken by the sight of her old friend; the contorted features, the fear in her eyes. The futile attempt to speak.

"Jimmy, go and get dressed. You must run for Doctor Ramsey. Tell him it's Miss Florence Bell. She's had a stroke."

Jimmy was dressed and running up the street in less than a minute.

Pauline straightened the pillows and blankets as best she could. "Don't worry, Florrie. I'm here."

Florrie tried to lift her head, her mouth gaping open, twisted to the left, her left eye sagging down, showing a red rim. Pauline held Florrie's hand with her right hand, gently stroking her forehead with her left.

"Jimmy has gone for the doctor. I'll stay right here, Florrie, I won't leave you on your own. Don't try to talk, just rest."

Pauline looked at the tired eyes in the wrinkled face. She smiled in an attempt to reassure her old friend. Florrie tried to smile back before closing her eyes. When Jimmy and the doctor arrived, Pauline didn't move until she was guided gently away by her son. The doctor lifted Florrie's wrist to confirm there was no pulse. A heart that had beaten for eighty four years beat no more.

Doctor Ramsey shook his head. "I'm sorry," he said, his voice low, two words laden with compassion. He had looked after Florrie and her legs for years. 'Young Doctor Ramsey', she had always called him. "Is there anyone we need to inform?" Pauline looked at him blankly. "Does she have any relatives?"

"Err, yes. She has nieces and nephews. They haven't been to see her lately. I think they live quite near, though."

"Will you contact them? I'll arrange for Florrie to be taken to the hospital for now."

Pauline went back to the bedside to fluff the pillow and tuck in the blankets.

"There now, Florrie." Pauline kissed Florrie's forehead. "No more pains in those old legs, love. No more pains."

She turned to leave, taking Jimmy by the hand. He looked over his shoulder, then pulled his hand from his mother's and went back to the bedside.

"Goodbye, Granny Florrie. I love you," he said.

He took the china cup and saucer with its cold tea from the bedside table. Doctor Ramsey followed Jimmy and Pauline into the kitchen. Pauline put the kettle on. Jimmy poured the cold tea down the sink.

"Susan will be here soon, Mum."

Florrie's battered old address book lay on the table. Pauline picked it up and flicked through the pages, then put it down, only to pick it up and flick the pages again, stopping occasionally to read.

"I know, love. I don't know how she'll take it."

"You know she goes out at night, don't you?" Jimmy was nervous.

"What do you mean?"

"When you go to The Orange Club, I'm pretty sure she doesn't go home. I'm worried about her."

"Where does she go? What about Chaz's house?" Pauline sounded alarmed.

Jimmy was beginning to wish he had never said anything. If he told his mum what he thought was going on, she would ask more and more questions. A small envelope fell from the address book. Jimmy could see the words *'For Pauline'* written in Granny Florrie's handwriting. Pauline tucked the envelope back in the book.

"I don't know, Mum, but I'm pretty sure her dad thinks she stays here. Are you going to open that envelope?"

Pauline was about to speak when the front door banged.

"Anybody home?" Susan shouted as she walked through the hallway. Her face fell when she saw Pauline and Jimmy in the kitchen. "What's wrong? Something's wrong, isn't it? Why are you sitting there looking so sad? Why aren't you next door?" Her voice escalated, she spoke quickly, panic rising in her words.

"Sit down, Susan," Pauline said.

"Not until you've told me what this is all about."

Jimmy stood up and walked over to her. "It's Granny Florrie, Susan."

Silence hung between them.

"No!" Susan screamed. "It can't be. Granny Florrie's always been here. She can't be dead. She's Granny Florrie…"

Susan ran from the room, up the stairs, across the familiar bedrooms and down into Florrie's house, shouting as she ran.

"Granny Florrie, it's me, Susan! Granny Florrie—"

She stopped at the doorway to the sitting room that had been Florrie's bedroom. The door was shut. Pauline and Jimmy had followed her through and stood behind her. Susan didn't need to open the door; it had always been open so they could hear Granny Florrie call. She turned to Pauline and burst into tears.

Pauline hugged her, both arms wrapped around Susan's shaking body. Jimmy stood to one side, not knowing what to do or say. His eyes met his mother's. Pauline nodded to him. Jimmy knew she would speak with Susan about her going out. She would do it when the time was right. Not now. Definitely not now.

* * * *

"You gotta admit it, Charlie. I know this bloody game better than anyone." He had taken Gloria to look round Number Three John Street. They were upstairs, in a large bedroom. "We've got five bloody good girls working, but they're not always busy." Gloria was moving from room to room. The layout was exactly the same as Number One, the houses symmetrical, their front doors at opposite ends of the frontage.

"I thought you wanted me to buy this place, put five more in?"

"I do. But since we spoke about it, I've been thinking."

"Oh, yes," he said, cautiously. Charlie didn't know if he liked the idea of Gloria thinking. She was right, though. No one knew the game better than she did.

"You're right, Charlie. We'll need to get a minder. I can't be in two places at once. And this place needs decorating. This wallpaper's shit. We also need to attract more punters."

Charlie looked around the main bedroom at the front of the house. The once pretty floral wallpaper, unsuitable, or 'shit' as Gloria put it, was peeling off.

"So, what do you have in mind?"

"We have to offer extras."

"Extras?"

"Dressing up. Uniforms. Whips. Handcuffs. Masks. All that sort of kinky stuff."

Gloria's enthusiasm amused Charlie. He smiled briefly. "And how much is that lot going to cost me?"

"Look, Charlie. I guarantee you will have your bloody money back in a year. Not the price of the house. I don't mean that, but the decorating, the extras if you like."

"Anything else while you're about it?"

"Yes, since you ask. I want part of this wall taken out." She pointed to the back of the room. "And a big one way window put in. This room will be the lounge, the viewing room you might say. Nice comfortable chairs." She walked into the adjoining room at the back. Charlie followed. "This is where the performance takes place. It will have to be equipped."

"Equipped? With the kinky stuff, you mean?" Charlie was intrigued.

"With whatever the girls need. It's called voyeurism. Some blokes just like to watch, and they pay a lot for it."

"What about the punter?"

"Same thing applies, Charlie. Some blokes like being watched. They will even pay extra for that. We win both ways. What do you think?"

Charlie scratched his balding head. He walked from room to room, trying to imagine Gloria's ideas for Number Three.

"What you say it's called?"

"Voyeurism."

"You're sure about this?"

"Have I ever let you down, Charlie? Believe me, we can make a lot of fucking cash here. There are cheap whores shagging away on the streets, so we have to offer something more."

Charlie liked Gloria's attitude to her business. Her chosen profession. She was good to the girls, too, perhaps because she hadn't always been the manager, as she liked to call herself. Gloria didn't like to be called a Madame. It sounded cheap. Charlie had paid for the delights of Gloria's body when he was younger, and she hadn't let him down then, either. In a manner of speaking.

She followed him into each room. He inspected the outdated bathroom before going downstairs. He walked from room to room, mentally adding up the costs involved in Gloria's plan, tutting and sighing as he went. Eventually, he turned and looked directly into her heavily made up face.

"Okay, Gloria. You're on."

* * * *

Keith Prentice had only one interest in life. He considered anything else to be either an irritation or a necessary evil. At thirty-three years of age, he had never been married or wanted to be. His family lived in Kent, and that suited him very well. He had his hair cut when it fell in his eyes and annoyed him and bought a new suit when the old one started to look a bit shiny. That was classed as a necessary evil. Customers expected certain standards. He expected them to dress smartly when they came to his club, so he could do no less himself. He was one of the lucky few who made money from a hobby.

He couldn't remember why he called it 'The Orange Club'. He used to get together with a few mates from university and play jazz. They would listen to records, and then try to copy the genius of the great players. At first, Keith rented the room above the present club, and then later he took the back room to store instruments. He could play the saxophone, trumpet, piano and drums. People said he was gifted. When the shop at the front became empty, he expanded his empire further and started to charge an entrance fee. The Orange Club evolved over the next ten years to become *the* renowned jazz venue in Leeds.

His latest member of staff was a stroke of luck. When the waitress said someone had walked in without paying, he expected trouble. Funny how things turn out. He'd sacked the previous receptionist for having her fingers in the till and was supposed to be watching the door himself that night.

Pauline was expecting to be chucked out and ended up with a job. He saw her tapping her feet and realised she was a fan, not just someone sheltering from the rain. She was good at the job, too. Reliable, honest and, best of all, she knew her jazz; they had talked jazz for hours that night. The trouble was he had fallen in love with her. That wasn't part of his plan. He tried to ignore it, but eventually had to admit the truth.

* * * *

The day after Florrie Bell died Pauline was in the waiting room of Botterill, Paterson and Lorrimer in Park Square. The gas fire hissed in the stuffy room as she turned the envelope over and over in her hands. Pauline had read and re-read the letter; Jimmy and Susan had read it too. There were no secrets.

Dear Pauline,

By the time you read this I will be gone. I want you to do me one last favour.

Go to see Mr Botterill in Park Square. His office is at number 11. He is a very kind man. He has my will and all the instructions for my funeral. It is all sorted out. He will contact my family.

With love, your friend,
Florrie.

Pauline jumped as the door opened. A tall man in a dark suit put his hand forward.

"Miss Hanson?"

Pauline nodded as they shook hands.

"I'm Harry Botterill. This way, please."

She followed him through to a tiny office. The wall to her left was covered by shelves, all stacked high with books and papers. His desk, equally occupied by books and papers, filled a third of the room. The floorboards creaked as they walked. He pointed to a chair, and she sat down, perching uncomfortably on the edge. Mr Botterill seated himself in a large leather chair at the far side of his desk, and she handed him the envelope. He carefully placed half-moon glasses on the end of his nose and read the little letter. He placed it on his desk and smoothed the creased notepaper with the palm of his hand. She thought he was probably about fifty, his thinning hair grey at his temples. He lifted his head slowly. Large, sad eyes looked straight at Pauline.

"I'm sorry to read this. It can only mean Miss Bell has passed away."

"Last night. She had a stroke. She was my neighbour." Pauline felt the tears fill her eyes. Her throat ached as she spoke of Florrie in the past tense.

"She came to me about five years ago to make her will. I remember it quite clearly." A smile crept across his pale, lined face. "She was quite specific about everything. Her funeral is all arranged and paid for. She didn't want anyone to have to go to any trouble. The details are in my safe."

"Will you be contacting her family then, Mr Botterill? She had several nieces and nephews."

"Oh, yes, yes. Like I say, she was quite specific. They'll all benefit from her will." He smiled.

Florrie had written in her note that he was a kind man, and Pauline could see it in his smile.

"I'll be on my way, then." Pauline stood up and turned to leave.

Harry Botterill moved swiftly around the desk to hold the door for her.

"How will I know when the funeral is, Mr Botterill?"

"Miss Bell gave me instructions for a small announcement in the 'Yorkshire Post', but I will write to you personally, Miss Hanson."

"Thank you. You're very kind." Pauline shook his hand. "Just like Florrie said you were."

She made her way out of the building, past the hissing gas fire and out into Park Square. A cold wind hit her cheeks, stealing the tears from her eyes.

Three days later, Pauline received a letter from George Botterill. The headed notepaper quivered in her hand as she read. The funeral was to take place the following Wednesday at the crematorium. Florrie had instructed her ashes were to be scattered in the Garden of Remembrance with no memorial. Pauline wasn't surprised. Florrie hadn't been a religious woman. She could hear her now.

'When yer gone, yer gone. Anyone as thinks different is kiddin' the'selves.'

The letter gave instruction that Pauline Hanson, Jimmy Hanson and Susan Fletcher were to choose something from 14 Vine Street to remember her by, if they so wished. The doorway linking the two houses was to be bricked up and the house was then to be sold.

* * * *

On Wednesday, 20th January, 1965, Miss Florence Bell was cremated at Rawdon on the outskirts of Leeds. Pauline stood between Susan and Jimmy at the back of the modern, impersonal chapel. The brick walls and plastic flowers gave a depressing air to the sad proceedings. Susan sobbed uncontrollably throughout the service. Pauline held Jimmy's hand to her right, her left arm around Susan's shoulders in a futile effort to comfort her. There were only twelve people in front of them. The vicar mumbled his platitudes, and eventually the red velvet curtains closed, taking the coffin from view and concluding the service. Pauline, Jimmy and Susan were the last ones to leave, taking their turn to shake hands with the vicar. Pauline thanked him for his kind words, and the three of them left, crossing the road to the bus stop. They sat together on the long seat at the back. Jimmy gave Susan a clean handkerchief. She wiped her eyes and blew her nose. A thin smile stole briefly across her lips.

"Thanks, Jimmy."

The trio walked up the hill from the bus station towards Vine Street, each in their own thoughts of Florrie. Pauline wanted to lift the sadness, but didn't know what to say, or what to do. Keith had given her the night off from The Orange Club. Wednesday was never very busy.

They passed the Odeon cinema where the marquee advertised the new Disney film, *Mary Poppins. 'Now being shown.'*

"That's it," Pauline said, with forced brightness. "That's what we'll do tonight. We'll go and see Mary Poppins. That'll cheer us up."

Jimmy and Susan looked at each other, then at Pauline.

"Are you sure, Mum? I'm not in the mood, really."

"Me neither, Auntie Pauline."

"Of course you're not in the mood. Neither am I." Pauline sounded cross. "But we can't sit about moping all evening. Granny Florrie would have hated that. Let's go home first." The anger subsided from her voice. "We'll do as she said. We'll each choose something from her house to be our special memento, and then we'll come back into town and go to the pictures."

They walked the rest of the way back to Vine Street in silence.

Jimmy chose a teacup and saucer. Susan chose a carved ivory brooch in a velvet lined box. Pauline chose the fireside chair.

"We'll have to call in at the Threlfalls and tell your dad we're going to the pictures," Pauline said as she locked the door. Jimmy stood behind Susan, at the edge of the pavement.

"No need. I, erm, I mean, he won't mind."

Pauline frowned at Susan, narrowing her eyes questioningly. "Still, Susan, he might worry."

Jimmy shook his head. Susan had confirmed, in those few words, that Jimmy was right. Susan didn't go home when his mother went to work. Of course, Charlie wouldn't worry. He wasn't expecting her.

Pauline and Jimmy enjoyed Mary Poppins, laughing at the funny bits, tears falling at the sad bits; their reactions exaggerated by raw emotion. Susan seemed determined to be miserable, but when Julie Andrews and Dick van Dyke danced across the rooftops of London, Pauline saw her smiling. They ate ice cream with funny little wooden sticks during the interval, and Susan felt obliged to cheer up a bit.

Pauline was trying so hard to lift their spirits. They stood up at the end for the National Anthem and filed out of the cinema with the happy crowds. When they stepped out onto The Headrow, their mood was dampened once again, by the cold, heavy rain and by reality.

"Jimmy and I will walk back to the Threlfalls with you if you like."

"It's okay, Auntie Pauline. There's no point in this weather. It's not far and the streets are well lit."

Her answer was casual. Susan wasn't going to make another mistake.

"You sure?"

"Positive. Thanks for taking me. It was good. See you tomorrow." She waved and was gone.

Pauline turned to Jimmy. "I think you're right, Jimmy. She's not going home, is she?"

"I don't think so, no."

"We could go to the Threlfalls now and ask Charlie—"

"No, Mum. Don't do that. It would only make things worse between her and her dad."

Pauline didn't answer. They walked side by side in silence, back to Vine Street, each trying to think of a solution to the problem. They hung up their coats behind the door and went into the kitchen. Pauline automatically made a pot of tea. Out of habit, she took a cup and saucer and two mugs from the cupboard. She stared at the cup and saucer for a moment and then gently placed it back in the cupboard with a deep sigh. Jimmy jabbed the fire with a poker, sending sparks up the chimney, lighting the soot on the fireback.

"Granny Florrie would have known what to do."

Pauline sipped her tea. She was sitting in the fireside chair from number fourteen. Jimmy turned to face his mother.

"Granny Florrie told me she thought Susan should get a job. I've tried to talk to her about it but there's no incentive. She doesn't need the money."

"Would it stop her going wherever it is she goes though?"

"I don't know, Mum, but it might."

"Maybe she just goes to see Chaz. Maybe we're seeing a problem that isn't there, Jimmy."

He shook his head. "Then why the secrecy? Chaz has told me she doesn't go there much these days, and if she does, it's always in the daytime."

"Maybe it's a boyfriend."

"No. She'd tell me if she had a boyfriend."

"I'll try to talk to her. She misses her mum. It's not that long since she died – only seven months – and now Florrie. It's as if she's grieving for her mother all over again. Susan didn't cry at Siobhan's funeral like she cried today. Maybe it's all coming out now."

* * * *

Maggie was standing outside the fish and chip shop when Susan turned up.

"You're late. I didn't think you were coming. You shouldn't walk up here on your own at night."

"Sorry, Maggie. I wanted to come earlier, but Pauline made us go to the flicks."

"The flicks? What did you see?"

"Don't laugh. We saw Mary Poppins."

Maggie laughed anyway. "I reckon Pauline had the right idea. Sometimes you need to do something silly."

"Maybe."

"Anyway, I got some news you need to hear, Susan."

"Oh, yeah? What's that, then?"

Susan wasn't interested in Maggie's news, not tonight. Maggie knew a whole load of interesting stuff, but Susan was beginning to wish she had gone straight home to The Threlfalls. She was cold and wet, and right now it seemed like everyone was getting to her. Pauline was acting like she was her mother. Jimmy knew too much, and Maggie had laughed at her when she asked her not to. Her dad gave her money to keep her out of the way, so he could go off with his fancy woman. He wasn't interested in her; Maggie was right about that. Susan disliked him even more now she knew he had been carrying on with another woman even when Mum was alive.

"I've been offered a job."

"Where? Doing what?" Susan was listening now. If Maggie stopped working the streets she wouldn't need a lookout.

"In a proper house. Same old game but in a warm house. I'm sick of standing on street corners in the freezing cold. You know how cold it was last winter. It's getting more dangerous out here too. I'll be protected from all that in the house."

Susan was speechless.

Maggie continued. "It's been there a while. Proper establishment. Expanding, you might say."

"But what about me?"

"Look, Susan, you're a good kid. Get yourself a job, not in this game, mind."

"I don't want a job. I want to work with you. You always said we are a team. A good team. I'm supposed to be dressing up as a lad, remember? Queer bait. What happened to that idea? I was going to dress up tonight if it hadn't been for Mary bloody Poppins. You told me you like your independence." Susan's words tumbled out in a hysterical rush.

"I'm sorry, love. And I'm sorry to tell you on a bad day, what with your Granny and all. I'm still keeping my room above the launderette. You can come and see me."

"She wasn't my granny!" Susan shouted. "She was better than any granny. She was Granny Florrie. She loved me and…and…" Susan sobbed.

"Come on, love." Maggie put her arm around Susan's shoulders. "Let's go back to my place. You've had a long day."

Susan pushed her away. "Forget it, Maggie. I thought you were my friend. I thought I could trust you."

"Susan…don't. I *am* your friend."

"Bye, Maggie. See you around."

Maggie shook her head in disbelief as Susan walked down towards the city centre and turned down a side street.

"Shit. Stupid, spoilt little cow." Maggie hadn't wanted to fall out with Susan.

* * * *

Susan waited until she saw the light go out in Jimmy's bedroom before letting herself into number sixteen. She wasn't in the mood to talk to Jimmy. She wanted to talk to Auntie Pauline.

"Hello, love, what brings you back here so late?" Pauline was sitting by the fire in Florrie's old chair, wearing her dressing gown and fluffy slippers. Susan sat beside her on the floor, staring at the flames.

"Auntie Pauline?"

"Yes."

"Can you get me a job at The Orange Club?"

"I could ask Keith—Mr Prentice. He's the owner. One of the waitresses handed in her notice last week, so we need someone. Why don't you come along with me tomorrow night?"

There was a pause. Pauline knew Susan well enough to know she was about to change the subject. It came as a relief when she said, "Is it okay if I stay here tonight, Auntie Pauline?"

"Won't your dad…?"

"No. He thinks I'm at Chaz's." Susan lied. The truth was her dad never knew where she was unless he could see her. That was the way she liked it.

"That's fixed, then. You come with me tomorrow and we'll talk to Keith, but please, Susan, you must stop calling me *Auntie*, especially if we're going to work together."

* * * *

The following evening, Susan took her transistor radio into the bathroom she and her mother had shared. She soaked in a bath full of bubbles and washed her hair. With a towel round her head turban style and a short silky dressing gown wrapped around her slim body, Susan walked along the landing, up the steps and past the big linen cupboard to her room. She pulled her thick wavy hair as straight as she

193

could, curling it under where it touched her shoulders, snipping tiny bits from her fringe so it wasn't quite in her eyes, but didn't show her eyebrows. Her makeup, blusher and eye shadow were carefully applied. She glued on her false eyelashes, and blended them in with her own lashes with mascara. She unzipped her Mary Quant dress and stepped into it so she didn't spoil her hair or makeup. It was brand new and bright orange with pink sleeves and hemline. She had bought it that afternoon from her favourite boutique, 'Guineas' in Albion Street. Susan wanted to impress Keith Prentice, and the orange dress would ensure that.

Chapter Twelve

March 1968

"Madame Fournier!" Susan came bursting into the kitchen. She never knocked.

"Susan, you made me jump. I was just t'inking about you."

"Oh, what about me?"

Susan loved being in Chaz's kitchen. Susan liked it when Chaz's Mum talked about their farmhouse in France. Madame Fournier would go all dreamy eyed when she spoke of her home. She had told Susan when Chaz finished university they could all return to France for good. Susan was dreading it. She hadn't seen much of Jimmy since he went to university in Durham and had become very close to the Fourniers. They had always gone to France for the summer holidays, but this time they wouldn't be coming back. The Fournier's kitchen always smelled of fresh bread and coffee. She liked Chaz's mum too, better than Pauline these days. Pauline was always interfering. Their relationship had changed forever that night Pauline took her to The Orange Club. Susan could look back now and realise it was a bad idea. Emotions were raw from Granny Florrie's funeral the day before. The way Pauline had said '*We* need a new waitress' and referred to her boss in such a casual way should have told her something was going on. She disliked Keith Prentice on sight. He was all over Auntie Pauline. Worse still, she was all over him, as if she was showing off that she had a man in her life. It was awful. Creepy. Made her shudder even now.

"Are you cold, Susan?" Jeanette asked. "You shivered."

"Sorry. I was miles away. Is Chaz home?"

Jeanette gave a small jerk. She didn't like the shortened version of her daughter's name, and Susan knew it. Charmaine preferred Chaz, but her mother thought it sounded ugly. Charmaine was such a pretty name. Anton, her father, occasionally called her Chaz, but not always.

"Not yet. She will be about ten minutes or so. Her father is working late, so she will be waiting for 'im."

"I'll wait if that's okay with you?"

"Of course it is. She won't be long. 'Ow is ze job going? Still enjoying your dancing? How's your daddy?"

If anyone else had asked her three questions in a row like that, Susan would have been annoyed. Somehow, when Madame Fournier spoke, it sounded different. Not nosey. Maybe it was the French accent. Certainly no one else called Charlie her 'daddy'.

"Dad's okay. We've been getting on a bit better lately. Now I'm twenty, he lets me work in the bar. He still misses Mum, though. I do, too, but in a different way, I suppose."

"And your dancing job at the disco…what is it called?"

"The 'In Time'. Love it! It's my sort of music, all the pop stuff. Stones, Beatles, Pink Floyd, The Who, Moody Blues. All the really good dance stuff."

"Do you have to dance all night?" Jeanette looked concerned.

"Not *all* night. I finish at one o'clock, and I get breaks. It's only Thursdays, Fridays and Saturdays. The bit I like best is when I climb into the golden cage and it's lifted up above the disco floor. I can dance and dance. Everyone watches, but they can't get to me—can't touch me. I'm 'The Girl in the Gilded Cage'. I love it. You should come and see me."

Jeanette smiled, but they both knew the truth. She wouldn't be going to the 'In Time'.

"It must be tiring, all zat…dancing, and then working in your daddy's pub…" Jeanette's voice trailed off. Astute as ever, Susan knew what she was thinking.

"You're thinking about Chaz, aren't you?"

Jeanette smiled in reply, her face softened by Susan's intuition.

"Maybe Chaz can't dance but she can drive, and she's clever, and she's going to be a teacher. She likes the music even if she can't dance."

"You are a clever girl, too, Susan. Wise beyond your years, I t'ink." She was about to say more, to tell Susan how pleased she was to hear about her improved relationship with her daddy, but the distinctive sound of Chaz's mini in the drive ended the conversation.

* * * *

Pots of paint, brushes, dust-cloths and ladders surrounded Pauline and Keith in the flat above The Orange Club. Pauline turned the heavy carpet samples, casually looking at the designs.

"I'll tell him when he comes home. Promise."

"What exactly will you tell him, Pauline?" Keith had had this conversation with his fiancé more times than he could remember. He loved this woman to bits, but she could be so exasperating.

"I'll tell him we're engaged."

"And…?"

"And we're getting married next year."

"And…?"

"And I will be coming to live here."

"And what?"

She knew exactly what Keith meant. He was the only person in the world who knew about her past. Siobhan had taken her secret to the grave.

He put his arms around her; a measure of how much she loved him, trusted him, she had told him everything. Times like this, she wished she had kept her secret, but then their relationship would be on a less than honest basis. It had taken a lot of heart searching and courage on Pauline's part. She told him one night after the club had closed. Soon after that, they became lovers. Keith made love to her in the most romantic, gentle and yet passionate way imaginable. Pauline hadn't known it could be like that.

"He's not a child, love."

"I know, I know. Maybe I'll get him and Susan together and tell her about Ireland at the same time. About her mum. I told her some bits, but not everything. If Jimmy is to know about his father, it might help them both to come to terms with things." She sighed deeply. "I sometimes think it's all best left. Ignorance can be bliss, you know." Pauline pulled away from Keith; she looked around at the gleaming paintwork and bright, bold wallpaper. She was looking forward to living here with Keith, after the wedding. Jimmy would have finished at university by then, and could live at Vine Street if he wanted to stay in Leeds. "I wish Susan would talk to me more. She thinks I interfere, I know she does."

"Maybe you do." Keith spoke softly. "You're not her mother, and she's twenty years old. I know you want to help, but maybe the best thing you can do is nothing. Just let her get on with her own life. Think what you were doing at twenty. Susan really isn't your responsibility; she has a dad, after all."

Pauline closed the heavy sample book and smiled at Keith as she put her arms around his waist. They kissed, giggling together like a pair of school children.

Pauline was happy with Keith; she loved him and he loved her. Maybe Susan didn't like Keith, but it was true, Susan wasn't her responsibility.

"I will speak with her, though. I won't wait for Jimmy to be there. She needs to know all I know about her mother. It'll be a weight off my shoulders. Tell you what, I'll meet her tonight, after she finishes work, and I'll ask her to come back home with me. I'm sure she will if I say it's about her mother." She smiled at Keith, and he smiled back. Pauline could tell he wasn't sure whether she would go through with it or not; his doubt made her determined to get it over with.

* * * *

Jimmy caught the coach in Durham and settled himself on the back seat for the journey to Leeds, his heavy rucksack on the seat beside him. There were never many passengers on the late coach; he would arrive in Wellington Street Bus Station at about eleven o'clock. He had packed a change of clothes and an extra jumper. The rest of his luggage was made up of his books and files. The train was quicker but much more expensive, and he had to watch every penny.

There were only a few more weeks to go before his finals, and he was looking forward to surprising his mum and Susan. Jimmy reckoned he could revise at home just as well, if not better, than in his digs. Many of his fellow students were busy campaigning against the war in Vietnam or for Czechoslovakian freedom of speech. Jimmy just wanted to study quietly.

He would wait up for his mum; she said Susan didn't stay overnight anymore, and she was getting on better with her dad. At least Mum had Keith as a friend and her jazz. He hoped his mum and Keith would get married one day, but maybe that was too much to wish for. She was happy with her jazz and her job, so that was something. Maybe he would see Susan and Chaz tomorrow.

The March night was dark, wet and miserable. The motion of the coach soon had Jimmy dozing. When he stirred, his neck was stiff, and he had pins and needles in his arm where he had leaned against the cold window. He thought the coach was still in the wilds of North Yorkshire, but when he wiped the condensation from the window with his sleeve, he recognised the landscape of Roundhay Park. He straightened himself and stretched as the coach travelled on towards the city centre. Familiar streets and buildings passed by.

Suddenly, his eyes widened in disbelief. The sight from the window brought his shoulders down; a paralysing sensation shot though his body like an electric shock. The coach travelled on, but Jimmy knew what he had seen. He only saw them for a couple of seconds, but it was long enough for Jimmy to know his mother and Susan were arguing. Standing on a street corner, arguing. They looked like a pair of scrubbers.

Jimmy felt sick to the core; a physical pain grabbed his guts. Had they no idea of danger? He knew Susan well enough not to be shocked by anything she did. But his mother? What was she thinking of?

Jimmy lifted the heavy rucksack to his shoulders and ran back along Wellington Street, along Boar Lane and up Briggate. He turned into Merrion Street. The weight of the rucksack cut into his shoulders, but he hurried on, not stopping until he got to the corner where he had seen his mother and Susan. He was soaked to the skin. Traffic swished past on the wet road, spraying through the puddles.

They were nowhere to be seen.

"You're a bit wet, mate. Can't come in 'ere like that." The bouncer at the 'In Time' looked at Jimmy as if he were the dregs of the human race.

"I just want to know if Susan is dancing here— tonight—is she here now? Susan Fletcher."

"That 'er name, is it? Fletcher? Never knew that. She related to Charlie, then?"

"He's her dad."

"Right, and who are you, then?"

"Jimmy. I'm a friend." He was becoming impatient. "Look. I'm freezing cold and wet through. I just want to know if Susan is here. I'm not bothered about coming in. I just want to know she's safe."

"Oh, right. Well, yes, then. She got 'ere 'bout ten minutes ago. Boss wasn't pleased she was late. Looked like a drowned rat, too, and upset. Yes, that's what she was. Upset. Not like Susan, that. If I know Susan, she'll be doing 'er 'air and makeup before she starts dancin'."

"Thanks. Tell her Jimmy's home, will you?"

* * * *

Charlie stood on his board behind the bar. He did his best thinking there. The Threlfalls was ticking over nicely again. He wished Siobhan and Tom were behind the bar. Everything looked the same, yet everything felt different since Siobhan died. Wishing never made anything happen, though. Siobhan was dead and Tom was a drayman. Tom Hicks was the happiest man he knew. Proud as a peacock in his red and gold drayman's coat. The massive shire horses pulling the drays were a part of Leeds. Tom sat up there, waving to the children as he delivered Tetley's Bitter, the happiest man in the world, always grinning his head off. Charlie envied him. Not the job he did; Charlie didn't like horses. No, not that. He envied Tom's contentment. Tom had achieved his lifetime ambition, whereas Charlie didn't even have an ambition.

"Evenin', boss."

The latest in a succession of students arrived for work. Dave and Adam had left; there was never any shortage of students wanting to earn a few quid. As one left, another would be there asking for a job.

"Evenin'."

Charlie nodded to them in turn as they took off their coats. Their timekeeping had improved since he knocked a bit off their wages for being late. Billy and Johnny liked these two well enough, so that was a good sign. Charlie's thoughts drifted, as they often did, to Susan. He liked Susan working behind the bar, and she came home every night now. Maybe she was growing up alright after all. He thought about going to see Pauline Hanson. Susan spent most of her time round there since Siobhan died; he felt obliged to offer something towards her keep. Susan had plenty of pocket money, but that wouldn't find its way to buying food. She was always home in the morning, but he had no idea what time she came in. He didn't check her room at closing time, or any other time, come to that. Whenever he spoke to her, it always ended up in a row, so he had stopped trying. Plenty of his customers would tell him about their daughters. Mini-skirts and boyfriends. Records and pop groups. Discos and cars. Charlie had heard it all. Susan was no different to the others. His mind drifted on to Gloria. A happier subject. She was doing a fine job in John Street. As promised, she found a minder to protect the business. Flint. It cost a fair bit to employ him, all cash, of course. All the refurbishments hadn't been cheap either, but Gloria was right. She knew her trade; business was brisk. She aimed, as she put it, for the *top end* of the market.

Professional men wanting a discreet service. Coppers, solicitors, estate agents... The list of regular clients was impressive.

"They want professional girls," Gloria told him. "They don't want some slag on a street corner."

Charlie never argued with Gloria. He smiled and pulled another pint.

Mrs Roberts had lit the fires against the chilly March wind. The reflecting flames danced in the brass pumps. The brewery had put in fancy chillers with electric pumps. He didn't see the point. It all just put up his electricity bill. Come summer, it might be different. People expected their beer to be cold these days, even in a heat-wave. He still had the hand pulled beer, but sales were dropping. It was hardly worth the bother of cleaning the extra pipes to the cellar.

The real difference was the customers. Billy and Johnny still came in, though not every night. Not since Siobhan died. Alf popped in from time to time, but not like he used to. Not every day, and not at the same time. Not since Siobhan died. Charlie sighed, a deep sad sigh.

These days most of his customers were students from the university. At least he hadn't the football crowds to put up with. Some of the pubs in town had been ripped apart, inside and out, on match day. Fighting too. If it hadn't been for John Street and Gloria, he would have gone mad. If Alf Lawrence had had his way, the business would have closed down years ago. It amused Charlie that Alf didn't know he was the boss. He hadn't cottoned on to why his superiors wouldn't do anything about it. He could see Gloria now, standing there with her hands on her hips and her head thrown back, laughing as she spoke. *'Don't you worry none about coppers, Charlie. Coppers is punters.'* She was always ahead of any trouble, saw it coming and sorted it out before it happened.

He admired that. Like now, she knew some girls were working the streets a bit too close by, so she was sending Flint to sort them out. Funny name that. Gloria said he was called Flint because he was hard and brainless. They would get a choice, 'come in the house and work, or move on'. They needed a couple more workers. It struck Charlie that John Street was the one thing that had been unaffected by Siobhan's death. John Street and the other little houses he bought. That side of things had always been a secret life. Charlie wanted life at The Threlfalls to go back to how it was before he met Siobhan, but all the wishing and wanting in the world wasn't going to make that happen. Sometimes, it felt as if the world had changed while he wasn't looking, with the exception of Gloria, of course. She never changed.

* * * *

"You sure he said he was called Jimmy?"

"Yep."

"And he knew my dad?"

"I'm not sayin' 'e knew 'im, I'm sayin' 'e knew your dad was Charlie. I didn't know that before."

"I don't broadcast it, Martin." Susan liked Martin. He wasn't the sharpest knife in the drawer, but he was good at his job. Definitely more brawn than brain, but he never forgot a face, never exaggerated the truth, and, unusual for a bouncer, didn't sell drugs. She was on her first break, and the news about Jimmy being home came as a pleasant surprise. She was already in a bad mood. More than a bad mood really, she was upset, but that was something Susan refused to recognise in herself, what with Pauline 'accidentally' meeting her on her way to work, expecting her to go to her house, just like that. Susan knew she had been waiting for her. The conversation, if you could call it that, kept spinning in her head.

"I want to tell you all I know about your mum," she'd said. Out of the blue, and then expected her to wait until after work. They had walked up Briggate and turned towards the Merrion Centre, crossing over Belgrave Street. Pauline gabbled on about the weather and jazz. Susan knew she shouldn't have yelled at her. Something had bubbled up inside her and thrown her into a rage she couldn't control.

"Get on with it, Auntie Pauline. Tell me now! I mean right now!" she had screamed. "I know what you're like,

Auntie Pauline. If you wait, you'll change your mind, just like you keep saying you'll tell Jimmy about his dad, but you never do." Tears had streamed down her face, mingling with the rain. She had barely noticed the rain, or the tears, her eyes were wild, her face and neck red with rage. Mascara and eyeliner ran down her cheeks.

"I don't want to tell you here—not now—standing on a street corner, and you in such a state." Pauline's voice had been calm, which made Susan even angrier. Auntie Pauline had known for years, especially since Siobhan died, that she craved the tiniest scrap of information about her mother. How could she have withheld anything?

"Tell me *now*!"

"Okay, Susan, have it your way. I'll tell you right here and now, on a street corner in the pouring rain, all I know about your mum. But let me warn you, you won't like what I have to say."

"Go on then."

"Your mum was from a village called Kilmain in Southern Ireland. She had lots of brothers and sisters. Her maiden name was O'Malley. Her father was a violent man. She ran away with some gipsies…"

"I know. You told me that years ago."

"There's more. She worked the streets of Dublin to get the ferry fare to Liverpool."

The words hung in the air like the ear splitting scream of a ghost, an apparition that could be neither confirmed nor denied. "Now you know all I know."

"When did she tell you?" Susan's voice had turned to a whisper. "When did Mum tell you that?"

"A long time ago, when you and Jimmy were little. We were good friends, me and your mum. We could talk about anything."

"Does my dad know?"

"I doubt it. She'd have been scared he'd chuck her out if he knew. I don't really know why she told me, but I never told anyone else."

"Not even your precious Keith?" There was a sneer on Susan's face; it made her look older, ugly.

"No, Susan. Not even Keith. He is a good man, Susan. I know you don't like him." It was Pauline's turn to feel anger. Her relationship with Keith was nothing to do with Susan. "You are wrong about Keith. We're getting married next year." Pauline struggled to keep her voice calm. She hadn't wanted to discuss Keith and was annoyed with herself for telling Susan her plans before she had chance to tell Jimmy.

"Why are you telling me all this now? What's the hurry, all of a sudden?"

"You were the one in a hurry, Susan. I wanted you to come back to my house after work, if you remember."

"That's not what I mean." Impatience and contempt filled her words. "Why tonight?"

"Does it matter?"

"No. I suppose not."

Susan turned and walked away. Numb with the knowledge that her mother had been a prostitute, she carried on walking to the 'In Time'. Once in her little dressing room, she peeled off her false eyelashes and stuck them to the mirror. She dried her hair and reapplied her makeup. She opened a drawer and took out a tiny tube of glue and stuck her eyelashes back on. She slid back the door of a small wardrobe and took the first dress she saw. She didn't care which one she wore. The transformation took about half an hour. The boss kept banging on the door, but she ignored it. When she stepped into her gilded cage, the cheers from the disco floor drowned the music. Susan smiled and danced like never before. She would go and see Pauline after work, apologise for shouting at her.

* * * *

Jimmy dropped his rucksack to the floor as he kicked the door shut behind him. He was exhausted, but knew he wouldn't sleep. He poked the embers of the kitchen fire before adding a shovel of coal to the dim glow. He sank into Grannie Florrie's chair without bothering to put the light on. Gradually, the fire gave heat and light to the little room.

As he waited for the kettle to boil, he saw a letter propped up on the mantelpiece; addressed to his mum, postmarked Sheffield a week ago. The envelope was good quality; he ran his fingers over the embossed surface as he turned it over in his hands. It was unopened. Printed on the back he read, *Andrews, Deighton and Wilcox, Solicitors.* He put the letter back where he found it.

His jeans were itchy and uncomfortable as they steamed from the heat of the fire. He stared at the glowing coals, his mind filled with the picture of his mum and Susan arguing in the street like a pair of tarts. That was putting it mildly; they looked like prostitutes. The door banged. He knew it had to be Susan coming in like that. He stood up and turned to the hallway as Susan came into the kitchen.

"Hi, Jimmy. What you sitting in the dark for?" She turned the light on.

Jimmy winced as his pupils adjusted to the sudden brightness. "Where's Mum?"

"I dunno. Probably with that Keith. What brought you home anyway? Didn't expect to see you 'til Christmas."

"I wanted to surprise you and Mum." Jimmy slumped back in the old armchair. "Susan…"

"What?"

"I saw you from the bus, you and Mum, arguing. What were you thinking of, out in the pouring rain? You looked like a pair of scrubbers. What were you doing there? I tried to find you and—" He broke off, swallowing the words that continued to build at the back of his throat.

She knelt on the hearthrug and looked up, staring him in the eyes, her jaw set tight. She tried to speak. She wanted to be angry with him for spying on her, but instead, she put her head on his knee. Jimmy stroked her hair and waited. Her breathing calmed and she lifted her head, staring at the fire as she spoke, knowing that if she were to look at Jimmy, she would cry.

"Did your mum ever tell you about your dad?"

"No, not really. She once told me she was from Sheffield, and *her* dad gave her this house."

"Mmmm."

"This isn't about my dad, is it?"

"No, it's not. It's about my mum. She was a prostitute in Dublin before she came to Leeds."

"What? No! I don't believe it! How do you know?"

"Your mum told me tonight. That's what we were shouting about when you saw us."

A silence fell between them. Susan crawled onto the chair with Jimmy. He put his arms around her and they sat together in the comfortable silence of long friendship.

"All the time I have wanted her to tell me all she knew about Mum, and now I wish she hadn't. But what I really don't understand is why she told me now."

"She'll be here soon. You can ask her."

"I think she must be staying at Keith's. They're going to get married, you know."

"No, I didn't, but I'm glad—happy for her."

"She told me tonight. I don't think she meant to tell me. She should've told you first. I sort of assumed you knew…I don't like him." Susan's tone was flat.

"I've only met him a few times—seems nice enough. As long as Mum's happy, it's okay by me." He smiled and turned Susan's face towards his, his forefinger and thumb on her chin. Susan gave a thin smile and rested her head on his shoulder. "Come on, Susan. Time we went to bed if Mum isn't coming tonight. It'll all seem different in the morning."

They lay as they had as children, holding hands across the little gap between the beds.

Chapter Thirteen

"You stupid fucking bastard." Gloria was incandescent with rage. Flint stood in front of her desk like a schoolboy caught truanting. Rainwater ran from his hair down the back of his collar. He couldn't have been more wet if he'd jumped in the river. Gloria turned slightly in the big black leather swivel chair. "How the hell do you think I'm going to sort this one, then? I'm not a fucking magician, you know. I can't make things disappear."

"I did like you said, Gloria." He knew as soon as the words left his lips it had been a stupid thing to say. Gloria stood up. Her tight black dress struggled to contain her wrinkled breasts as she leaned forward. Her fat little hands pressed down on the desk, her fingers, garnished with glittering rings and her trade mark nail polish, took such weight her knuckles whitened under the pressure.

"You could have fucking killed her. All I said was, give her the choice, come in or piss off. I never said anything about violence. I don't like violence."

"She started it."

"She started it?" Gloria repeated his words with disgust. "Is that all you can say? You sound like a spoilt kid. Look at the size of you. How big was she? Five foot nothing like me, I suppose."

"She was taller than you, Gloria."

"Course she was. Every bugger's taller than me, but she wasn't a six foot three lump of fucking lard like you, was she?" He didn't reply. "You say she kicked you in the shins and you pushed her away?"

"Yes, Gloria, that's all I did, honest."

"And she fell against a wall."

"Yes. That's just what happened—then she sort of slid to the ground."

"Was there any blood?"

"Didn't see any." He shifted uneasily from one foot to the other. The rain water oozed through the leather of his shoes.

"Christ knows what Charlie will say. You'd better hope that girl is okay." She sat down again, folding her arms as best she could. "Get out."

He closed the door behind him almost silently.

Gloria gave a deep sigh. She knew exactly what Charlie would say. '*You deal with it, Gloria. You know what to do.*' Except that this time, she didn't know what to do. It all depended on how badly that girl was hurt. Part of her said the coppers wouldn't care if a working girl was killed; part of her refused to believe it was true. It struck her then just how stupid that lump of fucking lard was. If he hadn't told her, she wouldn't have known that he had done anything wrong. Stupid fucking bastard. They don't come much thicker than that. She hadn't employed him for his intelligence, though, had she?

* * * *

Susan and Jimmy were awake, vaguely aware of each other. Neither of them had spoken or opened their eyes when their warm sleepy daydreams were shattered by loud banging on the front door. Susan sat up. Jimmy jumped out of bed and pulled on his damp jeans. A man's voice shouted through the letterbox.

"Anyone at home? Hello? Pauline, are you there?"

Jimmy opened the door to see Keith Prentice.

"Jimmy. I didn't expect to see you here. I thought you were in Durham."

"I came home last night. Come in, come in." Jimmy stood to one side as Keith stepped into the narrow hallway. Susan was coming downstairs; she was wearing Pauline's dressing gown and slippers. They went into the kitchen.

"Is your mum here, Jimmy?"

"We thought she was with you." Jimmy took a step backwards as he realised how things looked. "It's not what you think. Me and Susan. We're friends, that's all."

"I'm not concerned with you and Susan. Sorry. I don't mean that to sound rude. I came to see if your mum was okay. When she left last night, she was a bit wound up about things. I expected her back but she never came."

The three of them stood in silence as realisation crept upon them.

"Where would she go?" Jimmy looked at Keith.

"I don't know. She went to find Susan here." Keith and Jimmy turned to Susan.

"I don't know, either." She looked at Jimmy. "After you saw us from the bus, I went to work. You know that. I don't know where she went."

"I'm going to the Police," Keith said. "Something's wrong. I just know it is."

"Wait for us. We'll get dressed and come with you." Jimmy ran up the stairs as he spoke. Susan pushed past Keith and followed Jimmy.

"I'm not waiting for anyone."

Keith fled down the hallway and was gone. Susan only had her disco dress with her, but she didn't care. She threw it on and ran down Vine Street with Jimmy, holding hands as they went. When they got to the Police Station, Keith was shouting at the Desk Sergeant.

"She's missing, I tell you…"

"And I believe you, but she's not a child, and anyway, we would need next of kin here before I can fill out any forms."

"I don't want you to fill out any forms. I want you to find her for me."

"Sorry, mate. It's like I say…" The policeman spread his hands on the wide mahogany counter. He looked over Keith's shoulder at Jimmy and Susan. He was hoping for a distraction from this nutter who seemed to think Leeds City Constabulary would stop everything to look for a woman who had been missing for little over twelve hours.

"It's my mum." Jimmy was breathless from running. "He's talking about my mum. She was last seen near the Merrion Centre." A flicker of recognition crossed the sergeant's face, a slight frown. Only Susan noticed it. She stepped forward.

"You know something, don't you? What's happened to her? Where is she?"

"What was she wearing?" the copper asked.

"An orange mini skirt and—"

He didn't give her chance to say any more. "Wait here, please." He turned away from the desk and headed through a frosted glass door.

Keith, Jimmy and Susan looked at each other, fear spreading between them.

"He knows something," Susan said. "I could see it on his face."

Before Keith or Jimmy could reply, Alf Lawrence walked in. Susan ran the few paces between them and flung her arms around him.

"Hey, hey, Susan. Whatever's wrong? What are you all doing here? Jimmy? I thought you were still in Durham."

"It's my mum. She hasn't come home. We think something's happened to her."

"Have you spoken to anyone here?"

"Yes, the Sergeant. We think he knows something." Jimmy looked to the floor. Alf gently pushed Susan's arms from him as the sergeant returned. He seemed relieved to see Alf.

"What's going on, Sarge?" Alf asked.

"Do you know these people, Alf?"

"I do. I've known Susan here since she was born." He held her hand, aware of the frailty of her grip. Susan wasn't easily scared. Keith stepped forward to the desk.

"Sergeant. I'm Pauline's fiancé, Keith Prentice. Please, if you know anything, please tell me...tell us."

The sergeant looked over Keith's shoulder to Alf. "A word, please, Alf."

He beckoned Alf forward and lifted the flap for Alf to go behind the desk and into the room behind. They could see the two men talking behind the frosted glass. Alf nodded slowly, and came back to the desk. He walked straight to Jimmy.

"Your mum is in hospital. The sergeant is getting a car to take us there. It'll be quicker. Come on."

With sirens blaring and blue lights flashing, they travelled across Leeds in minutes. Alf sat in the front. Susan sat between Jimmy and Keith in the back. No one spoke.

* * * *

"Listen, Gloria." Charlie pointed his short, fat forefinger at her. "I leave you to run this business, and you do a good job."

They were in the office at John Street. When he was there, it was Charlie's office, and he sat in the big leather chair behind the desk. When he wasn't there, Gloria enjoyed the comfort of the leather chair. Whoever was in the chair was in charge.

"Thanks, Charlie."

She moved round the desk and put her hand on his knee. She gave a big, Gloria, lipstick smile. Her fake smile, the one she kept for punters. She pouted her lips to kiss him on the cheek. She couldn't help it, even now when she was so worried, it came as second nature to flirt in the company of a man.

"Shut up. And don't smile at me like that." He pushed her away. "I don't want to fall out with you, and you don't want to fall out with me. We need each other whether we like it or not, and I'm telling you, you're wrong."

Her smile gone, Gloria squeezed into a tub chair near the window. "What if she dies, Charlie? That's murder."

"Let me remind you of a few things, Gloria. Number one, she most likely isn't dead." Charlie counted the numbers before her on his fingers to emphasise his reasoning. "Number two, whoever she is, she's a prostitute. Number three, because she's a prostitute, the police won't bother too much to find out who did it. Number four, as you have told me many times, coppers is punters, so they won't look here."

He sat back in his chair. Charlie rarely came to John Street during the day; he didn't want to be here now. Gloria had phoned him at ten in the morning, something else he didn't like. Gloria thought all this more serious than he did. She pushed herself up, more comfortable standing in her daytime slippers than squashed in the little chair. She walked to the window and gazed blindly into the overgrown garden at the back of the house.

"I don't like it when you call them prostitutes. They're my girls."

"Maybe that's why we see things differently." Charlie was irritated by Gloria's way of thinking. For some reason it made him uncomfortable.

"You don't even know their names."

"That's how I like it, Gloria. I have to keep a distance. I'm the boss."

"Oh, yes, you're the boss." Gloria felt her anger rising. She felt protective of her girls. Charlie was being a shit. "I know that, Charlie. I never forget that. What *you* forget is that this is my home. If we fold, you'll find some other way to make money." She was shouting now. "You could even sell these houses and just walk away with thousands in your pocket, while I would have nothing. Not even a roof over my head. Think about it, Charlie. Do you wonder that I'm worried?"

"For Christ's sake, Gloria, shut up, will you. I'll say it again. Number one, she may not be dead." He counted on his fingers again. "Number two, she was a prostitute. Number three, the police won't care. Number four, they won't look here."

He stood up and walked from the room into the hallway and outside, slamming the door behind him. He took a deep breath of cold morning air as he stood on the top step. He made a mental note to tell Gloria she must sweep the leaves from the path. Silly cow. Still, she had been right about one thing, he could sell these houses in John Street and make a killing. He had bought them and a few other little houses for peanuts and house prices were on the rise.

He walked towards Briggate; opening time in fifteen minutes. No need to rush. Susan would open up if he wasn't there. The streets glistened in the late morning sun, low in the sky and still wet from the downpour of the night before. Puddles lay in the uneven pavements, damaged by the frosts of winter and still not repaired. The roads were no better; a stream of rainwater ran in the gutter. Charlie considered walking down to the market when a bus passed by, the spray soaking his shoes.

"Shit," Charlie muttered and turned the corner into Briggate.

A newspaper vendor was setting up his stall, struggling with a sheet of plastic in a vain effort to shelter himself and his newspapers from the rain. Charlie never understood how the Yorkshire Evening Post came out at lunchtime. Not that he ever bought a newspaper as a rule, but the vendors' shouts of "Evening Post" could be heard all over town by eleven-thirty. The headline in the placard caught his eye. His step faltered.

"Murder in City Centre."

Charlie bought a paper and hurried home.

* * * *

From years of experience, Alf knew a female victim of violence would be taken to Ward 4. His uniform caught the attention of the Ward Sister. In turn, her dark blue dress with white apron and cap gave her authority and respect.

"We've come to see Pauline Hanson, Sister."

She frowned. She knew her patients' names and there was no Pauline Hanson.

"She was brought in last night. We believe she was attacked and brought in by ambulance."

She paused for a moment. "Come with me." She led them into her office. "Please sit down." There were only two chairs; Susan and Jimmy took the seats, Keith stood behind them, one hand on the back of each chair. Alf stood by the door. The Sister sat behind her desk, several piles of neatly stacked papers in front of her. "Are you relatives?"

"She's my mum. Where is she? I want to see her." Jimmy said.

The sister replied slowly and carefully. "A woman was brought in here last night suffering from a head injury. She had no identification with her, so I don't know whether or not she is your mother. Can you describe her to me?"

Jimmy was about to speak when Susan interrupted. "She's really nice with beautiful red hair and green eyes, and we were wet with the rain and—"

"You said 'we'," the sister said. "Were you there when she was injured?"

"No, no, I'd gone. Is she here, then? Is Auntie Pauline here?"

The Sister didn't reply, but looked towards Keith. "Are you related to Pauline Hanson?"

"No, not related. She's my fiancé."

She stood up and asked Keith to follow her. She took him to a side ward; the curtains to the room were closed. Once inside, Keith's worst fears were realised. She gently folded back the sheet. Pauline's beautiful pale face, her red hair stuck to her cheeks, her eyes closed in everlasting sleep. He turned to the Sister and nodded.

"I thought it best you identify her rather than her son."

"Thank you. Yes. She is Pauline." Keith took a deep breath and followed the Sister back to her office. He couldn't look at Jimmy or Susan. He turned to Alf and shook his head. Jimmy and Susan sat motionlessly, all colour drained from their faces.

"I'm so terribly sorry," the Sister said, her eyes on Susan and Jimmy. "She passed away just before you arrived. She never regained consciousness. She had a massive blow to her head."

* * * *

Today wasn't turning out well at all for Charlie. He hated being woken by the phone, Gloria insisting he went round. Stupid cow. Then he got soaking wet thanks to that bloody bus, it would take days for his brogues to dry out properly, and now on top of all that there was no sign of Susan, and he had to cope with lunch time trade on his own. He wanted to read the paper; see if there was any link with the murder and what Gloria had told him about Flint pushing some tart against a wall. It was pretty unlikely, but still, he'd like to know. He called 'time' and was pushing the bolts down in the big doors when he saw Alf Lawrence's shiny shoes. Charlie straightened himself.

"You're a bit late, Alf. Or is it a bit early?"

"I'm not here for a drink, Charlie. Best close up. I've got bad news."

Charlie didn't like the sound of this. He followed the policeman into the best room.

"Is it Susan?"

"No, Charlie. It's not about Susan. Can we sit down?" As he spoke, Alf was pulling a chair from one of the tables by a window.

"Not here, Alf. We'll go into the kitchen. I need to turn the lights out in here or some bloody copper'll think I'm serving after time."

Alf hadn't been in the kitchen since the night Siobhan died. Nothing had changed. The armchairs were still there, either side of the fireplace, the big table, the long, high cupboards, the gas stove and the kettle. Charlie sat by the fireplace and waved towards Siobhan's chair. Alf shook his head and pulled a wooden chair from the table. He had just walked from Vine Street and would have welcomed the comfort of the armchair and a cuppa. It didn't seem right though, and Charlie didn't offer to put the kettle on. The newspaper lay on the table. Alf picked it up and pointed to the headline. *"Murder in the City Centre."*

"It's about this." He handed the paper to Charlie. He read it as if seeing it for the first time; the paper slipped from Charlie's hands to the hearth, his mind racing. He was sure now that Flint had killed the prostitute, but how had Alf made the connection with him so fast? His face was ashen.

Alf continued. "She was Jimmy Hanson's mum, Pauline."

Charlie rested his head back on the worn chair. Relief washed over him like a warm tide.

"Your Susan's with Jimmy at Vine Street. Poor lad's holding up well, but it's a hard knock for him. Thought I'd better tell you."

Charlie sat forward again. "Thanks, Alf. Good of you to tell me. Yes."

Charlie was trying desperately to collect his thoughts, to sort out what it all meant. Flint had shoved a prostitute into a wall. Not Pauline Hanson. That must have been a separate thing. Someone else.

"It explains why Susan wasn't here at lunchtime, Alf. She's doing alright now, you know. What with her dancing and all. Siobhan and Pauline were friends; she was always going round to Vine Street for a natter."

Alf gave him a curious look. He knew Charlie Fletcher and his sort well enough to know he was hiding something.

"Yes, I know. I saw her at Siobhan's funeral. I'll be off then, Charlie. Keep your ear to the ground. You might hear some pub gossip about this one. Far as we know, Pauline had no enemies."

They walked back through the bar. Charlie unfastened the heavy bolts and let the policeman out. He leaned heavily on the back of the closed doors and sighed deeply. Charlie went back to the kitchen and made himself a cup of tea before sitting down at the table, the Yorkshire Evening Post spread out in front of him.

A woman, in her mid to late thirties, was found lying on the pavement near the junction of Wade Lane and Belgrave Street. She had sustained a severe head injury and died later in Leeds General Infirmary. At the time of going to press, she had not been identified. The police are treating her death as murder and ask anyone who was in the vicinity last night to contact them.

"Shit."

Charlie pushed the newspaper away. Right area. He was sure now. Flint had killed someone. What he couldn't be sure of was that he had killed Pauline Hanson. Charlie walked back into the bar and dialled Gloria's number.

She answered as she always did. Her soft, sexy 'telephone voice' said everything, and nothing.

"Number One John Street. How can we be of service?"

"Gloria. It's me. What did she look like? The woman he shoved?"

"Hang on, he's right here. I'll ask him." Charlie heard her call to Flint, and he heard his reply in the background. There was no need for Gloria to repeat it.

"I heard that Gloria. Red hair."

"What's wrong, Charlie? Did she die?"

"It's worse than that, Gloria. She wasn't a worker, and, yes, she died."

"Fucking hell, Charlie. The coppers'll be like flies on shit."

There was a pause. Charlie wasn't going to tell Gloria he knew Pauline. That was on a need-to-know basis, and Gloria didn't need to know.

"He's got to go, Gloria. Flint. Pay him off. Tell him to get out of Leeds and not come back. We don't want this coming back on us."

He hung up. Charlie looked down at his hands and, turning the wedding ring on his finger, slowly climbed the main staircase. Walking through the ballroom to the back of the stage and up the narrow staircase, he pulled the cloth from the bureau and unlocked the drawers; he felt safe here, in control. He lifted all the papers out of the bottom drawer of the bureau and sorted them into piles. There was all the Threlfalls stuff, two sets of deeds for John Street, and then all the other houses. He liked being a man of property. When the profits built up, he bought another terraced house for cash. Six altogether. The solicitor in Manchester sorted it all out, even the leases. Nice, that. If he sold up in John Street, he would still be okay. He was a rich man. Susan would get it all one day.

Susan.

She must never link him with Pauline Fletcher's death. He was pretty sure the coppers wouldn't dig too deep at John Street, as long as bloody Gloria kept her nerve. The police would be looking for some pissed off curb crawler in the streets for Pauline's killer. He put the papers back in the drawer in their neat piles. He locked the bureau carefully and put the key in his inside pocket.

* * * *

"I'll go if you want me to." Keith wasn't sure if his presence in the little kitchen was making things better or worse for Jimmy and Susan.

"I don't know what I want," Jimmy said. "I want Mum to be here. I…I don't know anything anymore."

Susan put her arms around him. They clung to each other in silence.

"I would like you to stay," Jimmy said.

Keith's face relaxed, he pressed his lips together and nodded; the closest thing to a smile he could manage.

"You really did love her, didn't you?"

"I loved her more than I can say. She was everything to me."

"I know." Jimmy stepped away from Susan and offered his hand to Keith. As they shook hands, Keith patted Jimmy on the back. "I suppose I'd better open this." Jimmy tore open the letter, and the stiff white paper shook in his hands.

Andrews, Deighton and Wilcox,
20 South Church Street
Sheffield
Yorkshire

1st March, 1968

Dear Miss Hanson,

It is with regret that we write to advise you of the death of your father on 14th February 1968, at 16 Willowbank Road, Sheffield.

We are instructed to obtain probate of your father's estate and Mr Deighton of this firm has been appointed as executor.

The will provides for you to be sole beneficiary, and we are taking steps to wind up his estate.

As soon as the final estate accounts are ready for your approval, we will notify you, but in the meantime, if you wish to discuss the matter further, please contact Mr Deighton's secretary to make a convenient appointment.

Yours Sincerely,
Andrews, Deighton and Wilcox

He handed the letter to Susan. She read it and handed it back to him.

"What does it mean, Jimmy?"

He shrugged and handed it to Keith. He read it and handed it back to Jimmy.

"You'd better sit down, Jimmy."

"Why? What is it?"

"There was never going to be a good time to tell you this."

Jimmy sat down in Grannie Florrie's chair. Both he and Susan were mystified.

"I know your mum wanted you to know, but was scared you might not be able to handle the truth. But it's my guess you're going to find out soon enough anyway. Perhaps it's better from me than from a stranger. I don't know."

"What are you talking about, Keith? I know Mum was from Sheffield. I know her dad gave her this house."

"Pauline told me her dad was a bad man," Susan said. "Was he in prison or something like that?"

"No. Nothing like that. There's no easy way to say it."

"What? No easy way to say what?" Jimmy asked.

"This letter means your Grandfather has died."

"I realised that much." Jimmy was beginning to feel annoyed.

"What you don't know is that he was your father, too."

Susan gasped, putting her hand to her mouth.

Keith continued. "He raped her on the day of her mother's funeral."

Jimmy stared into the glowing ashes; he struggled to speak. "You mean…incest?"

Keith nodded. Susan sat on the rug in front of the fire. She held Jimmy's hand and put her head on his lap. They stared in silence at the fire, as they had the night before, each deep in thought. After a few minutes passed, Keith broke the silence.

"Jimmy, you know where to find me if you need me for anything. Anything at all."

"Thanks. And thanks for telling me. I had to know sometime. It explains a lot."

Keith closed the front door quietly as he left.

Susan stood up and put the kettle on. She made some toast, but neither she nor Jimmy could eat.

"I used to nag her to tell you about your dad." Susan spoke quietly and steadily. "I understand now. I understand why she couldn't bring herself to tell you and why she never wanted a boyfriend until she met Keith. I always thought your dad must have been a criminal. You know. A burglar or something. This is worse. Much worse."

"If it tells us anything, it tells us Keith is really special. He made her happy."

"I was wrong about him. When I first met him, I just didn't like him. I thought he was just after your mum for sex. I was a stupid kid who thought she knew everything."

"It doesn't matter now, Susan."

"Yes, it does. I sort of fell out with your mum a while ago." Tears fell from her swollen eyes and Susan spoke in stifled sobs. "We never actually argued before last night. It's just that I thought she was trying to be my mum. Oh, Jimmy, she was kind and loving and…"

"Shh…" Jimmy held her to him. "We can't go back. Mum worried about you, that's all. We have each other and—"

He was interrupted by a loud knock on the door.

Alf Lawrence stood on the doorstep, a briefcase in his hand.

"I need to take statements from you and Susan."

Jimmy stood aside as the policeman stepped inside. "I persuaded C.I.D. to let me come. Seems you were the last people to see your mum."

"I saw Mum from the bus. Susan was talking to her."

"Yes. We had a row, Alf. She told me stuff about my mum."

Alf sat at the little table. He took a pen and some paper from the briefcase. First Jimmy, then Susan, told him everything that had happened the night before. He wrote slowly, taking down every word. In all his years, he had never heard the like. They signed their statements, and Alf put the papers back in the briefcase.

"Take a little advice from an old copper. Don't answer the door unless you know who's there, and keep it locked. The press will be round before long, you can count on it."

"Thanks, Alf," Susan said. "You've always looked out for me, haven't you?"

The policeman nodded. "You're a good girl, Susan." He paused on the doorstep. "You know where I live, don't you?"

"Are you still at the Police House?"

"Yes, for now, but I'm retiring later this year. Me and Mrs Lawrence will have to move then. I'll let you know. If ever you need me, you'll know where I am."

As he stepped out into the street, a mini pulled up and parked outside number 16.

"I'll be off, then." Alf said. "I know this visitor will be welcome."

"Come in, Chaz. We're in the kitchen."

The look on her face told Jimmy she had heard about his mum.

"Jimmy…I heard it on the news. I brought the paper."
Chaz had a copy of the Yorkshire Evening Post. "It's in the
late edition. It's too awful." She hugged Jimmy, then Susan.
"What does it mean, mistaken for a prostitute?"

Jimmy grabbed the newspaper from Chaz.

*The murdered woman has been named as Pauline
Hanson. She was an unmarried mother who worked at The
Orange Club on Chapeltown Road. Police believe she may
have been mistaken for a prostitute.*

Jimmy's shoulders sagged as he read. The article made
his mother sound cheap. She *had* looked like a prostitute, he
had said as much to Susan. '*You looked like a pair of
scrubbers.*' It amounted to the same thing.

"Mum says you must come to our house. Both of you.
I've got my car outside. Please say you'll come."

Jimmy didn't know whether he wanted to go or not. He
shrugged his shoulders in a non-committal way. He hadn't
the strength to make a decision.

Susan thought about it for a moment. "Well, I think it's
a good idea. We can call at the Threlfalls, and I'll get some
clothes. Get your stuff, Jimmy."

Two students were behind the bar at the Threlfalls.

"Where's my dad?" Susan asked.

"Dunno. He opened up then went through the back."

Susan didn't want to talk to her dad, so she went up the
main staircase and packed a few things. Jimmy and Chaz
were waiting outside in the mini. They were soon in the
welcoming kitchen of the Fournier's home. Madame
Fournier had set the table for five. A large tureen of

steaming soup was placed in the middle of the table, home-made bread rolls in a basket.

"Now zen, you poor darlinks. Zis is a terrible day. I know you will be 'ungry, and I t'ink you can manage my special soup."

Susan and Jimmy each managed a thin smile. They said a quiet "thank you" and sat down.

"My wife is right, of course. First, we will have some soup, and then we will talk."

The soup was delicious. Susan and Jimmy had no appetite, but they ate the bread and drank the hot soup gratefully. Afterwards, they went into the lounge. Madame Fournier brought coffee and almond biscuits.

"Now," Anton said. "Tell us, Jimmy. Tell us about your mother."

Susan, Jimmy and Chaz sat on the sofa together. Susan was in the middle. The three friends held hands. Jimmy told the Fourniers how he had come home on the bus to surprise his mum and Susan, and how he had seen them from the bus. Susan took over and told how Pauline had spoken of her mother. Between them, they related the staggering events of the last twenty-four hours. They sobbed and hugged as they spoke, at times unable to speak at all. Jeanette gave them handkerchiefs to wipe their reddened eyes. The Fourniers listened in horror. Jimmy showed them the letter from Sheffield.

"Your mo'zer was a good mo'zer." Jeanette tried to hold back tears. Her husband put his hand on her shoulder. The overwhelming sadness permeated the walls of the room.

Anton moved forward and pulled a chair close to the sofa. "On Monday, Jimmy, we will telephone this solicitor in Sheffield. There is nothing we can do today or tomorrow."

He pointed to the letter. "First thing Monday, we will start to sort this out. I will take a day off work. They can do without me for one day."

"I'm supposed to be dancing tonight," Susan said.

"Then we must telephone your club and tell them you won't be in. I'll do it if you like."

Susan nodded in assent.

"Does your daddy know where you are?"

She shook her head.

"Then I will telephone him, too."

Anton was relieved to be able to do something useful. The calls were brief and he soon returned to the lounge.

"Well, that's all sorted out." Anton looked at the clock on the mantelpiece. "We should try to get some sleep." He turned to his wife.

"I will boil ze kettle and make 'ot chocolate for you cheeldren. I will give you each ze 'ot water bottle, too. Anton eez right. We must try to sleep."

* * * *

The cold morning crept through the curtains. Jimmy didn't want to wake up. He hadn't slept until after three o'clock, and then only fitfully. Dozing and waking every half hour with the jolt of reality. The soft duvet nestled around him. He had only slept under sheets and blankets before. He didn't want to get up. If he got up, he would have to face the day, and he didn't want to. He thought about his mum, the way she had worked at the bakery and then in a bad part of Leeds. She had done so much for him. Everything. She could have had him adopted. That's what most girls did when they had a baby before they were married, especially in 1948 when he was born. Who could have blamed her under the circumstances?

Memories of his happy childhood filled his head. School, Susan and Chaz, birthday parties. Grannie Florrie's kitchen and the door connecting their houses. His reverie was shattered by the memory of Grannie Florrie's twisted face, as she lay dying, flashing before his eyes. His mum went to see a solicitor, and they had chosen their mementoes after the funeral. He would have to organise his mum's funeral now. Her cold body would be lying on a cold slab somewhere. He didn't even know where she was.

The smell of fresh coffee coming from the kitchen helped him push the duvet back. He took a dry pair of jeans and a jumper from his bag, ran his fingers through his hair and dressed. Anton was sitting at the kitchen table, The Sunday Times spread out before him.

"Ah, Jimmy. There you are. My wife has gone to church. She likes to go to Mass, but she has left us some warm croissants in the oven, and there is coffee in the pot. Help yourself."

"You're both very kind. I…"

"Don't mention it. We are your friends. We do what any friends would do."

Jimmy poured a mug of coffee and sat down. Anton folded his newspaper.

"Goodness knows when those girls will put in an appearance. They were chatting half the night. I will wake them soon. The police have been on the phone."

Jimmy looked up. "What did they want? Have they found who killed Mum?"

"No. Nothing like that. I just confirmed you and Susan will be staying here for a while. It will be better for you."

Susan and Chaz came downstairs just as Jeanette returned from Church.

"It's all my fault, Jimmy." Susan wiped tears from her cheeks as she hugged him.

"Your fault? How is it your fault?"

"Me and Chaz were talking about it last night after you went to bed. Your mum came to meet *me.* The only reason she was there was because of *me.* She wanted me to talk to her after work, but I ranted on and made her tell me about Mum. We walked and talked for a bit. That's why we were there, up by the Merrion Centre."

"Susan!" Jimmy held her by the shoulders. "Stop it! Mum was in the wrong place at the wrong time. That's all."

"But that's just it, Jimmy. She was in the wrong place at the wrong time because of *me.*"

"You must stop this. Mum wouldn't want it. You mustn't feel guilty about it."

"You two aren't falling out, are you?" Chaz came into the room, carrying a plate of biscuits. "Mum's just made these. I warn you now, she'll be feeding you all day."

The tension diffused and the moment passed.

The day wore inexorably on. Anton reiterated his promise to help all he could. He would contact Jimmy's professor in Durham to explain his absence. He would contact the solicitor in Sheffield. He would go with Jimmy to Vine Street to see if they could find a will. He would help organise the funeral. As Chaz had predicted, Jeanette offered an endless stream of food.

Two days later, Jimmy travelled by train to Sheffield. Anton offered to drive him there, but Jimmy wanted to go on his own. The Fourniers' kindness had been overwhelming. Jimmy was grateful for everything they had done. For

Madame Fournier's wonderful food, and for Monsieur Fournier's practical guidance.

The train stopped at Wakefield Kirkgate, then travelled on to Sheffield. South Church Street was in the city centre. Richard Deighton's secretary ushered Jimmy into a bright modern office. The golden teak furniture smelled of wax polish, and Venetian blinds filtered the dazzling March sunshine.

"Your grandfather's will is very simple, Mr Hanson. He left everything to your mother, and, in the event of her being pre-deceased, everything goes to you."

Jimmy nodded. It was all so unreal. He had never been addressed as 'Mr Hanson' before, and to hear this man talking of his grandfather just didn't sound right. Grandfather? Father? He had never known him, so what did it matter? Jimmy couldn't think of him as family or even as a distant relative. He was George Hanson.

"You say you have your mother's will with you?"

Jimmy nodded and handed an envelope to Richard Deighton.

"Mum left everything to me," Jimmy said.

The solicitor didn't reply straight away. He read Pauline's will and then handed it back to Jimmy.

"Your mother's death, and may I offer my sincere condolences, doesn't complicate the matter too much. You say she died very recently?"

"Yes. The funeral is Friday, next week." Jimmy saw no reason to explain the circumstances of his mother's death. It would make no difference to George Hanson's will. "Mum hadn't opened your letter. I did. I think maybe she was scared of what it might contain. She hadn't been in touch with her father for a long time, you see. I never met him."

Richard Deighton sat back in his chair, his hands touching at his fingertips. He didn't know why George Hanson had been estranged from his daughter, but he had been in practice long enough to know not to ask. It was none of his business.

"You are fortunate indeed that your mother made a will. Not many people of her age have taken the trouble to do so. It makes my job much easier, and you will receive your inheritance more quickly. I understand your mother's solicitor was Harry Botterill of Park Square in Leeds."

Jimmy nodded. "He was Granny Florrie's solicitor. From the date of Mum's will, she must have made it soon after Grannie Florrie died."

"He is executor of your mother's will. In due course, Mr Hanson, your entire grandfather's estate and your mother's estate will come to you. Your grandfather stipulated that his house in Willowbank Road be sold, so that may take a little time. You are a rich young man, Mr Hanson."

On the journey back to Leeds, Jimmy realised that if Keith hadn't told him the circumstances of his birth, he would never have known. Mr Deighton didn't appear to know, and George Hanson wouldn't have told anyone. He was glad he knew. He understood why his mother had never been able to speak of it.

* * * *

Pauline's coffin was covered in orange chrysanthemums. Jimmy had wanted to speak at his mum's funeral but knew he wouldn't be able to do it. The service

235

would be mercifully short. At Jimmy's request, Keith Prentice gave the eulogy.

What is it that we remember when we think of Pauline? Everyone who knew her will have their personal memories, but we all remember her kindness, her selflessness and her beauty. Pauline was one of those rare people who was beautiful inside and out. She came into our lives like a breath of fresh air, never hinting at any troubles of her own. To say that her sudden and tragic departure has left a hole in our lives is an understatement. She was so proud of Jimmy and was looking forward to seeing him in his cap and gown later this year. As most of you know, her love of jazz brought us together. Pauline and I were to be married next year. Now, we must all carry on in life without this wonderful woman who touched us all. But go on we must, knowing we are better people for having had the privilege of knowing Pauline.

Jimmy stood at the doorway of Rawdon Crematorium, Keith at his side. Susan, Chaz and Monsieur and Madame Fournier behind him. He shook hands with strangers and thanked them for coming. Jimmy didn't know half of the people who were there. Keith introduced him to musicians and customers from The Orange Club. Others introduced themselves as having worked with his mum at the bakery. Susan's dad came but quickly left. There were no neighbours from Vine Street. They still hadn't forgiven her for being unmarried. Keith had arranged a reception at The Orange Club after the service where he had arranged for some food to be served. Apart from Keith, the Fourniers and Susan, Jimmy didn't know anyone.

Everyone tucked into the food and had a few drinks, and then slowly the room emptied.

It was over.

Pauline's ashes were to be scattered in the Garden of Remembrance where those of Grannie Florrie had been scattered four years earlier.

Chapter Fourteen

May 1968

Life drifted into a routine for Susan. She worked every lunchtime and Monday to Saturday evenings at the Threlfalls. When she finished at the Threlfalls on Thursdays, Fridays and Saturdays, she went to the 'In Time' and danced in her gilded cage. Sunday evening was her only time off. Of course, she still had mornings to do what she wanted. Sometimes she went to see Madame Fournier, and Chaz, if she was at home. Sometimes she just slept.

Jimmy had gone back to university, and the house in Vine Street was locked up. Monsieur Fournier had eventually persuaded him to go back to Durham and take his finals. Jimmy had wanted to pack it all in and travel. There had been no progress in finding Pauline's killer, and the press had lost interest. Whenever Alf called in for his half of Tetley's, Susan asked the same question.

"Any news, Alf?"

"Still nothing." Alf shook his head and sipped his beer. He looked into his glass and, without raising his head, said, "You see, Susan, no witnesses have come forward."

"I know that. I was the last person to see her alive. It was all my fault."

"No. No, it wasn't. Feeling guilty isn't going to help. C.I.D. now think it may have been an accident and not murder after all."

"They'll just say that so they don't have to keep looking." Anger boiled up inside her. "Of course it was murder."

"Listen, Susan. When Pauline was found, they thought she was a prostitute, so no one took much trouble to investigate the scene. When it was realised she was a good, hard-working mum, they went back the next day to look for clues, but the rain had washed the pavement clean. They found some blood on a wall, but nothing else. There was no evidence of rape or anything like that. They think she may simply have lost her balance and banged her head. No one will admit it, but it's true, and for all I know, they're right. I'm telling you this because this is my last night on the beat." He looked at the clock. "In three hours time, I'm retired. That's it. No more a copper." He pulled a piece of paper from his jacket pocket. "This is my new address. I wrote it down for you. Come to me if you ever need to. I mean that."

"Thanks, Alf."

He finished his drink and left.

Susan watched him go. There was something about the way he said 'if you ever *need* to; not if you ever *want* to'.

She worked in the bar all evening. Wednesday night was never busy. When there was no one to serve, she filled up the fridges and collected glasses. Charlie stood on his board at the end of the bar, chatting to customers and smiling at her whenever he caught her eye in that 'proud father' way she hated. It meant he was talking about her. By closing time, she had convinced herself that Alf thought C.I.D. were wrong, and that Pauline's death was no accident. She decided there were two things she needed to do. The first wasn't connected to Pauline's death but it was something she had thought about for a long time. The bar closed promptly at ten-thirty. Charlie sat at the kitchen table counting his takings. Susan made two mugs of tea and handed one to Charlie.

"Thanks, love. You worked hard tonight. Right proud of you, I am."

"I'm off upstairs for a bath, Dad. See you tomorrow."

Charlie called after her, "'Night, love."

"'Night, Dad."

She took her tea up the back stairs and into the little bathroom. She put the plug in the bath and turned on both taps before walking along the landing, up the five steps and into her bedroom. She put on her black boots and a black coat, sipping her tea as she waited for the back door to bang. As soon as she heard the familiar sound, she ran along the landing, turned off the taps and ran down the stairs two at a time. She opened the door to the yard just as Charlie closed the big gate behind him.

The streets were quiet. It wasn't hard to follow Charlie's trilby hat despite his small stature. Susan concentrated on the figure in front of her. She kept about thirty yards behind him. Had he no idea how ridiculously old fashioned he looked? Susan knew her way round Leeds. She knew where the shop doorways were so she could hide if he turned round. She followed him to John Street. Three women stood on the corner smoking. Susan knew they were prostitutes from her days as look out for Maggie. They watched the cars, waiting for one to slow down. Charlie walked straight past, into the first house and down the side passageway. A red light glowed dimly in the front porch. Susan was riveted to the spot. This had to be the brothel where Maggie worked. She had expected him to meet someone. Give them a package and accept an envelope in return. She had suspected for years that her father dealt in stolen goods.

"You dirty old bastard," she whispered. "You even sneak in the back door of a brothel."

She thrust her hands deep into her pockets and walked home, deep in thought. Her dad had been sneaking out after closing time for as long as she could remember. Shagging prostitutes even when her mother was alive. Maybe even shagging Maggie. Maggie had been right about one thing: he was sneaking out to be with another woman. Turned out to be any woman. Susan wasn't sure if that made it better or worse. The thought made her face distort, her mouth twisted in disgust.

She hadn't seen Maggie for about four years, not since they fell out. Maybe she would go and see her, but then, Maggie probably didn't have her flat any more. Maybe she lived at John Street, and Susan had no intention of going *there*. No. She had accomplished what she set out to do tonight. It wasn't what she expected, but she knew now what her father had been up to after closing time.

She wondered how much Alf knew about John Street. He would know about it for sure, but did he know her dad was a customer?

Susan let herself in to the Threlfalls the way she had come out and went upstairs. She refilled the bath with hot water and was still soaking in the bubbles when she heard the door bang downstairs. Her dad was home and would have no idea she had been out. Susan was planning her next move. Knowing what her dad was up to both simplified and complicated her next move. It was a good job Jimmy was away. He would have tried to stop her. Not that she would have told him what she was doing. Better he was well out of the way, though.

* * * *

"Put the kettle on, will you, Gloria?" Charlie threw his hat onto the kitchen table. Gloria set out a tray with two cups and saucers.

"I got some good news and shit bad news, Charlie. Which do you want first?"

"Oh, Christ. I was in a good mood 'til you said that. Go on, get the bad stuff over with."

"We got more girls on the streets trying to pinch our trade."

"I know. I saw them at the end of the street. Three of them. What's the good news?"

"I found a replacement for Flint."

"Oh. Yeah." Charlie sounded sceptical. "Has this one got more than one brain cell?"

"Maybe two. Point is, this guy is a real frightener."

"What d'yer mean? Frightener?"

"Just that, I hope. He's big, black, and strong. Hands like shovels. He'll do as he's told. To be fair to Flint, he got unlucky. He didn't mean to harm that bloody woman. Anyway, that's all in the past, and we got away with it. You wanna meet this one?"

"Nah. What's he called?"

"Dunno. Not his real name anyway. They never use their real name. He calls himself Winston. He'll go and talk to them. Offer them a job or piss off. Same as before. I've told him no violence, but I can't guarantee it. He says he leaves no marks, whatever that means."

"When's he starting? I want rid of those scrubbers at the end of the street. They bring down the tone of the neighbourhood."

Gloria knew what he meant. They had no trouble in John Street and didn't want any.

"Tonight. Trust me, Charlie."

"I always do, you old tart." He still liked Gloria. She was an honest sinner. Bit like himself, really. They laughed together. Life and business was good again.

* * * *

Susan got up just after ten o'clock the next morning and went out. Charlie was still in bed, and Mrs Roberts was cleaning in the bar.

She went to the market and bought some cheap clothes. Not her usual style, but exactly what she wanted. She put them in an embroidered shoulder bag and made her way to the makeup stall. Max Factor pan stick, pale porcelain, grey and bright blue eye shadow, and some cheap bright orange lipstick. Rimmel 'Mandarin'. There was no point buying expensive stuff. With a bit of luck, she would only wear it once. Anyway, cheap was what she wanted. She put the makeup in her bag and wandered around the stalls for a while before walking back up Briggate. She timed it so she arrived at the Threlfalls as Charlie opened the doors. It was going to be a long day. She worked lunchtime and then rested in her bedroom before working the evening behind the bar. She then went to the 'In Time' and her gilded cage.

The same thoughts ran through her head all day. The police weren't finding Auntie Pauline's killer. Weren't even looking. As for that crap about it being an accident, that was just an excuse to do nothing. She knew how to find the bastard. Her stomach had been in a knot, and she hadn't been able to eat anything. If she had, she knew she would throw up. She took the embroidered bag from the little wardrobe in her dressing room. The black bra pushed her breasts up, giving her a cleavage. The crotchless knickers were uncomfortable with scratchy elastic. She pulled on the fishnet stockings and fastened her suspenders. The leopard print jacket and tiny mini-skirt were perfect. She sat at the little dressing table and backcombed her hair. She applied the pale panstick makeup thickly. The bright blue eye shadow went on next, then her usual black eye liner, but with a much wider line. Her false eyelashes could stay on. She then took the grey eye shadow and applied it under her eyes, streaking it downwards. Perfect. She looked worn out, older, weary. High stiletto heels, and she was ready.

"G'night, Martin."

The doorman at the 'In Time' was waiting for the last few customers to leave as Susan left. "Where you goin' dressed like that, Susan?" Martin couldn't believe his eyes. "You look like a…you look…"

"Like what, Martin? Like a prostitute?"

"Well…yes."

"Good."

He shook his head. "You be careful, Susan."

"I will."

She walked a few paces in the cheap uncomfortable shoes then turned and came back. Martin was still staring at her.

"Do me a favour, Martin. If I don't turn up for work tomorrow, call the police. Okay?"

"What you doin'…?"

"Never you mind. Don't ask any questions. Please, Martin. There's something I have to do."

She turned and walked away in the opposite direction to the Threlfalls. The last customers left, and Martin went inside and locked the door behind him. He went to the office and took the telephone directory from the shelf. Threlfalls Hotel, Briggate 62538. Charlie Fletcher would want to know about this. Martin looked at his watch. Quarter past one. He dialled the number. No reply. He replaced the receiver. He would call the Threlfalls again in the morning to make sure Susan got home in one piece.

* * * *

She stood on the corner of John Street.

The streets were deserted. The cheap shoes had rubbed blisters on her heels and she was scared. Very scared. A car pulled up. Susan's knees shook as she stepped forward and leaned through the open window. She wanted to turn and run, but knew she had to do this. If she was going to find Auntie Pauline's killer, she had to do it. If her mum could do it to get away from her father, then she could do it for Auntie Pauline. She gritted her teeth and smiled.

"How much, love?"

In the yellow haze of the street lights, Susan saw an unshaven, lined face, dirty fingernails. The car smelled of alcohol and tobacco. He was about fifty. She tried to remember what Maggie used to charge, cursing herself inwardly for not having thought this through properly. What was she thinking of? Had she imagined she would just stand here and a bloke would walk up to her and she would miraculously know he was the one who had killed Auntie Pauline? How stupid was that?

"Depends what you want."

"Just straight sex."

"Thirty quid."

"You must be joking. What's so special about you? You a fucking virgin or something?"

"That's my price."

"Fuck off." He wound the window up and drove off. Susan stepped back into the shadows and leaned against a stone wall with her eyes closed. Shit. Fuck. Bollocks. He was right. She was a virgin. She felt dizzy. Madame Fournier would be cross with her for not eating anything. She smiled at the thought. Madame Fournier would be very cross with her if she knew what she was up to.

Susan didn't hear them approach. In a split second, there was a hand over her mouth, another arm grasping her round the waist lifting her from the ground. She bit the hand, hard. He yelped in pain.

"The bitch bit me."

The other two grabbed her and threw her over the wall, then all three of them scrambled after her. Before she could stand, she had her arms twisted up behind her back.

"See what you did to my hand, you bitch?" He pushed his bloody hand in her face, smearing his blood on her cheek. "You're gonna pay for that, big time."

The two who held her laughed as he pushed her skirt up and grabbed her crotch.

"Well, what we got 'ere, slag? Open door, ready for business. Well, we mustn't disappoint the little lady, eh?" He unzipped his jeans and pushed her legs apart with his knees.

Susan screamed in pain as he thrust himself inside her. The two behind her backed her into a tree so they could watch as he raped her, his hands around her neck so she couldn't scream. When he finished, he let her drop to the ground.

"Fuck me, lads. I reckon I just had a virgin."

"You lucky bastard."

The stronger one picked her up and turned her round. He threw her down onto her knees. He raped her from behind, while the other two watched and laughed. The third man crouched in front of her, taunting her, holding out his hand, pushing leaves in her mouth.

"Here, little doggy. Want some more, little doggy? My turn next, little doggy."

Susan's arms collapsed. She was unconscious when the third man raped her.

* * * *

"Night, Winston."

"Night, Maggie." He checked his watch. Ten-to-four, Maggie was the last to leave. It had been a quiet night. A party of coppers had been in the voyeur room. Weird party, that. They were celebrating the retirement of a bloke who wasn't there.

He thought this job might be boring, and in a way it was. Not a lot for him to do but plenty to see. He had moved on the three girls from the end of the street hours ago. They wouldn't be back. It had been quiet since. All he had to do was watch the customers go in and out. Gloria nodded from the hallway to let him know they had paid, and that was it.

He decided to check the street one last time when he saw Maggie running towards him.

"Winston…you gotta come…there's someone in the garden down the street."

"Whatcha mean? Someone in the garden?" He followed her towards the end of John Street and round the corner.

"I heard someone crying. I think she's hurt."

"Did you see anyone, Maggie?"

"No. I daren't go. There could be anyone there."

"Where?"

Maggie stopped and pointed over a wall towards some trees. "Here. Listen."

Winston put one hand on the top of the wall and leapt over, landing quietly in the leaves, disappearing into the dark garden. Moments later, he emerged with Susan in his arms, her bloodied face smeared with dirt, leaves stuck around her mouth. Her clothes were ripped, she had no shoes on, and her knees were covered in mud and leaves. He sat on the top of the wall and swung his legs round, holding her easily in his arms as he landed on the pavement. Maggie couldn't believe her eyes.

The shock on her face irritated Winston. "What d'you expect? A lame dog or something?"

"I know her. She's a friend of mine."

"So what you want me to do now? Take her to Gloria?"

"No. Not there." Maggie thought for a few moments. "Will you carry her to my place, Winston? It's about ten minutes away."

"Okay, but we'd better be quick. Gloria will think I've done a runner."

He carried her with ease. The streets were quiet as Maggie walked a few paces in front of him. They stepped into doorways as cars passed by. No one saw them. Maggie had her keys ready as they approached the launderette. She unlocked the side door and Winston carried Susan up the stairs. Maggie let them into her room, and Winston laid Susan on the single bed.

"Gotta go, Maggie. You'll be alright, yeah?"

"We'll be fine, thanks. I owe you. Keep this quiet, okay?"

Winston nodded and left. Maggie ran some warm water in the sink and started to bathe Susan's face. Susan murmured and opened her eyes.

"It's okay, Susan. You're safe. You're with your old friend, Maggie."

Susan tried to lift her head and fell back on the pillow. Turning on her side, she curled up in a ball. Maggie made her a cup of tea with plenty of sugar, and helped her sit up to drink the hot, sweet liquid. She took a clean towel from the cupboard and helped Susan out of her torn clothing, helping her to wash, and gave her a dressing gown. Maggie asked no questions. Susan could only say "thank you" to every kindness. They sat on the edge of the little bed together, Maggie with her arm gently around Susan's shoulders. She spoke quietly.

"When I was a kid, I was in an orphanage. They said my mother left me on the doorstep. Dunno if that's true or not. Then when I was sixteen, they were going to send me to Australia, so I ran away. This woman set me on as lookout, like you used to do for me. She looked after me 'til I got this place." Maggie poured more tea and gave Susan a biscuit. "I don't mind all that, it's just how it is. I'm independent, and I have my freedom, and I do what I want—and I've never been raped."

They sat in silence for a while. Susan wrapped her hands round the mug of tea, staring into the comforting drink.

"It's okay at John Street. Gloria runs it. She's quite something, is Gloria. We girls can work as much as we want, the bosses take a percentage. It's better than standing on street corners in winter. I missed you, though. Missed our friendship."

"I did it for Auntie Pauline. I wanted—still want—to find her killer. The police have stopped looking."

Maggie lay back in the bed, her head propped against the wall. "And you thought you could find him by working the streets?"

"Yes. Stupid me, eh, Maggie? Stupid Susan."

"I heard about your Auntie Pauline. Everyone did. I thought about going to her funeral. Didn't know her myself, of course. I thought her boy…Jimmy, isn't it? I thought he wouldn't like me being there, so I didn't go."

"Jimmy's at Durham University, he finishes soon, doing his finals."

Daylight was starting to filter through the thin curtains. Susan shivered and yawned.

"We both need some sleep, Susan. You lie by the wall. It'll be a squash but we'll be warm."

Susan pressed her body against Maggie. It made her feel safe.

* * * *

Charlie shuffled across the kitchen in his slippers and dressing gown. He had slept in and needed a cup of tea before he shaved. Susan would open up at twelve. He rubbed his eyes to focus as he picked up the note on the table. It was from Mrs Roberts. He hoped she wasn't handing her notice in; he could do without the hassle of finding another cleaner.

Dear Mr Fletcher,
The phone kept ringing but I didn't answer it.
Irene Roberts.

He screwed it up and threw it into the fireplace. He was filling the kettle when the phone rang. He walked through to the bar and lifted the receiver.

"Is that Charlie Fletcher?"

"Who wants to know?" Charlie was annoyed and suspicious.

"You don't know me. Ah'm Martin. Ah'm t'bouncer at t'In Time' where your Susan dances. Did she come 'ome las' night, Mr Fletcher?"

"Yes. I suppose so. I expect she's in bed. Why? What's the fuss?"

"Ah'm just a bit worried. Summat she said as she lef' las' neet. Can you check on her?"

Charlie held the receiver away from his face and looked at it as if the telephone had gone mad.

"Okay. I'll check. She should be down soon to open the bar up." He replaced the receiver and shuffled to the bottom of the back staircase.

"Susan! You up yet?" he shouted.

Charlie went upstairs and knocked on her door before opening it. Her bed hadn't been slept in.

251

"Bloody hell."

Charlie looked at his watch. Ten-to-twelve and he hadn't even shaved yet. He dressed quickly in the clothes he had taken off the night before and ran his electric shaver quickly around his face. The doors of the Threlfalls opened at two minutes after twelve.

Susan.

She'd let him down again. She was getting as bad as these bloody students.

By three o'clock, Charlie had had time to think about the phone call from this Martin. Presumably, he was the one who had been calling all morning. As he walked toward the doors to lock up, a tall man, casually dressed in jeans and a checked shirt, walked up to the door.

"I'm closing." Charlie pushed the door towards him.

"Ah'm Martin. Ah rang yer. Is she back, then?"

"Er, no. No, she's not. She'll be at her friend's house. She was supposed to work this lunchtime. I'm not best pleased with her right now. She should've rung me." Charlie put the bolts down on one of the doors and went to close the other.

"Can Ah come in, Mr Fletcher? Ah dunt want a drink. Ah want ter tell yer what she said. Ahm reet worried." Martin shifted his weight from one foot to the other.

Charlie paused. There was something about this big man that made him feel uneasy. He held the door back, and Martin stepped inside. Charlie bolted the second door and gestured for Martin to go into the best room. They sat at one of the tables.

"She didn't tell me ter come ter yer, Mr Fletcher. She told me ter call t'police if she didn't get to work toneet. Ah didn't want ter a wait that long, yer see."

"Police? Why would she say that?" Charlie was baffled.

"Ah dunt know. It was the way she were dressed, yer see. Tha's what worried me. She were all done up like a tart."

Charlie leant back in his chair. "Well, Martin. I have to thank you for coming. For your concern about my daughter. Susan's no fool, and it's my guess she was going to a party. Fancy dress, one of these Tarts and Vicars things. Something like that. That's what it will've been, but I tell you what, I'll phone her friend, Chaz. Most likely she's at her house."

Charlie stood up and walked to the door.

Martin turned to Charlie as he stood on the doorstep. "Ah hope yer reet, Mr Fletcher, but Ah think yer wrong."

Charlie sat at the kitchen table and counted the lunchtime takings. He could do it without thinking. Instead, his thoughts were on the strange conversation he had just had with this Martin bloke. He looked up the Fournier's number in the telephone directory and dialled the number.

"Non, Monsieur Fletcher. We 'ave not seen Susan. She was 'ere on Tuesday morning. She 'ad coffee and…"

"Thank you, Madame Fournier. I must go. Thank you."

Charlie hung up. There was no point continuing the conversation. He hadn't meant to be rude. There was one other place he could try. He put on his hat and coat and walked as quickly as his short legs would carry him to Vine Street. He didn't need to knock on the door. Cobwebs across the door frame to the handle told him Susan wasn't here. He went to the police station.

"And you say, sir, that the last time she was seen was last night, leaving the 'In Time'."

"Yes, that's right." Charlie was getting impatient. He didn't like this copper's attitude. "Is Alf Lawrence here?"

"Alf? No. He's retired. You'll not see Alf here. You know him, then?"

"Yes."

"And you're told she was dressed like a tart, walking up towards the Merrion Centre?"

"Yes." He was acutely aware how this was sounding.

"She's twenty."

"Yes."

"And she often stays with friends?"

"Yes."

"Well, sir, I think we should wait a bit longer before we all start panicking. It's my experience these girls turn up sooner or later. Usually sooner."

"Like Pauline Hanson did, you mean?" Charlie could barely believe what he had said. He was worried stiff about Susan now and would say anything to get some reaction from this fool of a copper.

"Now then, sir. That was an accident. Let's not get all het up. Maybe you could check the hospital if you're worried."

"Course I'm worried. She's my daughter, and she's missing, you bloody fool." Charlie didn't wait for an answer. He was on his way to the Casualty Department at the Infirmary.

* * * *

Susan was awake as soon as Maggie swung her legs out of the bed.

"You won't leave me alone, will you, Maggie?"

"Listen, love. You're safe enough here. Only me and Winston know you're here, and he won't tell anyone. It's half past twelve. I don't know about you, but I'm starving." Maggie dressed as she spoke. "I'll get us some fish and chips. I won't be long. Find yourself some clothes in the cupboard."

Susan got up slowly. Her whole body hurt. She ran some hot water in the sink and took off the dressing gown. She washed herself slowly from head to foot, and then washed the soil from her hair. The cracked mirror over the sink reflected bruises around her neck. Her face was swollen. It was like looking at a stranger. For a second, she saw Pauline's face smiling in the mirror; she felt her presence. Pauline knew what she was going through, what she had been through. There were bruises on her legs and arms, her knees grazed, soil stuck in the wounds, too sore to wash away. She patted her body with a towel. Her skin was too sensitive to rub. She found a baggy jumper at the back of the cupboard and some track bottoms.

"I got specials with mushy peas." Maggie unwrapped the fish and chips from the newspaper. "No expense spared for my best friend. I got bread and marg and some jam for later if you want it, and some fresh milk."

Susan hadn't realised how hungry she was until she smelled the food.

"Funny, isn't it," Maggie went on. "Fish and chips smell lovely when you're hungry and awful when you're full."

Susan smiled thinly. "I don't remember much about last night. There were three of them. I think I must've passed out."

Maggie had a chip half way to her mouth. She froze for about five seconds while Susan's words sank in.

"Three of them?"

Susan nodded.

"You want to go to the police?"

"No, Maggie. I still want to find Auntie Pauline's killer."

"Jesus, Susan. I thought I was tough. You can't seriously be thinking of going out on the streets again?"

"Look, Maggie. It's my fault she was murdered. She came to see me, and I argued with her and left her there. I have to find her killer. I just have to."

"Okay, okay. I get all that, but there has to be a better way. Do you have any idea how many punters are out there? How will you know when you find her killer? You think he's gonna have 'I killed your Auntie Pauline' tattooed on his face?"

"You got a better idea?"

"No. I don't. But I know who will." Maggie finished her meal and screwed up the greasy newspapers. She threw them into the waste paper basket. "You stay here. Promise?"

"Where are you going?"

"Out. I'll be about an hour. Promise me you'll stay here."

"I promise."

* * * *

Gloria was dozing in the kitchen when someone knocked on the door to the hallway. She pushed her bunioned feet into her slippers and opened the door. It was Maggie. Good worker, Maggie. No baggage with her.

"Can I have a word, Gloria? It's important."

"Come in, love. You not thinking of leaving, are you?" Gloria couldn't think of any other reason for Maggie wanting to speak to her. Maggie followed her into the kitchen.

"No. It's not that. It's to do with Pauline Hanson, you know, the woman who was murdered."

Gloria stopped in her tracks and turned quickly, her face pale despite the heavy makeup.

"It wasn't murder. It was an accident. The coppers say so." Gloria's eyes darted over Maggie. "What the fuck do you know about it?"

"Nothing. I have a friend who thinks it was murder and the coppers aren't doing anything."

"Who is this friend?" Gloria's question was an accusation.

"She says we are all at risk until he's found. I think she's right."

"Well, she's bloody well wrong, whoever she is."

"You know something, don't you, Gloria?"

"Me? No. But I know when to keep my fucking trap shut, and you'd do well to do the same." Gloria's cheeks had gone from drip white to bright red. Maggie was convinced now that Gloria knew something.

"You know there was gang rape at the end of the street last night?"

"A what?"

"You heard, Gloria. Gang rape. Three of them. Could be the ones who killed Pauline Hanson."

"Oh, no. No, it wasn't."

"How d'you know that, Gloria?"

"I don't. I don't know fucking anything. I'm just sayin' what the coppers say. Your friend been to the coppers, has she?"

"Not yet. Tell you what, Gloria. I'll bring my friend to see you. If you can convince her, then that's good enough for me. We'll be here at eight o'clock. Right? She's the one who was raped." Maggie slammed the door behind her.

Before she was out of the house, Gloria was dialling the number of the Threlfalls Hotel.

"Charlie. We got trouble. Bad trouble. You gotta get round here."

"What now? What's it about that won't wait?"

"Pauline Hanson."

"Shit." Charlie had been on the phone to Leeds General Infirmary and St James' Hospital. There was no sign of Susan.

Gloria gasped for breath as she repeated her conversation with Maggie. "I'm worried, Charlie."

"I've got my own problems right now, Gloria. Susan's missing."

"You gotta fucking well be here at eight, Charlie. If this stupid bitch goes to the coppers, the whole Pauline fucking Hanson thing could kick off again."

"I've got a missing twenty year old daughter, and I've got a pub to run. How the hell—?" Charlie was shouting.

Gloria shouted back. "Your Susan's gone off with her mates before, and you'll have to leave your precious bar to your staff for one night. Be here, Charlie."

* * * *

Susan tried to sleep. If she could sleep, she could escape the thoughts in her head. She remembered the car pulling up, and she remembered saying 'thirty quid', then three featureless faces, but nothing after that until she woke up on Maggie's bed. That's the way she wanted it to stay, but her mind kept pulling her back like a magnet. When she did drift off, she saw a child's hand with a silver coin pressed into it. The smell of alcohol and tobacco pervaded her dream.

"Wake up, Susan."

Maggie was back. Susan hadn't heard her come in. She was relieved to wake up, to get out of the dream.

"Gloria knows how your Auntie Pauline died. I'm sure of it. We're going to John Street at eight o'clock."

"I can't go *there*."

"Why not? What's the big deal?"

"It's my dad."

"Your dad? What's it to do with him?"

"He's a customer there. Your customer for all I know. Remember, you said once he most likely had another woman, even when my mum was alive? Well, he still goes out some nights after closing. The night before last, I followed him, and he went to John Street. He went in the back door."

"The *back* door, you say?"

"Mmm. Yeah, the back door, sneaking in like a rat."

"Then your dad's not a punter. Gloria wouldn't have punters coming in the back. Your dad must be the boss."

The silence which followed was electric. The idea was impossible. Susan didn't want to believe it, but couldn't deny it was a possibility. The more she thought about it, the more everything fell into place. This was what he had meant

259

by his business. This was what had paid for her clothes, records, makeup. Everything. She felt sick.

* * * *

Gloria had it all worked out, more or less. As luck would have it, the voyeur room wasn't booked. She put the young kid in there with Maggie. The kid was in a bad way; Maggie hadn't lied about the rape. She would talk to them, and Charlie could watch. It was about time he saw how hard she had to work to make this place run smoothly. She wasn't quite sure yet what exactly she was going to say, but that had never been a problem before.

Charlie wasn't keen on the idea. His mind was on his daughter, but that would have to wait. She'd help him find her when this was sorted out.

There were twelve chairs in the room. Each had a full view of the red velvet furniture, bondage equipment, and costumes hanging from hooks in the voyeur room. A four poster bed was in the centre; mirrors hung from the ceiling and walls.

Charlie sat before the one way window and looked up. His body went rigid, the breath knocked out of his body with the hammer blow of shock as he saw Susan standing before Gloria. He started to shake; he felt blood rising to his face as if it would burst. He stood up slowly, putting his hand to the arm of the chair to steady himself. He took small steps to the doorway and onto the landing. Susan turned when she heard the door open.

"Hello, Dad."

"Get out, Gloria."

"Oh, no, Dad. I think Gloria here should stay. You see, she was just starting to tell me a load of lies about how Auntie Pauline fell against a wall."

Charlie and Gloria looked at each other. Gloria opened her mouth to say something; Charlie put his hand up, signalling her to keep quiet. His face was ashen as he leaned against the back of a chair.

"You see me and my friend Maggie here, we've worked it out. Maggie works here, Dad. Did you know that? She's been telling me all about the way you recruit new girls. You and the lovely Gloria here. Funny how Flint disappeared the day after Auntie Pauline died."

"Susan." Charlie struggled to speak. "You don't understand…"

"But I do understand, Dad. That's your problem, isn't it?"

"No, you don't, Susan. Gloria and I look after these girls. If it wasn't for this house, they'd be on the streets." He sat in the chair he had been leaning on. "Ask your friend if you don't believe me."

"I don't need to ask anyone about the streets, Dad. Look at me. I was raped by three men last night. The only reason I was out there was to find Auntie Pauline's killer, and all the time it was *you.*" Tears of rage streamed down her face.

"Me? I didn't kill her."

"As good as." She pointed her finger in his face. "You stay right here. I'm going home. I'm going to pack my bags. You won't see me again, Dad, so take a good look at my bruises and remember how I got them. Just give me an hour. C'mon, Maggie."

Charlie put his head in his hands as she left the room.

Susan poked her head back in. "Oh, yes, and one other thing. The night she was murdered, Auntie Pauline told me how Mum earned the money for the ferry from Dublin to Liverpool. Work it out for yourself, Dad."

Charlie barely had the strength to look up. By the time he did, she was gone.

Chapter Fifteen

September 1968

Susan closed her eyes; the sun warmed her face.
Songbirds filled the air with their optimistic music. The
bruises had faded. Physically, she had recovered.

Chaz sat at her side, reading. Susan dozed. The bad
dreams hadn't disappeared, but they were less frequent. She
felt her body relax, the warm breeze from the lavender fields
healing her mind with its hypnotic scent.

She had been in Provence for ten weeks.

Maggie had written to her.

Dear Susan,

*I hope you're feeling better. Guess what? I got a
proper job, not on the game anymore. I didn't want to go
back to John Street, even if your dad and Gloria would let
me. I had a bit put by for a rainy day, and after you left, it
was pretty much pissing it down when I met that old copper
friend of yours. He sends his love and says he will write
soon. He told me I should take a leaf out of your book and
get out of Leeds. Did you know that Keith Prentice has shut
The Orange Club? I heard he's gone touring, playing his
jazz. Anyway, I took your friend's advice and a number 44
bus and got out of Leeds. I work on Barnsley market selling
second hand books. When it's not busy, I read. I like the love
stories best. I've got a council flat with central heating.
Posh, it is. You did me a big favour.*

Love from your friend,

Maggie.

Susan smiled to herself every time she thought about Maggie. She would go and see her in her flat one day. But not yet. Her thoughts drifted back to the Threlfalls. When she had gone back there with Maggie that night, they had gone up to the top floor. She stuck a screwdriver in the lock of the bureau and pulled the drawers out, scattering papers everywhere. Just to piss him off. She took her birth certificate and her Post Office book. There was only one entry. Monday, 16th August, 1948. Deposit. Seven shillings and sixpence. Next, they went to her bedroom. She took the money she earned from dancing from under the mattress and placed it at the bottom of a suitcase. In the top drawer of her chest of drawers was a little box. Susan showed the carved ivory brooch, nestling in velvet, to Maggie.

"This was Grannie Florrie's."

Maggie said nothing, just smiled.

Susan threw a few clothes in the suitcase before snapping it shut. She made Maggie promise not to tell her dad where she was going, though he would probably guess she would be with either Chaz or Jimmy.

Madame Fournier brought cakes and lemonade into the garden. Only Maggie and Alf had the address in Provence.

In the end, there had been a compromise. Monsieur Fournier told her dad she was with them, and they would be travelling, and that she would contact him when she was ready to do so.

Susan sat up and squinted into the bright light. She could make out the figure of a man standing next to Chaz, his outline in silhouette. He had a large bag slung over his shoulder.

She recoiled in fear. Susan didn't want any men around her, except for Monsieur Fournier. Her wounds were deep. The stranger put his bag down and moved towards her, kneeling on the grass at her feet. Relief swept her in a wave. She threw her arms around his neck.

"Jimmy! Oh, Jimmy, you're here at last. Where have you been?"

"Hey, steady on, Susan. You're squeezing me to death here."

Monsieur Fournier joined them. Laughter rippled through the garden. Susan couldn't let go of Jimmy's hand. He had to eat his cake and drink his lemonade with one hand.

"If you just let go of my hand for a minute, Susan, I want to show you something."

She smiled as she released her grip. Jimmy unfastened his bag and pulled out some photographs. They were recently taken, in colour. He handed them to Susan one at a time. Smiling faces looked out at her. Lots of them. Susan was puzzled. She had never seen any of these people before.

"I've been to Ireland, Susan. To Kilmain." He saw a doubt in her eyes. "Your grandfather is long gone, Susan. These are all good people. The O'Malleys. They are your family. They want to meet you."

Susan ran her fingers over the faces. These strangers were her family—her mother's family. They could tell her about her mother as a little girl, and she could tell them about her wonderful mother.

"Will you come with me, Jimmy? You too, Chaz?"

Chaz hugged her. "We thought you'd never ask."

About The Author

Barbara Phipps was born in Liverpool in 1950. Her earliest memory is of moving to the West Riding of Yorkshire in 1953. The family travelled by train, few people had cars in those days. She attended Sandal Endowed Junior School and Wakefield Girls' High School, leaving in 1967 with a handful of 'O' levels, perhaps notably including English Language and Literature. Apart from a disastrous eight year marriage, when she lived in Norfolk, Barbara has lived in Yorkshire ever since. She re-married in 1982 and has a son and a daughter.

She describes her career as that of a serial assistant to the medical profession, having assisted doctors, pathologists, vets, dentists and pharmacists, all of which have been very interesting and very badly paid. Now retired, she has been a Magistrate in West Yorkshire since 2000.

Her hobbies include reading, cooking, walking and gardening. She shares an allotment, growing vegetables with limited success.

She has written several short stories. 'The Threlfalls' is her first novel.

Lightning Source UK Ltd.
Milton Keynes UK
UKOW030609250512

193223UK00001B/2/P